"I'd like you to think better of me," he said, and rather tentatively, his hand came out and touched her cheek. "Please?"

The words "I think you're perfect now" trembled on her lips, but she moderated them. "I don't think badly of you, Cousin Chart," she said, his knuckle against her cheek like a hot coal.

"I'm not your cousin," he said sharply. His hand spread to rest along her jaw, and she leant into it like a bird settling into a nest.

There was a moment of silence. The birds were still and quiet; if the others were talking in the drawing room, it was inaudible. . . . His hand slid around to the back of her head and tilted it. He lowered his lips to hers.

They both sighed as their lips touched. She stretched her arms round the rough texture of his jacket and felt the hard power of his body beneath.

Voices became louder.

The curtain hissed back.

"Mr. Ashby!" exclaimed Cressida. "Juno!"

A REGENCY VALENTINE

Jo Beverley
Carola Dunn
Ellen Fitzgerald
Sheila Simonson
Kitty Grey

FAWCETT CREST • NEW YORK

A Fawcett Crest Book
Published by Ballantine Books

Library of Congress Catalog Card Number: 90-24392

ISBN 0-449-22081-8

This edition published by arrangement with Walker and Company

Manufactured in the United States of America

First Ballantine Books Edition: February 1992

Contents

A Walk Through Valentine Parva   1
   Kitty Grey
If Fancy Be the Food of Love . . .   8
   Jo Beverley
An Afternoon Gardening   66
   Kitty Grey
A Maid at Your Window   71
   Carola Dunn
A Gentleman Calls   119
   Kitty Grey
April When They Woo   122
   Sheila Simonson
On The Church Porch   177
   Kitty Grey
A Maiden All Forlorn   180
   Ellen Fitzgerald
A Talk with Toby   230
   Kitty Grey

A Walk Through
Valentine Parva

"I THINK IT IS the utmost foolishness, my dear Mrs. Trent. If the good vicar were alive, he would never countenance it. Taking on a parcel of girls at your age—the minxes will run you off your feet."

Cressida was certain that Mr. Trent would have approved wholeheartedly, for he had always enjoyed the company of young people. Cressida had sometimes wondered if his proposal, following so hard on the deaths of her parents, had more to do with Mr. Trent's wish to see her and her younger brothers provided for than any strong regard for her. Certainly, he had understood that was the reason why she had accepted him. But she had always been a good wife, and he a fine husband. Nearly three years of marriage had led to a deep affection between them and Cressida still missed him.

However, it was unwise to contradict Mrs. Warren. In the complex hierarchy that governed the village of Valentine Parva, only the resident who was both the sister of a bishop and the relict of a dean felt she had the authority to chastise a woman who was the widow of the canon who had been the previous incumbent of the Church of St. Valentine, particularly as the widow was the niece of an archbishop and the daughter of a vicar as well. Rather than annoy Mrs. Warren, Cressida contented herself with saying, "I am only four-and-thirty, and Toby does not tire me out."

"Tobias is only five," Mrs. Warren said repressively. "If only you had asked my advice sooner. Still, if the first of them arrives tomorrow, there is nothing you can do but encourage them to cut their visit short."

Cressida had waited until today to tell Mrs. Warren, making her call upon that lady early enough so that she could have the pleasure of spreading the news, but too late to try to bully her into withdrawing her invitations. She had not told Mrs. Warren the reasons behind the young ladies' visits, for she did not wish her guests to be the subjects of vicious gossip. "How true," she said as she stood to bid Mrs. Warren farewell.

She walked home, for she did not keep a carriage. It was a cold afternoon, so her pace was brisk as she walked past the church and turned down the lane that would take her to Hugh's Grange. It was silly, in many ways, to continue to live in the large house now that her brothers no longer made their home with her. It would be far more practical for the house to be let to a subtenant, but she liked the thought of living in a saint's barn.

She knew the old legend that St. Hugh had kept his grain in the house was ridiculous. The building was Elizabethan—not nearly old enough—and it was a most unbarnlike structure. But Mr. Trent had agreed that it might well stand on the site of a granary once belonging to the first bishop of Lincoln. In the far distance, Cressida could just see the towers of the cathedral. Seven miles was a long way to carry corn, but one never knew.

Cressida had come to Valentine Parva six years ago—a year after her marriage—when Mr. Trent's increasingly poor health had forced him to resign his duties as a canon of Lincoln Cathedral and take on the less demanding responsibilities of a small parish. At the time, Cressida had thought a village full of retired clergymen would make a rather demanding congregation: the standard expected of sermons would likely be very exacting.

A few months after their arrival, Cressida found herself with child. Mr. Trent had been delighted. Declaring that the tiny vicarage was too small for themselves, Cressida's two brothers, and a family of young Trents, he had, with the optimism that endeared him to Cressida, taken a ninety-nine-year lease on Hugh's Grange. Alas, he had died a few weeks after Toby's first birthday. And, soon after, Cressida's brothers had left for university.

Since then the house seemed very empty. Of the servants, only Cressida's maid, Maudie Brick, lived at the Grange. The cook, Mrs. Barleyman, and her son, John, who did the gardening and odd jobs, lived in a cottage nearby. Kate and Eliza, the young maid-servants, walked to the house from their father's farm.

It would be nice to have the house full of visitors. Despite Mrs. Warren's words, Cressida thought there was nothing wrong with girls who had just come out. Of course, for some it was a difficult time, especially if they were given to fancies. . . .

She recalled herself at sixteen. She had still been a child, with her yellow hair down her back. Next year, she would put it up, and magically be a young woman. The Loops, despite the fact Mrs. Loop's family moved in high circles, were not the sort of people who took their daughter to London, or even to Bath, for a Season, but her aunt Wells had promised to take Cressida to the Assemblies. As the eldest child of an impoverished clergyman, Cressida had thought life could hold no greater joy, until she met the Marquess of Chelmly.

He had been visiting his aunt Susan, Lady William Ashby, who thought the fact that her husband provided Mr. Loop, who stuttered to such a degree that he often could not preach a coherent sermon, with his living gave her the right to summon Mrs. Loop or her daughter as unpaid companion whenever she wished. Cressida had known the marquess was in the house for some days before they met. She had arranged the flowers for the dinner that had welcomed him, his parents, the Duke and Duchess of Tyne, and the dozen other guests. Servants' gossip, to which Cressida was privy, said that his family hoped the country would make him more at ease, and romantically inclined. Although he was only two and twenty, his father the duke wanted a secured succession.

Cressida had not seen him or any of the visitors. She did not have any expectations of seeing them. She crept around the house taking care to avoid meeting people, since Lady William was capable of scolding her and making unkind remarks to her mother if she thought Cressida was putting herself forward.

Cressida was writing invitations in the back parlour when she first met Chelmly. When the door opened, she jumped to her feet in case it was Lady William, even though it was more likely her ladyship's footman coming with another list of names.

She did not expect to see a young man step inside, shut the door quietly, then put his ear to it.

Perceiving he thought he was alone, Cressida awkwardly said, "Good afternoon, sir." The "good afternoon" came out almost as a whisper: the "sir" as a squeaky shout.

"Shush!" the young man cautioned. Then he looked up and said, "I beg your pardon. I thought you were one of my cousins."

"I am Cressy Loop, sir. The vicar's daughter."

"How do you do, Miss Loop. I'm Chelmly . . ."

"I beg your pardon." Cressida swallowed hard, then added, ". . . my lord." It was the correct form of address for Lord William: she believed it was also correct for a marquess. "I shall be gone directly." Lady William believed in the lower orders keeping in their place. If she objected to Cressida playing with her children, doubtless conversing with her nephew was also forbidden.

"It is I who should beg your pardon. I did not mean to intrude. You seem very busy."

"I am writing invitations, my lord." Lady William had impressed upon her the fact it sounded common to speak in incomplete sentences. "These are for Lady William, my lord. Most are for the ball she gives at the end of your parents'—I mean, their graces' visit. The rest are for dinners the fortnight before. Lady William likes everything done in advance."

"You did all this today?"

"Yes, my lord."

"Well done. With your permission then, I shall retire to the garden. I overheard plans for a sketching party driving to the lake, with your humble servant meant to judge the young ladies' efforts. I prefer to decline the honour."

To Cressida's amazement, he flung open the window and agilely jumped through. Cressida stepped to the window and fastened it after him. Lady William did not like open windows. When a footman put his head around the door a few moments later, Cressida was assiduously bent over her task. She heard doors open and shut along the corridor, then the sound of carriages being brought around to the front of the house. She wondered if the marquess had made his escape, and if she would ever know.

She was vastly surprised when a footman brought her a tray with a nuncheon of pigeon pie and cream cakes. Lady William had never before shown any such consideration. She was even more surprised when Chelmly came to share it with her. He asked about the ladies carved into the mantelpiece, and Cressida explained that they were likenesses of virtuous women from the Old Testament. Soon they were talking quite easily.

When they had finished eating and the footman had cleared away the plates and withdrawn, leaving the door wide open, Chelmly surprised her yet again by taking up a quill and asking her to show him how far she had got with the list.

"My lord! It isn't proper ... Lady William—"

"—need never know. I like doing this sort of thing. At least, I think I shall. I've always found that having a list to follow makes life much easier."

Cressida was not sure when she'd fallen in love with Chelmly. For the three months of his parents' visit she gazed at him in church, treasured the memory of that afternoon in the back parlour, and the few other words they'd exchanged since. She spent hours sitting hidden in the elm tree in front of the vicarage, hoping for a glimpse of him passing along the lane. Her heart had been broken when he had called upon the Loops to take his leave—a courtesy typical of him—and she'd been out. She was certain that she meant nothing to him.

Christmas brought remembrances from him to the whole family: books useful at school for the boys, a paisley shawl for Mrs. Loop, and an inkwell for Mr. Loop. Cressida recalled mentioning that her father could only fill his half full, for the glass had cracked, and Mr. Loop had felt it too luxurious to replace it. And for her, he had sent a beautifully illustrated book of country flowers.

She had kept the book until she had married. At the time it had seemed wrong to keep any remembrance of a long-ago and half-forgotten love, and so she had given it to her goddaughter. So foolish of her to remember now . . .

As Cressida opened the gate in front of Hugh's Grange, she firmly turned her thoughts to the visitors who were coming tomorrow, and put the marquess out of her mind.

If Fancy Be
the Food of Love . . .

THE HONOURABLE CHARTERIS ASHBY sauntered along
Oakham High Street feeling both noble and dis-
gruntled. On the one hand, here he was immediate
on his arrival in the area, hurrying to attend to his
uncle's dying wish. On the other hand, it was a glorious day for January, the hunt was out, and the
scent must be running breast high.

He consoled himself with the fact they seemed
in for a spell of mild winter weather ideal for the
hounds and it should only take one visit to assure
himself that Aunt Araminta's daughter wanted for
nothing.

Chart Ashby, eldest son of the younger son of a
duke, was a pink of the *ton*, a renowned huntsman
and the despair of matchmaking mamas. Even now
he couldn't resist throwing a winning smile at a
charming young miss tripping along beside her parent. The girl coloured in confusion.

She was doubtless destined to dream of the dashing
young man with the dark wavy hair and long-lashed
grey eyes, but Chart allowed her to slip from his mind
as easily as she had entered it.

Sheer bad luck had him wasting a fine day's
hunting. First he'd arrived at Tyne Towers on
Christmas Eve to be greeted with the news that the
ailing duke was finally at death's door. It had
seemed necessary to pay a farewell visit to Uncle
Arthur, but he had felt safe in the knowledge that

the duke had not spoken in over twelve hours and he need only sit by the bed for a few minutes looking solemn.

Once in the depressing bedchamber, however, Chart had found the silence distasteful, and had felt compelled to start a one-sided conversation. He was known for his easy address. He'd survived dinners beside deaf bishops, and evenings with tongue-tied debutantes, so talking to a dying man was no great challenge.

He had started with the weather and local affairs, then passed on to juicy on-dits and his plans for the hunting season—a stay with Terance Cornwallis, who had the great good fortune to have a comfortable little place in Rutland, convenient for the Quorn, Belvoir, and Cottesmore.

And the old gentleman had revived.

"Rutland? Rutland, you say?" the duke muttered in a weak, breathless voice. "That's . . . Minta's gel is. Ju . . . Julia?"

The doctor had hastened forward. "Nothing to be concerned about now, your grace," he murmured. "Just rest."

"Rest! Old fool. I'll soon have all the rest I need. Give me a drink." With a sigh, the doctor poured something into a glass and assisted the duke to drink it.

The duke coughed a little, then looked at Chart again. "What was I saying?" The old man squinted at Chart in the dim light, and so he leaned a little closer.

"That's better. You're not a bad 'un, Charteris. Better than your father. William's a nasty streak to him. He'd have cut Minta off without a shilling. I was duke, though. I told him, 'I'm duke and I'll do as I please.' "

The duke's eyes fell closed, and he wheezed. Chart was thinking of slipping away when his un-

cle opened his eyes again and whispered, "Daugh-
ter . . . Judith . . . Minta's dead now. Died with that
Rathbone on the way to Boston. Cheer the end of
British rule. Daughter."

He lapsed into silence again, staring into shadows
and perhaps seeing them all when younger—himself;
his younger brother William, who had always re-
sented not being the heir to the dukedom; and strong-
willed Araminta.

She'd eloped at the age of thirty when Chart had
been scarcely breeched. He had only the vaguest
recollection of her, but that was how she was always described. Strong-willed. She'd have to be to
run off with Jeremy Rathbone, supporter of the
French and American revolutions, author of the in-
famous pamphlets *In Praise of Revolution* and *The
Great Call for Equality on English Soil.*

Lord, thought Chart with a grin, he'd have liked
to have seen his father's face when he heard he was
brother-in-law to Rebel Rathbone.

"Always liked Minta," rasped the duke. "Should
have done something about the gel." His breath
wheezed in and out a few times. "Look her up,
m'boy. Lives in Oakham. Look her up. See she's
right and tight. Minta's gel . . . Always liked
Minta . . ." With that he drifted to sleep again,
and this time it lasted.

Chart had been glad to escape and had thought
little of the duke's ramblings. But when he rose on
Christmas morning it was to the news that his uncle was dead and those had been his last words. The
request had assumed the nature of a sacred, deathbed mission.

One that was costing him a fine day with the
hounds.

At least this street was reassuring. The terraced
houses were solidly prosperous, with fresh paint

and shining brass speaking clearly of comfortable
circumstances.

Chart came to a stop before Newington House,
three stories of warm brick. The windows gleamed,
the paintwork was pristine, and the brass knob and
knocker shone in the sun.

His mission was as good as completed.

He ran lightly up the steps, rapped on the door
with the silver head of his riding crop, and set up
a whistle as he waited.

The door was opened by a middle-aged maid who
was the picture of responsible servanthood. Just the
ticket, thought Chart, seeing yet more evidence of
comfortable respectability. He handed over his card
with his most charming smile.

"Charteris Ashby to see Miss Juno Rathbone if
she is available." At the very dubious look on the
woman's face he added, "You might add that we
are by way of being related. Cousins, in fact."

At this he was admitted and led somewhat grudg-
ingly to a small reception room. "I will enquire,
sir," the maid said, and left.

Chart looked around and was confirmed in his
expectations. The furnishings were all high quality
and eminently dull. After all, his cousin Juno was
the offspring of Aunt Araminta and her radical revolutionary husband. After their death the girl had
been raised by Rathbone's sister, Clarabel, an ar-
dent follower of Mary Wollstonecraft, author of *Re-
flections on the Revolution in France, A Vindication
of the Rights of Men*, and *A Vindication of the
Rights of Woman*.

Chart was sure his cousin found this dull, stolid
room just to her taste.

Juno, he mused.

Junoesque.

Juno Rathbone was doubtless a strapping young
lady with a strong will and very blue stockings.

"Mr. Ashby?" It was a soft, melodious voice.

Chart turned to face the door and a petite lady, almost a girl, with delicate features and ash-blond hair. She came forward and extended a hand.

"Juno?" he blurted out in amazement, and then got a grip on himself. "Do I have the pleasure of meeting my cousin, Juno?"

"If you are indeed my cousin, sir," she said with distant coolness. "As Mama's family cast her off, we have never taken heed of her family tree."

She took a seat and waved him towards another. Chart sat, revising his opinions. This was no stern revolutionary. She was young. She was fragile. She could almost be called pretty. She was appallingly dressed in some grey thing, and it looked as if someone had hacked her hair around her shoulders with a blunt knife.

"Will you take tea, sir?" she asked. At his assent she rang a small bell and gave the order to the hovering maid. She then sat in silence, small pale hands in her lap, and waited for him to make the next move.

Shy, thought Chart indulgently, relaxing and crossing one leg over the other. *Poor little thing. I wonder where militant Clarabel is.* "I'm the eldest son of your mother's brother," he explained kindly. "Not the duke. The younger brother, William."

"Oh," she said with supreme disinterest. "Well, I don't suppose you have any reason to lie about such a thing." She looked at him in a disconcertingly direct way and added, "I do not intend to be impolite, Mr. Ashby, but is there a purpose to your visit? We have done very well without contact with your family for a good many years."

Chart blinked. It occurred to him that little Miss Rathbone seemed no more aware of him than she would be of the visiting vicar. He was not a man used to being ignored by young ladies.

He leant forward and smiled more warmly. "But these family quarrels shouldn't be allowed to go on from generation to generation, Cousin Juno. In fact, I am here as a result of the deathbed wish of my uncle, the duke." He let his voice drop to an intimate tone. "He asked me to make sure that you were comfortably situated."

A touch of colour did invade her cheeks—and very becoming it was, too—but instead of looking down in confusion, Juno Rathbone's only reaction was to move back slightly. Her gaze never wavered from his. "Then your mission is over, Mr. Ashby," she said flatly. "I am perfectly comfortable."

At that moment the tea tray was carried in, and she turned her attention to it.

Juno was grateful for the distraction. Perfectly comfortable. What a bouncer. Her heart rate was quite alarmingly fast, and she was aware of the man across the low table as if he were a shining beacon on a dark night.

Cousin Charteris. She had never given thought to the younger members of her mama's family. From the little Minta had said, her brothers Arthur and William were typical examples of the male aristocracy—arrogant, repressive, and dictatorial.

Juno slipped a surreptitious glance at the very large, amazingly handsome man who had invaded her quiet world. Arrogant would doubtless fit. And, she told herself firmly, handsome is as handsome does.

She passed him the tea, pleased to see her hand was steady. "Am I to gather the duke is dead, then?" she asked.

"Well," he said with a smile. "The duke is dead, long live the duke and all that. My cousin James, the former Marquess of Chelmly, is the duke. Our uncle Arthur is no more."

"And this is a recent event?"

"Christmas Day."

"You have my condolences," Juno said, struggling to maintain a calm demeanour. What she wanted above all was for him to leave, to take away the disturbance he brought. It was essential, however, that he leave satisfied that all was well. She had no intention of brooking interference in her life by male relatives who were strangers to her.

"So," he said as he put down his cup. "Will I have the opportunity to meet your aunt?"

Juno looked up, startled. She had thought that at the root of this visit. She sought for an evasion, but found none. "My aunt Clarabel died last spring, Mr. Ashby."

"Did she?" he remarked, and added, "Then I offer you my condolences. Who lives with you now?"

Juno could feel herself tensing. "I have an excellent staff."

He sat up straighter. "Come now. You're what? Seventeen? You can't possibly live all alone here."

Juno found her hands tight on one another and relaxed them. "I have three maids and a housekeeper, and I am eighteen, Mr. Ashby."

He rose abruptly and looked at her with a slight frown. "We'd be off to a better start if you'd call me Cousin Chart," he said. "It simply will not do, you know. I don't know how matters came to be left like this."

Juno too rose, wishing not for the first time in her life that she had eight or nine more inches. "It will do perfectly," she retorted with all the dignity she could command. "Matters were left this way intentionally. My uncle Augustus is my guardian, and he has no qualms about my situation. Let it be perfectly clear, Mr. Ashby, that my life is no concern of yours!"

"Of course it is," he said sharply. "You're my cousin. What will people say?"

"If by 'people' you mean Society, the *ton*, I don't care *that*!" Juno punctuated this with a resounding snap of the fingers—a skill of which she was very proud.

Colour touched his cheeks. "Well, as one of your male relatives, I can't just snap my fingers, my girl. We'll have to decide what's best to do—"

"No, you will not!" Juno stated, and when he paid no attention she picked up a Minton plate and smashed it against the edge of the table. At last she saw him look fully at her.

"What in the—"

"You will not," she continued forcefully, "because, one, I deny your right to rule over me simply because you are male and I am female. And, two, because, thank God, I am no blood relative of yours, sir!"

"I beg your pardon?"

Juno became suddenly aware of the anger in him. Her heart instinctively began to race, and the temptation to hide was frighteningly strong. Her conviction in equality was unshaken, but she had never had to shout it at a large and hostile man before. His outrage, she told herself, was proof of the pudding.

She swallowed and kept her chin up. "You have been misinformed, Mr. Ashby. Your aunt was my mother in the true sense of the word, but she did not bear me. My father was a widower, and I was six months of age at the time of the marriage." She stalked over to the open door and stood beside it. "I'm sure I should thank you for your concern, but I cannot bring myself to do so. Good day."

He picked up his curly-brimmed beaver, his leather gloves, and his crop and walked towards her. He stood there for a moment looking down at her—far too large, far too male. . . . There was a slight frown on his handsome face, not of anger but rather of puzzlement. Juno could feel a tremble in her legs. She had no idea what he might do.

In the end, all he said was, "Good day, Miss Rathbone." And then he left.

Juno stood for some time after his departure, because she seemed unable to mobilise her body in any meaningful way. She was still upset from the brief battle, but that wasn't the main problem. Something much more strange was tilting the world and making it spin. When he had stood before her it was as if waves of something, something warm and wicked, were washing over her and turning her giddy.

Charteris Ashby was the first man she had ever encountered who made comprehensible Mary Wollstonecraft's warnings against attractive men.

Juno moved at last and went to her library to take down her well-worn copy of *The Vindication of the Rights of Woman*. She easily found the place.

"Men of wit and fancy are often rakes; and fancy is the food of love. Such men will inspire passion. Half the sex in its present infantine state would pine for a Lovelace, a man so witty, so graceful and so valiant. . . ."

With a sign, Juno knew she was in danger of pining. She skipped a few lines.

"Women want a lover and protector; and behold him kneeling before them—bravery prostrate to beauty!" The mere thought of Chart Ashby kneeling before her made Juno dizzy.

She had always been troubled by that particular passage in the book and always read it with a guilty trace of longing. Now she understood her feelings a great deal better.

She thrust the book back firmly into its place on the shelf. Thank heavens she had sent the man to the rightabout and would see him no more.

* * *

Chart Ashby made his way back to the inn where he'd stabled his horse, swinging his cane and reviewing the extraordinary encounter. Who'd ever heard the like? Still, she had spirit, for all she was a tiny thing. Juno! It reminded him of a hound he'd named Hercules, only to have the beast turn out to be a runt.

Not that Juno Rathbone was a runt. Ariel would suit her. There was an ethereal quality to her—until she started smashing china, snapping her fingers, and spouting all that nonsense.

He laughed out loud briefly. She certainly appeared able to take care of herself. Since she was content with her lot and apparently no relative of his, he was a free man.

That evening, when Chart had to endure Terance Cornwallis's rapturous retelling of the day's chase, he consoled himself with the thought that it was a foretaste of many wonderful runs to come. Eventually Corny, having consumed what appeared to be a whole hind of beef and downed two bottles of claret, thought to ask, "Did you settle the cousin, then?"

Unsettled, more likely, thought Chart with a grin. "Well enough," he replied. "She's not in need, and in fact it turns out she's not my cousin. She's my aunt's stepdaughter."

"Oh. That's all right, then." Corny raised his glass. "To foxes and fine weather!"

Chart heartily echoed the toast and drained his glass.

Two nights later, Corny looked across the table soberly—in the sober manner of a man who's drunk large amounts of claret, port, and brandy—and said, "Something up, Chart?"

"What do you mean?" asked Chart, who had also consumed a great deal of wine.

"Have to say this, old friend. Style's a bit wonky. Haven't seen you up with the leaders. Dammit, you almost came off at that ditch today, and my grandmother could jump it." After a moment's consideration he added, "Without a horse."

"Surrey was startled," Chart protested. After a moment he admitted, "I keep thinking about ... about Miss Rathbone."

Corny blinked. "But you said. Not your cousin. Happy enough there with her aunt and her books."

"That's the thing, Corny. No aunt."

"No aunt?"

"Died last year."

Corny raised his glass. "To the aunt!"

Chart frowned. "Don't think you're supposed to toast the deceased, old boy."

"No ... ? Probably right. But what's the problem? Someone else instead of aunt. All settled."

"No one else instead of aunt."

"All alone?"

" 'Three maids and a housekeeper,' " Chart quoted, remembering delicate features, flushed cheeks, and eyes sparkling with anger.

Corny shook his head. "Won't do, old boy."

Chart slammed down his glass. "*I* know it won't do. *You* know it won't do. She thinks it's right and tight."

"Dicked in the nob?" Corny suggested.

"No, she's not dicked in the nob," Chart snapped. "She's a damned proponent of women's rights!"

"Rights to what?" asked Corny blankly.

"God knows. The only right that bothers me is the right to live by herself with just servants for company."

Corny kindly filled his friend's glass. "Not your problem, old boy. Leave well enough alone."

Chart stared at the wine moodily. "But is it well? I think she's lonely."

Corny shook his head. "Lots of friends. There's dull bluestockings all over the place these days."

"No way for an eighteen-year-old girl to live."

"Chart, old boy. Put your mind to your horses."

"Can't. Not until I settle poor little Juno."

Terance looked at his friend with deep concern. "Going to ruin the hunting season," he warned, then came up with a suggestion. "Find her a companion."

Chart shook his head. "She wouldn't take one. Doesn't think she needs one. Dammit, if I was eighteen and alone in the world, *I'd* have a bear leader."

The candles burned low and began to gutter as the two men considered the matter through an alcoholic haze.

Chart suddenly sat upright. "Make it a good deed," he declared. "Find someone who needs a home!"

Corny nodded. "That's the ticket. Who?"

Chart slumped down again. "Damned if I know. Thought the world was full of indigent females."

He thought Corny had sunk into a stupor, but he must have been thinking, for he suddenly stirred and said, "Cousin Cressida."

"Juno," Chart corrected.

"No. *My* cousin. Cressida Trent."

"Indigent?"

"Course not," said Corny with a frown. "What sort of loose fish do you think I am to leave my cousin indigent?"

"Sorry," Chart apologised. "But then, what good is she?"

"Widow. Lives quietly near Lincoln with her young son. Bound to be cast down. Get Miss Rathbone to go and succour her."

"That's the maddest idea I ever heard!"

"Not. They'll get on like nobody's business. Daughter of a parson, widow of a canon. Very book-

ish and serious, Cressida is. Nice old thing, though.
A knowing one, all right."

"How old?"

"Oh, well over thirty."

Chart thought of poor little Juno stuck in that
dull house with no friends. "I'll do it," he said.

A few days later Juno was in the kitchen, a favourite haunt these days. She sat at the deal table, chin
on her hands, a slim volume open in front of her
but ignored.

"There's no reason," she said, "why I shouldn't
travel. I could go to Italy."

Mrs. Davies, the cook, didn't look up from the
cake she was beating. "If you say so, Miss Juno."

Juno accurately translated this to be disap-
proval. She had long had the habit of bringing her
thoughts to Mrs. Davies for reaction. Aunt Clarabel
had not liked it, saying the woman did not have an
improved mind.

Since her aunt's death, Juno spent more and more
time in the kitchen; the only other occupations she
had were her Latin, mathematics, and pistol practise. Now, with the troubling thoughts stirred by
Chart Ashby, she was trying to work round to the
subject of men. Mrs. Davies, after all, had been
married twice and had two grown sons.

"But what am I to do?" she asked.

"What do you want to do, miss?" responded the
cook without obvious interest.

"Something." Juno sighed. "I can't stay here for
the rest of my life."

"Well, there's nothing stopping you," said Mrs.
Davies. It was one of her offerings that Juno found
both irritating and stimulating. Stopping her from
going, or from staying? Talking to Mrs. Davies was
rather like talking to the Delphic Oracle, and any

attempt to demand precision inevitably led to busy silence.

Juno tried a bold tack. "Do you think I should marry, Mrs. Davies?"

The cook looked up. "A young lady with a comfortable independence shouldn't marry unless she wants to."

"But should I want to?"

Mrs. Davies reached for a handful of sultanas and dropped them into her batter. "Not until you meet him."

"Who?"

"Bellarion."

Juno looked in puzzlement at the book before her. It was *Castle Blood*, by Mrs. Delamare. The heroine, torn from her loving family by the evil Count Grosmark, was praying her true love, the dashing Marcus Bellarion, would arrive in time to save her from a fate worse than death. Bellarion was of course the true Count Grosmark, having been defrauded of his inheritance by his uncle. Even though the novel was dangerously seductive, she hardly thought the hero would sweep into her own life and solve all her problems.

In truth, he was part of her problem.

Novel reading had begun so innocently. After all, Mary Wollstonecraft had written that "the best method that can be adopted to correct a fondness for novels is to ridicule them." When Juno had discovered Mrs. Davies victim of a taste for such weakening literature, she had felt obliged to read them and put an end to the rot.

Each week Mrs. Davies would get a new one from the circulating library and each week Juno would read it and discuss it with her—or at least give the cook the benefit of her comments. As Mrs. Davies had little time for reading, Juno began to read to her as she worked.

It was very strange, but soon the critical commentary became excited speculation as to the likely development of the story. The "unnatural and meretricious scenes" and appeal to sensation so abhorrent to Mary Wollstonecraft were not so to Juno. They harmonised with the yearnings of her young heart. Knowing she was as foolish as an opium eater, Juno delighted in her secret vice even as she concealed it from her aunt.

Now there was no one to disapprove, and yet she was still guiltily aware that her taste for fiction was a vice and she was an unrepentant sinner.

"I can't marry Bellarion," Juno pointed out. "He's only a character in a book."

Mrs. Davies began to spoon her mixture into tins. "Maybe. Maybe not."

Before Juno could pursue this, Elly came bursting into the kitchen. "He's back!" she gasped.

Juno leapt to her feet, in no doubt as to who "he" was. "Chart Ashby?"

Sensible, middle-aged Elly laid a hand on her ample, heaving bosom. "Handsome enough to die for!" she declared.

"Say I'm not home," Juno commanded.

"Oh, never do that, Miss Juno," Elly protested. "He's doubtless come a terrible long way."

"Happen she's scared of him, Elly," murmured Mrs. Davies.

Juno looked at the woman and stiffened. "I am not. I've sent him to the rightabout once, and I can do so again. I suppose we had better offer him tea, Elly."

As she swept to the door, Juno could swear she heard Mrs. Davies mutter "Bellarion." She did hear her say, "Not the Minton this time, Elly."

Juno sniffed. There would surely be no call for china-smashing again. Mr. Ashby must have realised she was not a woman to discount.

She paused before a mirror in the hall and considered her appearance, telling herself it was to assure herself there was no smut on her nose.

There was absolutely nothing wrong with her practical round gown of blue-grey bombazine or the knitted grey shawl wrapped around her shoulders for warmth. How silly it would be to be flimsily dressed in January.

However, she couldn't even try to convince herself that her hair was acceptable. Aunt Clarabel and she had always trimmed each other's hair, keeping it short for practicality's sake. Since her aunt's death Mrs. Davies had reluctantly taken over the task, always telling Juno she should call in a coiffeuse to do it properly. Juno, however, was all too aware of her weaknesses and knew that would be the first step towards a debilitating obsession with appearance. She would just have to hope that the cook grew more skilful as time went by.

She ran her fingers through her pale curls in an attempt to make some of the more wayward tufts stay down. It was useless, and so she ignored it and went resolutely forward.

When she walked into the front parlour her breath caught in her throat. He was even more handsome than she remembered. Moreover, she realised, he was the image she had carried in her mind as she read *Castle of Blood*.

He was Bellarion.

"Miss Rathbone."

"Mr. Ashby." Could he hear the betraying tremor in her voice? Juno knew she should offer her hand, but she took a seat and indicated one for him.

"Thought I'd drop by again," he said, seeming a little uneasy. "After all, we must be stepcousins or something."

"I suppose we must."

There was a silence broken only by the crackle

of the coal fire and the ticking of the massive gilt mantel clock.

"Fact is," he said at last, "wanted to apologise. Had no idea, of course, that you weren't my full cousin."

Juno decided not to point out to him that she would have objected to his interference even if they had been blood relatives. "I'm sure your intentions were of the best, Mr. Ashby."

"Look here," he said with that devastating smile that tugged up the right side of his mouth and crinkled his fine eyes. "Can't you bring yourself to call me Cousin Chart?"

"Very well," said Juno with a little sigh. "Cousin Chart."

She was rewarded by another smile. "Very cosy house you have here, Cousin Juno," he said cheerily. "Comfortable."

"Very comfortable."

"Must be a bit lonely for you, though, since your aunt died. But you'll have a great many friends here in Oakham. School friends and such."

Juno was suspicious, but she also sensed a genuine concern in him that weakened her. "I was educated by my aunt," she admitted.

"Oh. Still, you must know lots of people here."

"Yes, I suppose I do," Juno replied. The trouble was, she thought, that they were all of her aunt's generation. Aunt Clarabel had been a lively companion, and Juno had never felt the lack of friends her own age until her aunt's death.

The tea tray came. Juno made the tea and poured it into the plain cups, which were clearly an unnecessary precaution. She was a little disappointed. It had been strangely stimulating to cross swords with him the last time.

"Fact is," said Chart Ashby nonchalantly as he

accepted his cup, "I was wondering if you'd be able to tear yourself away for a week or two. Or longer."

Juno looked up in astonishment. "To go where?"

"Lincoln," he said, which didn't lessen her bewilderment.

He explained. "My friend Terance Cornwallis has a cousin. Widow. A Mrs. Trent. Lives in a village near Lincoln. Thing is, he's beginning to think she's a bit low. Keeping him awake at nights, off his feed. Just last night we were saying that his cousin Cressida needs a visitor. Someone to cheer her up, encourage her to get out a bit. Thing is, we don't know anyone suitable, and then I thought of you. Bit of an imposition, but I just had this feeling you're a woman who would like to help another woman."

"Of course," said Juno blankly. "But would this lady welcome the intrusion of a stranger?"

"Well, now," Chart said, "she'd probably welcome anyone. But I had it in mind, if you'll permit it, to tell her *you* were feeling a bit low. Make it easier for her to accept help, don't you know."

A new place. New people. A noble purpose. The strange project was suddenly immensely appealing. Juno took an impulsive decision. "If this poor lady agrees, Cousin Chart, I would be happy to do my best to help her."

His smile was positively dazzling. "What a wonderfully kind nature you have, Cousin. On Corny's behalf, I thank you. I'll set it all up in no time."

Juno was enraptured by the excitement of impending change, the knowledge of noble purpose, and the glory of Chart Ashby's approval.

Which is how, one week later, she came to be rolling through the frosty countryside towards the village of Valentine Parva, near Lincoln.

A few days later, Mrs. Davies unfolded a letter from her employer and read it to Elly.

Dear Mrs. Davies,

My journey was without untoward event, and I am now at Hugh's Grange in the village of Valentine Parva. Everyone here is most kind and welcoming, but matters are not quite as I expected.

Mrs. Trent is not alone, for she already has two young ladies staying here, a Miss Aquila and a Miss Philomena Ware, whose father is recently deceased. They are sisters and very fashionable, though Philo, as she prefers to be called, is of an easy nature. Aquila I find rather haughty and she seems to have formed the intention to make me fashionable, which, as you know, would be against my principles.

Moreover, another young lady is expected daily. I did demur about extending my visit in these circumstances, but Mrs. Trent, or Cressida as she has directed me to call her, insists nothing delights her more than a houseful of young people. In truth, she herself is not as I expected, for she does not appear very old or cast down. She has a young son called Toby, who is a pleasing child.

I read most of *The Spectre of Marsh Hall* during the journey and found it lived up to all our expectations. Imagine my delight when I found Hugh's Grange to be the very image of the Hall, except for having only one tower, not four. It is covered with ivy just as the Hall is, and has a heavy oaken door that creaks no matter how much oil is applied. Imagine my further delight to have been offered the room at the top of the tower. Of course, I took it: it is just like the one in which Seraphina was incarcerated!

I confess this has at times made the story a little too believable and I have taken to reading in the sitting room, using my old disguise—Lord Montboddo's *Of the Origin and Progress of Lan-*

guage. I know you disapprove of this deception and you are doubtless correct, but my Secret Vice is such a betrayal of all Aunt Clarabel's teaching that I feel compelled to maintain the deception.

I have finished *The Spectre* and will send it to you as soon as I have the opportunity. It is fortunate that the other guests also enjoy novels and there are any number lying around . . .

Mrs. Davies finished reading the letter aloud and put it down. "Foolishness," she said.

"But you like those books, Gertrude."

"That's not what I mean," said the cook, frowning thoughtfully. "Fetch me a piece of the writing paper, Elly."

"What, the good stuff!"

"Yes, the good stuff. I'm not going to shame Miss Juno by sending a letter on rough, am I?"

And so, the next day, Juno unfolded a sheet of her own embossed paper to read a letter from Mrs. Davies. It contained a brief, creatively spelled account of the running of the house and a rambling story of how Mrs. Davies had drowned her sorrow over the death of her first husband in endless charitable works. It ended with "That Miss Aquila doubtless would benefit from occupation to take her mind off her grief, but principles are principles."

Juno had not quite considered matters in this light. Balancing principles with charity was obviously a great deal more complex than she had thought. But as the Bible said, of all the virtues "the greatest is charity." Therefore, the next time Aquila said, "My dear Juno, please let me do something about your hair," Juno swallowed and said, "Very well."

After a shocked moment, the enterprise became a cause for excitement to all the young ladies, the number of which now included Katherine Tilbury.

In fact, it was Katherine who had been the final straw for Juno. She was a porcelain beauty with exquisite clothes. The Gray sisters, being in half-mourning, had not made Juno feel too like a crow, but next to Katherine she did and found she disliked it intensely.

Juno was given no time to change her mind. Aquila quickly found sharp scissors and began her work.

"Don't cut it too short, Aquila!" Juno protested as the scissors scrunched close to her scalp.

"You have always said you like it short for practicality," Aquila pointed out. "I am merely going to make it *stylishly* short."

Juno winced with each cut. There seemed to be a great deal of hair falling to the floor. At last Aquila said, "There!" and Juno was hurried off to the big cheval mirror in Katherine's room.

"Good heavens!" she whispered.

She heard Philo calling, "Cousin Cressida! Do come and see Juno. It's a transformation!"

It was indeed. Curling tendrils framed her face, which seemed suddenly to have developed more contours. Her eyes looked larger and her chin narrower. She turned her head and saw that the tendrils were longer about the nape of her neck. From the neck up at least, she looked like a heroine ready for a dashing hero.

She wanted to throw her arms around Aquila and thank her, but that would be to betray her upbringing. She really didn't know how to react.

"It . . . it should be practical, I think," she said at last. "Thank you, Aquila."

It wasn't clear whether Aquila found this thanks lukewarm, for at that moment Cressida came in and was as admiring of everyone's efforts as anyone could wish.

She seemed to understand Juno's feelings too, for

she said in her kind way, "You will find it much easier to take care of now, Juno, for it will always look tidy. Really, Aquila, you have a talent. If you are ever in need of the means of survival, you will have the whole *ton* at your door."

"Then let me practise my talent further," said Aquila, a glint in her eye. "Next, Juno, your clothes."

Juno was about to protest when she remembered Mrs. Davies's advice. She really wouldn't want Aquila's grief to overwhelm her. She soon, therefore, found herself the borrower of two of Philo's gowns—Philo being the only one of a size with Juno and professing to be happy enough to give the garments up as they did not suit her darker colouring.

And so Juno tried on the dark lilac wool with a cream satin frill at the collar, and a grey cloth gown with a pinkish stripe.

"I think we should trim that up with pink ribbons," said Aquila, assessing her with an appropriately eagle eye. "It will suit you wonderfully. You are almost out of mourning, after all."

"I have never been in mourning," said Juno. "My aunt did not approve of ostentatious grief."

Aquila stared in disbelief. "Are you saying you were wearing those dull clothes from *choice*?"

"They are practical," Juno defended.

"Pink is no less practical than grey," retorted Aquila.

"Pink ribbon is," Juno pointed out, "if you have to iron it."

Philo laughed. "She has you there, Aquila. Kate is always muttering about the difficulty of caring for fancy clothes."

"As long as you are here," said Aquila, "Kate will care for your clothes, and that dress cries out for pink ribbons."

And so Juno, out of the kindness of her heart,

found herself with a very becoming hairstyle and two charming gowns. It seemed that sometimes virtue need not be its own reward. When the grey dress was trimmed with pink ribbons, Juno stole a further opportunity to study herself in the mirror. Honesty compelled her to admit that she appeared almost pretty. She almost looked like the sort of young lady an evil villain would want to spirit away to a bleak castle; the sort of young lady a dashing young aristocrat would risk body and soul to rescue and make his own. . . .

All unbidden, the image of Chart Ashby sprang into mind. What would he think to see her so transformed? Very little, she told herself firmly. She was nothing to him.

She wrote to tell Mrs. Davies of her charitable endeavours and received yet another reply that seemed mainly to do with Elly's concerns about her sick sister's welfare and that ended, "I suppose that Mr. Cornwallis might be worried about his cousin. I wonder if she writes. Of course you couldn't write to a strange gentleman, but you could write to your cousin, Mr. Ashby."

The thought of writing to Chart Ashby made Juno's heart pound, and it wasn't from fear. Perhaps she should have written when she first arrived at the Grange, but it had seemed so bold. Now, however, she could see it as a charitable duty.

Juno was writing this letter and had just described a visit to Lincoln when Aquila walked into the sitting room and demanded, "Who has taken the last volume of *Masqued Valentine*?"

Philo said no. Juno, after a guilty glance at *Of the Origin and Progress of Language*, muttered no.

Katherine said anxiously, "It was I who lent it to you, Aquila. I had already read it three times."

"I thought you had finished it, Aquila," Juno said.

"I had," said Aquila with a sigh. "But I wished to refer to the St. Valentine's Day customs mentioned there. I know *you* wouldn't have it, Juno. You only ever read that book, over and over again. I don't know how it can be so fascinating."

Before Juno was forced to reply, Katherine exclaimed, "Oh yes! It will soon be Valentine's. We should try some of those quaint ideas."

Philo looked up from the charts on which she recorded the progress of her canaries. "Eating eggshells filled with salt and writing in blood? Not in your style, Aquila."

Aquila subsided onto the faded chaise. "Country life is so tedious, Philo, I will try anything for amusement."

"Do people really do such things?" Juno asked. "Writing in blood?"

"According to *Masqued Valentine* they do," drawled Aquila. "The heroine, Heloise, writes her name in blood and puts it into a box along with the names of the other ladies present. But it isn't her true love who picks it, but Baron Jarlsberg. Of course, he has arranged it so." For a moment she had almost been animated, but she carefully smoothed such disturbance away and gave a slight yawn. "The most utter nonsense, of course, and pointless for us, deprived as we are of any male companionship."

"We could try the 'names on the water' one," broke in Katherine excitedly. She turned to Juno. "That is where Heloise finds the name of her true love, Arthur Montdragon. Each lady writes the names of the men she knows on pieces of paper and wraps them in clay. Then she throws the clay into a pot of water. Whichever name breaks free first and rises to the surface will be her true love. He will then appear within the month and they will be happy ever after. Oh, do let's try it!"

There was a hiatus as the young women eyed one another, then Aquila smothered another yawn and said, "Oh, why not? On Valentine's Eve, then. I will write the name of Prince Igor Pushkin," she announced with a smile. "I do know him, but if he rides up to the Grange within the month I'll climb on a broomstick and fly away!"

On Valentine's Eve, therefore, they all gathered for the ritual. After a great deal of work, even Cressida had been prevailed upon to join the "game."

Katherine had pointed out to the other young women that to exclude her might imply that there was no possibility of her ever finding another husband. Admittedly she was old, but there was still hope. Squire Brokelby was a widower, though goutish, and Mr. Ulverstone, a scholar living in Valentine Magna, had shown some interest at church the last few weeks. He could not be more than fifty, and his poor health doubtless meant he was on the lookout for a wife to care for him.

With this in mind, all four of the girls had badgered Cressida to take part. Now, however, she frowned at the wide copper bowl full of water and the four candles standing around it. "This smacks dangerously of superstition," she said.

"It's just fun," said Philo quickly. Juno had noticed that Philo did not seem quite her normal self this evening. Did she take this too seriously?

Juno didn't. For one thing, she hardly knew any men whose names to write. She had listened enviously to Aquila and Philo mulling over a huge list of acquaintances from three continents in an attempt to whittle them down to five, the number decided on. Juno had only the heroes of books to write, and she was embarrassed to admit to that.

"I think," she said as they all set to writing their

slips of paper, "we should agree now not to reveal the name that floats up. It will be more exciting."

"Will it?" asked Katherine doubtfully, but Philo quickly agreed and neither Aquila nor Cressida seemed to care.

Juno therefore felt safe writing the names Bellarion, Arthur, Cyrillus, Hector, and then, in a spurt of daring, Chart Ashby. She rolled them up tightly and coated them with the sticky brown clay.

When they were all done, they gathered round the copper bowl, which the candlelight gifted with mysterious fiery depths.

Aquila went first, and let her names languorously fall to sink to the bottom. Very quickly the clay softened away and three pieces of paper floated up. With surprising speed for Aquila, she snatched the first then gathered the rest and threw them to sizzle in the fire.

She looked at the name with no expression at all. "As I supposed." She sighed. "Nonsense. You're next, Cressida."

"I could hardly think of anyone to write," Cressida admitted as she tossed her offering in. Perhaps she had been more thorough with the clay, for it took a little while for one to break free. Eventually it did, however, and all alone a piece of paper came up, uncurling as it rose.

Before Cressida could grasp it and hide it in her hand, Juno at least had seen the name.

James.

Cressida had unusual colour in her cheeks. Juno wracked her brain for a James in the area and could think of none of Cressida's station in life. She surely could not have a passion for the elderly sexton.

Katherine went next, giggling a little. She seemed surprised but pleased by the name the water returned to her. Then it was Juno's turn. Her main preoccupation was that the water not play the

trick it had on Cressida and reveal all. Most of the
names would be possible, but if Bellarion was re-
vealed, the novel readers could hardly fail to realise her secret.

As soon as the paper began to rise, she grabbed
it, then held it tight without looking. "Your turn,
Philo."

Philo almost seemed reluctant. She held the
pieces of clay-wrapped paper above the water for a
few seconds before releasing them, then she
watched with such intensity that Juno could not
help but do so too.

Eventually, a piece of paper rose and was taken.
Philo read it, and a brightness came to her face.
After a moment she composed herself and said, "I
must just check on the canaries."

They all shared a look, but Aquila appeared the
most puzzled of all. Juno took the opportunity to
glance at her own, impossible name.

Chart Ashby.

That evening, Chart and Corny were sitting down
to a very tasty dinner at the White Hart in Lincoln,
looking forward to St. Valentine's Day. The reason
for their presence in Lincoln was the lack of good
hunting weather lately, along with Juno's dutiful
letter.

The previous evening, facing another day without a meet, Chart had suggested they trot off to
Lincoln to see the cousins.

"Cousins?"

"Juno and what's her name . . . Cressida. See how
they're doing. Tell you what," he added with a grin,
"know what tomorrow is?"

"Cottesmore meet," said Corny morosely. "Or
would be."

Chart shook his head. "Valentine's Day. And
there the cousins are in Valentine Parva. It's

tempting fate. My sisters make a big thing of it back home. Look," he said, leaning forward, "what if we go to Lincoln. Then at first light we nip into Little Valentine and leave something on the doorstep—flowers. That's what you're supposed to do. With a verse."

"A verse!" exclaimed Corny as if Chart had suggested high treason.

"It's easy. 'Violets are red . . .' That sort of thing. I've had lots of practise. Sisters, you know." He got a sheet of paper, thought for a moment, then wrote, reciting as he did so:

> *"Sweet Cressida so tall and fair,*
> *I love the colour of your hair.*
> *Your eyes are such a wondrous blue*
> *I'm forced to tell you I love you."*

Corny looked at him with stunned admiration. "Just like that! You're as good as that Byron fellow."

"Oh, not quite," said Chart modestly. "Now for Juno." Another moment's thought and he produced:

> *"Little Juno, mild and sweet,*
> *I worship at your tender feet.*
> *Smile at me just once today*
> *And I will your trusty lover stay."*

"Last line's a bit wonky," judged Corny.

"Depends how you say it," defended Chart.

Corny still looked doubtful. "I say, Chart. It's not like making an offer, is it? I mean to say, marrying cousins ain't that clever anyway, so I'd have to marry your blue-stocking and you'd end up with Cressida, who's a nice enough old thing but way past her prime."

"We're not supposed to sign them," Chart pointed out, "and no one takes valentines seriously. And she's not really my cousin."

He had, in fact, been surprisingly put out by the notion of Corny's having to marry Juno Rathbone. "Here," he said, and passed over Cressida's verse. "You copy this out. If anyone does guess, there'll be no problem if we send valentines to our cousins."

So here they were, valentine verses neatly written and hothouse roses in water in their room, ready for the next day's jape.

At Hugh's Grange, similar plans were underfoot. After the "names in water" Philo and Cressida had disappeared, but Aquila, Juno, and Katherine had discussed the event and decided that Cressida must have an admirer. It would surely encourage her if she were to receive a valentine offering from him the next day.

"If he were up to snuff," said Aquila, "he would have flowers on the doorstep with a verse."

Katherine sighed. "I wish someone would do that for me."

"Well," said Juno. "Why don't we leave flowers for her? I saw the name she got—"

"Don't tell us!" exclaimed Katherine. "It would break the spell. Anyway, valentines should be anonymous."

"Why?" Juno asked. This sort of delicious nonsense had not been part of her education.

"It's just the way it is. Philo was telling me all about it. But I think it's a wonderful idea to leave flowers. We'll have to get up early tomorrow and pick crocuses or snowdrops. There isn't much else."

"We could make paper flowers," said Aquila. "I know a way that produces very pretty ones."

This was seized on enthusiastically, and soon Katherine and Juno were following Aquila's guidance and making a colourful bouquet of poppies for

Cressida. When it was finished they composed a verse, and it was decided Katherine would creep down to put it on the doorstep at first light.

When the flower-making was over, Juno made an excuse and slipped out of the house. She found the place she wanted and uprooted several snowdrops with plenty of earth and returned to the house. She would pot them up. If Katherine wanted a valentine she would have one, and Aquila since she had been so kind, and Philo so she wouldn't feel left out. And she would have to make one for herself or it would be obvious who had done it, and that, apparently, would spoil it.

She tried to pretend that this was all Christian Charity again, but she knew she was finding it wickedly exciting and, despite all rationalization, the fact that the water had sent her Chart Ashby's name was making her heart sing. She remembered the way his mouth turned up on one side when he smiled in a certain way, the mischievous glint in those grey eyes, and the overpowering excitement she had felt when he had stood close to her that once.

When Arthur took Heloise in his arms and pressed his lips to hers, Juno could not help but think of Chart Ashby doing the same to her. It made her feel warm and soft; it made her yearn. It was all nonsense and dangerous and in direct opposition to all she had been raised to believe, but she was as helpless as if she had contracted galloping consumption.

As she returned dreamily to the house she encountered Philo, coming out the front door.

Philo started guiltily. "Where have you been, Juno?" she asked.

With her hands full of snowdrop bulbs, there wasn't much point in Juno prevaricating. She quickly explained her charitable work and found

Philo mildly enthusiastic. "Yes, Katherine would be thrilled. I don't know about Aquila. But you better not bring those into the house, you know."

Juno looked down at the snowdrops. "Why not?"

"Superstition. If anyone brings snowdrops inside before St. Valentine's Day, all the unmarried ladies in the house will remain that way for the year."

"Well," Juno said, "marriage is a trap most women would be best to avoid anyway."

"That may be your opinion," said Philo, "but I hardly think all of us would agree. I'll fetch some pots. We can leave them by the side of the house. They'll be safe enough, and then tomorrow you can just move them to the front step."

This was soon accomplished. Juno went up to her room and composed verses. As the house settled for the night, she heard Katherine creep down with Cressida's valentine. She got up ready for her own mission but heard more footsteps.

When everything was finally quiet she made her way downstairs, trying to avoid the creaking steps. She had to freeze when Cressida crossed the first-floor landing. She was still dressed, which was unusual. Perhaps Toby was restless.

Finally, however, Juno made it to the kitchen unobserved and slipped out the back door. She collected her pots and carried them round the house to the front. There she stopped in amazement.

In addition to Cressida's paper posy, there were half a dozen paper lilies, some scrolls of poetry decorated with more poppies, and some pots of crocuses. She started to laugh. Everyone in the house must have had the same idea. She added her collection.

The make-believe didn't bother her, as she had never thought to receive a true valentine. The kindness behind the pretence touched her. She had friends.

* * *

Chart and Corny were astonished when they finally crept up to Hugh's Grange at first light to see the doorway resembling a flower barrow.

"Thought your cousin lived quietly," Chart said.

"House full of young women," Corny pointed out, clutching his bouquet. "They must all be smashers."

They sneaked up and deposited their colourful bunches of roses alongside the little pots and paper flowers, making sure their verses were tucked into each one.

"Wish I could see their faces," Chart said with a grin when they'd achieved a retreat. "Why not?" he immediately asked. "That house is within sight of the churchyard. We could hang about there."

It was a nippy vigil, but they endured it, fortified by the brandy flask Chart had brought. Eventually the door was opened by a maid, who stared, then shouted something.

In a moment a number of young women rushed out, exclaiming and picking through the offerings. An older woman and a child soon appeared.

"That's Cressida," said Corny. "And little Toby. Mind, he was unbreeched when I saw him last. Which is Juno?"

"I think," said Chart bemusedly, "she's the one in the pinkish thing. She's done something with her hair."

"Pretty little thing," said Corny.

"Yes," said Chart, aware of a painful stab of jealousy.

When they got back to the inn to collect their horses, he said, "I don't see why we don't go and call now we're here."

"What? But it was all supposed to be secret. They're bound to guess if we come waltzing up."

"They'll guess anyway. They'll only need to ask

to hear we've been in the village. We'll just go up and admit to it. It's all fun, anyway."

"What about the rest of those flowers?"

"Yes," said Chart. It had not escaped his eye that at least three of the valentine offerings had been for Juno.

Juno had been up with the dawn and dressed by daylight, ready to see the reaction to the valentine display. When she entered the dining room, she found everyone already there full of excited amusement. Even Philo, who tended to break her fast in the kitchen with Toby, was there, drinking a cup of tea. Each was eying the other, wondering who would speak first, when Eliza let out a shriek.

The four young women were up and out of their seats on the instant, and truth to tell, Cressida was not far behind. Everyone exclaimed at the offerings, some more so than others, depending on when they had placed their own there. The flowers and scrolls were all quickly and evenly distributed, except that there were two extra—one for Cressida, one for Juno.

"Good gracious," said Juno, looking at the beautiful golden hothouse roses, her heart racing. No one in the Grange had the opportunity to buy such things. She gingerly unrolled the scroll and read out the verse.

"Juno, you sly thing," said Aquila. "You have an admirer!"

"No," Juno protested. "Honestly!" The name Chart had sprung into her mind, but it was ridiculous. He was miles away. "And what about Cressida?" she asked.

Everyone looked at their hostess, who appeared utterly bemused. "I have not the slightest idea," she said, holding the pink roses as if they might explode. "But perhaps," she said briskly, "now the excitement is over, we can do more justice to Mrs. Barleyman's pancakes."

She and Juno, however, took the time to arrange their flowers in water.

"Someone else sent me pink roses once," Cressida murmured. "It is very strange. I haven't thought of him above once or twice in years. . . ."

She broke off her musings and said, "But this admirer is obviously the merest acquaintance, for he does not even know the colour of my eyes." She walked briskly away from her flowers. Juno watched her, wondering about someone called James.

By the time Juno got to the table and the delicate breakfast pancakes, the excitement was mostly over. Apart from Cressida and Juno's bouquets, the valentines were quickly explained and everyone seemed to take it as Juno had, as a pleasing sign of friendship. Philo took Toby out for a walk, Aquila went off to write letters, and Katherine settled down to a sketch.

Juno took her bouquet to her tower room to muse on yellow roses. In no time their perfume filled the air, making her mind swim. No one had ever given her flowers before. She found it didn't seem to matter who the donor had been, or that the blossoms appeared soft and fragile; they were as powerful as a storm, as music, as fire. They stirred her almost to madness.

She touched the petals soft yet strong, curling out from the secret heart. She felt the cool firm buds curled tightly on themselves and yet ready to soften and open. Like her heart.

Imagine if these had been sent by a man she loved.

Little Juno, mild and sweet,
I worship at your tender feet.

Smile at me just once today
And I will your trusty lover stay.

She found the failed metre in the last line as endearing as a stray dimple. It made the sender human.

Then, out of her window, she saw two horsemen riding down the lane towards the Grange. They were fashionable men on fine horses.

One of them was Chart Ashby.

Heart pounding madly, Juno flew to her small mirror and dragged a comb through her hair, blessing Aquila a thousand times. She tried to see her gown and could not, so she rushed down the stairs, knocked, and then, hearing no reply, nipped into Katherine's room to use the full-length mirror.

Thank heavens she was wearing the pink dress. Despite the chill in the old house, she ruthlessly discarded her grey woollen shawl.

Then, seeking composed dignity, but almost dizzy with excitement, she made her way downstairs even as she heard the hollow sound of the knocker.

As Eliza opened the door, Juno was in place to go forward with pleased surprise. "Cousin Chart," she said, and extended a hand that only shook slightly. "What a pleasant surprise."

It was only as she was introduced to Mr. Cornwallis that the thought struck her. If Chart was in Valentine Parva, *he* could have sent the roses.

She turned from Mr. Cornwallis and looked up at Chart.

He smiled and winked. "Happy Valentine's, Cousin." Then he frowned and said, "No, dammit, not cousins. Happy Valentine's, Juno."

It was happening again, that something special was washing over her. She was sure, strange though it seemed, that he was going to kiss her. . . .

But then Cressida was there, followed by Katherine and Aquila, and Juno knew she had been imagining it.

In fact, she told herself in a little while, she was in danger of making a great fool of herself. The two young men soon confessed to having sent valentines to their cousins and treated it all as a great joke. The roses clearly meant nothing.

Moreover, it did not escape Juno that Chart paid particular attentions to Aquila and Katherine, and that was hardly surprising as one was so poised and handsome, the other so pretty. He was a pink of the *ton* and used to young women of that sort, not self-conscious bluestockings with secret romantical afflictions.

And so she made a few lightly scathing comments about foolish Valentine's Day practises, supporting them with Wollstonecraftian quotations in favour of rational thinking.

After that she started a weighty discussion of the implications of the establishment of the Portuguese Empire in Brazil. No one, however, took it up with any enthusiasm, and soon the talk moved again to social matters and fashionable gossip, with Aquila leading the way and the two gentlemen happily doing their part.

As soon as the men left, Juno went to her room with the express intent of throwing out a bunch of yellow roses, or at least taking them down to the church.

Her hands wouldn't obey her, and instead she sat and wept. She no longer knew what she wanted, what was right, what was possible. She just knew it was all unutterably painful.

Riding back through Valentine Parva, Chart looked at the cloudy sky and said, "More rain."

Corny morosely agreed.

"Don't seem much point in going back to your place," Chart said.

"Ain't much point in staying here," replied Corny.

"Like to have a word with little Juno," Chart admitted. "Didn't seem happy."

"Seemed well enough to me," Corny rebutted.

Chart shook his head. "Seemed put out. Probably because I sent her those roses. Probably doesn't believe in that kind of thing. Why don't we send for our stuff and rack up at the Heart and Arrow for a day or two? If the weather's going to be foul, it will be more fun to be here than in the Shires."

Corny agreed, but gave his friend a very worried look.

The next few days were torture for Juno. It rained continually. When Cressida discovered the young men had decided to stay in the village, she made them free of the house and they took her up on it. Straight after breakfast they ran down the lane in heavy cloaks and then stayed all day at the Grange, chatting with Aquila, Katherine, and Philo, playing card games, admiring the canaries. . . .

They were affable with everyone, Juno felt, except with her. For some reason she felt Mr. Cornwallis disapproved of her; he doubtless did not believe in women's rights. Chart almost seemed to be avoiding her, so seldom and so awkwardly did he speak to her.

When she saw his easy address with the other young ladies, the light compliments he paid them, the almost flirtatious tone he often used, and compared it with the stiff way he talked to her, she felt like crying again, but was determined not to make a fool of herself.

Then it got worse. The number of gentlemen was increased by the addition of Sir Anthony Overton, who had made Katherine's acquaintance during a visit to Lincoln Cathedral. It seemed Sir Anthony was always with Katherine—he was even teaching her to ride now that the weather had improved—and Mr. Ashby was inclined to hover over Aquila. It was true that he had asked Juno if she cared to try riding his horse, but she had wanted to so much that she had felt obliged to say no.

The weather improved. Juno expected Chart's immediate departure and longed for it, even though it would break her heart. But in the end, Mr. Cornwallis went while Chart stayed behind. He gave a rather sheepish explanation of having hurt his leg and being unable to hunt for a few days. No one believed him, as most of the time he forgot to limp.

Whatever his reasons, he stayed in the village for one week, then two. He accompanied them on walks, read aloud from their favourite books, and played spillikins as cheerfully as whist. Katherine and Aquila were both charmed by his easy address; only Philo seemed immune, and she was definitely not herself these days.

Juno was sure he had fallen in love with Aquila, for she was the one with whom he seemed most relaxed. She was of good family, she was rich, she would make a wonderful society hostess. Juno hated her.

She went to great pains to make her adherence to Mary Wollstonecraft's ideals crystal clear as often as possible, until one day Aquila said, "Dear Juno, we know your lofty ideals, but do spare us the sermons."

Katherine added timidly, "Some of us would like to be cossetted by the man of our dreams."

Juno was silenced, not knowing what she could say that would neither offend nor give away the foolishness of her heart. When the conversation split and she found herself apart with Chart for a

moment, she would have fled if she could have
found a pretext.

"Are you perhaps unhappy here, Juno?" he asked
seriously. "I can see your mind is not in accord with
the other young ladies'."

"Oh no," she said quickly, feeling mean-spirited.
"I find it very pleasant. Truly. Everyone is most
kind. Not that I must not return home soon, of
course," she babbled. "Mrs. Trent cannot be expected to house me for ever."

"She assured me she is delighted with the situation. You must not concern yourself and, at risk
of having my nose bitten, I must say I cannot be
happy at your returning to living alone." He looked
very ill at ease. "My parents would be willing to
have you visit them, but to be honest I wouldn't
advise it. I go home as little as I can. . . ."

Juno stared at this frankly unfilial attitude.

"However," he continued, "my cousin Lord Randal and his wife will be in London for the Season.
They would be delighted to have you visit, and they
are great fun. . . ." He flashed her a concerned look.
"That is, if you don't object to fun. . . ."

There was nothing Juno wanted more than to go
to London, to enjoy the theatre, to dance at balls
under glittering chandeliers. Her rational side tried
to deny the offer, but she found herself saying, "I
don't know . . ."

"Of course," he said quickly, "there's lots of
philosophical stuff going on there, too. Royal Society. Readings. Museums . . ." He looked round the
drawing room and said desperately, "It's a little
warm in here. Why don't we go into the conservatory? The canary song is charming, isn't it?"

It was not particularly warm. In fact, Juno had
been wishing vanity had not made her leave off her
shawl; she was sure she'd heard Chart mutter about
the infernal din Philo's canaries made; but she was

not about to object to anything that would give her a few moments almost alone with him.

With the heavy red curtain hung to block the draught dropped between them and the drawing room, it was alarmingly intimate in the small glass room. Juno turned and clucked at one of the canaries, which promptly trilled.

"Don't get them going," Chart said.

Juno bit her lip as she turned and raised a brow. "Charming song?" she queried, then thought to turn away again. He was so close, and she felt dizzy. She'd noticed Mr. Cornwallis did not have this effect on her.

"Juno," he said hesitantly. "I know I'm a frippery sort of fellow. Can't seem to get interested in philosophy or even much in politics unless it's going to affect my own interests. I will try to improve."

Juno stared. "Improve?" she echoed. How did a paragon improve?

"I'd like you to think better of me," he said, and rather tentatively, his hand came out and touched her cheek. "Please?"

The words "I think you're perfect now" trembled on her lips, but she moderated them. "I don't think badly of you, Cousin Chart," she said, his knuckle against her cheek like a hot coal.

"I'm not your cousin," he said sharply. His hand spread to rest along her jaw, and she leant into it like a bird settling into a nest.

There was a moment of silence. The birds were still and quiet; if the others were talking in the drawing room, it was inaudible. . . . His hand slid around to the back of her head and tilted it. He lowered his lips to hers.

They both sighed as their lips touched. Juno felt as if she had been walking in mist that suddenly cleared to reveal sunshine and glory. She leant against him, and his arms came round her. She stretched her arms round the rough texture of his jacket and felt the hard power of his body beneath.

She tasted him on her lips and tongue, and it was strange; it was something she had always known.

The birds began to sing.

Voices became louder.

The curtain hissed back.

"Mr. Ashby!" exclaimed Cressida. "Juno!"

They broke apart, but not very far. Behind Cressida stood Aquila, Philo, and Katherine, all staring with shock and perhaps some envy. Standing in Chart's arm, Juno looked up and saw him red-faced and dazed but looking blissful. She suspected she looked the same. She certainly didn't feel as if she had done anything wrong.

That was clearly not Cressida's opinion. "Juno, you are in my care here. I cannot countenance this. Please go to your room and wait there for me to speak to you. Mr. Ashby. Come into my sitting room."

Brought down to earth, Juno looked up an apology for having got him into trouble. He smiled, winked, and gave her a squeeze before releasing her. Heart floating again, Juno went up to her room, grateful for a chance to digest and savour the memory of that kiss.

Sometime later, Cressida came in and sat with a sigh. "Oh, Juno. I had never expected you to be a foolish one."

"Foolish?"

Cressida sat more upright. "Juno, Chart Ashby is a handsome man. He is also rich and very well born. He could marry anyone, and his family will look much higher than you."

Marriage. Juno had not really looked beyond the marvellous present, but now she did and found it glorious. "He is of age. He can do what he wants."

Cressida sighed again. "Juno, the Ashbys are one of the first families in the land, and believe me, they are aware of that fact. Think how they behaved when your stepmother married your father." She looked down and fiddled with her wedding band. "I too," she added hesitantly, "had experience with their haughty ways. I once knew an Ashby . . ."

She looked away into the fire burning in the small grate. "It was nothing serious, of course, but we liked each other I think. It was made perfectly clear to me by his aunt that I was unworthy to join the family." She looked up and said with great seriousness, "That aunt was Chart Ashby's mother. Even though he says he wishes to, my dear—and I fear he is not a serious-minded young man—he would never be allowed to marry you."

"He wants to *marry* me?" Juno gasped.

"Juno," said Cressida sharply, "I had thought you a rational woman. Of course he had to say he wanted to marry you when he was caught kissing you in such a manner. . . ." To Juno's surprise Cressida went quite pink, obviously embarrassed at what she had interrupted. It had all seemed perfectly natural and wonderful at the time.

"He *doesn't* want to marry me?" she asked, confused.

"He may want to marry you at this moment," Cressida said reluctantly, "but it cannot run deep. And think, Juno. What do you have in common? You have such a serious, studious nature and you believe so strongly in women's rights. He finds his pleasure in society, dancing, hunting. . . . You would be at one another's throats as soon as the honeymoon was over, my dear."

Cressida was not a woman whose words could be ignored. Juno felt something begin to break painfully. "It would be bad for him if we were to marry?" she whispered.

"Yes," said Cressida gently. "His family would disapprove. I doubt they would cut themselves off from him entirely, but they would never accept you and that would make you both unhappy. In addition, you would soon find no conversation or activities to share. He is handsome," she added kindly, "and has turned your head. This happens to all young women at least once. A little sober thought will soon show you that there is no future in it."

Juno swallowed tears. "Is that what happened to you?" she asked.

Cressida stood. "Yes," she said. "And as you can see, my life has not been shattered as a result. I had a good marriage based on mutual repect. I have a lovely child." Then she sighed, and Juno heard the loss in it. But the next moment her hostess was her usual brisk self. "I have been forced to tell Mr. Ashby he may not visit here again. I hope I can trust you not to communicate with him."

"Of course, Cressida."

Cressida left, and Juno sat in thought. It was sad but true. She could not possibly make Chart a good wife, and she would be in agony to come between him and his family. She, who had never really had family, valued it all the more.

It was terribly painful to think she would never see him again, but it was for his good, and at least she had that one kiss.

Then she realised that he might still feel obliged to her in some way. She must go away where he could not find her. She would go to Uncle Augustus in Wales. Chart would soon give up any pursuit and find a more suitable wife. Someone like Aquila perhaps. Juno made a firm resolution not to hate Aquila Ware.

Perhaps one day, like Cressida, Juno would find

a quiet, sober gentleman to marry; one who would enjoy discussion of philosophy and politics. . . .

She started to pack, tears leaking down onto her clothes as she worked.

At Tyne Towers in Shropshire, the new Duke of Tyne was attending to correspondence with the assistance of his secretary when his brother, Lord Randal Ashby, walked in dressed for travelling.

The duke looked up with a smile. "Ready for off?"

"Just about. Wanted a word with you before we leave."

At a look, the secretary bowed and left the two brothers alone. They were alike, yet unalike. Both fair and slim, Lord Randal's component parts came together to make a glittering kind of beauty, whereas his older brother was merely pleasant-looking. Perhaps it was a lifetime of dutiful hard work that had made the duke a little paler, a little less defined. He was also nearly ten years older than his thirty-year-old brother.

James poured wine for them both and waited. Randal and his wife, Sophie, had come to the Towers for Christmas, and then, after the old duke's death, had stayed on until matters were straight again. There had been no shortage of time to talk, so why this sudden need to see him?

"I'm going to be a trifle intrusive," said Randal with an unrepentant smile. He responded to his brother's look of query with one word. "Marriage."

"Ah," said James, and studied his claret. "Yes."

"I just thought I would point out to you, in case it has escaped your notice, that Sophie and I have been married for over two years with no sign of little Ashbys. And I assure you," he said with a grin, "that it's not for want of trying."

"I'm sorry," said the duke.

"No need. It doesn't concern us unduly. However, if one of us is going to produce an heir to the dukedom, it is unlikely to be me."

"I see." The duke rubbed his head pensively. "I've nothing against matrimony, you know. I just never seem to meet someone to my liking. Marrying a person one can hardly tolerate sounds like hell."

"I agree with you there. However, may I point out that perhaps you haven't met anyone to your taste because you never go anywhere."

"I go to London occasionally, and on visits."

"To London out of Season and visits to bachelor households. You need to meet eligible young ladies. You're one of the major matrimonial prizes in England."

The duke shuddered. "Don't remind me. Whenever I do go to a social event, I think I hear hunting horns."

Randal laughed. "More than likely." He looked at his brother curiously. "Have you never met anyone you found even promising?"

His brother looked back thoughtfully. "Once, perhaps. But we were very young and it didn't last. . . . I remember I didn't feel shy with her and she made me feel quite a dashing fellow. . . ." He sighed. "It was a long time ago."

Randal looked a little disbelieving at the whole story, but said, "If there's one like that, there's bound to be more. But you'll have to go and look or Chart will end up as duke, and though he's a fine enough fellow, father would turn in his grave."

The old duke had disliked his brother and not wished Lord William or any of his sons to succeed him.

"Speaking of Chart," said the duke, picking up a letter. "I have a steaming letter here from Uncle

William complaining that he appears to be in the toils of Aunt Minta's radical daughter.''

Randal frowned and then picked the name out of the family tree. "Cousin Juno Rathbone. What would Chart want with her?"

"Father sent him to check on the girl, since Chart was off for his usual stay in the Shires. Chart wrote and told me he'd found her in comfortable circumstances but without a suitable companion, and arranged for her to live for the time being with an elderly cousin of a friend near Lincoln. The girl isn't apparently a blood relative, anyway. She's Rathbone's daughter by his first marriage."

"So what has Uncle William in a stew?"

"He's discovered Chart's spending rather a lot of time in Lincoln."

After a blank moment, Randal got the point and grinned. "In hunting season? It must be love."

"That seems to be Uncle William's fear. He's always loathed the slightest connection to Rebel Rathbone. The thought of his son marrying the man's daughter is plainly driving him to apoplexy. He wants me to play Head of the Family and order Chart home."

"And will you?"

"Of course not. However, since you are going east . . .''

" 'Fraid not," said Randal firmly. "We are going to Melton to stay with Ver. I'll check on matters in Oakham if there's any point, but Lincoln's an extra day's journey north." With a mischievous twinkle he added, "Why don't you go?"

"If you haven't noticed," said the duke, "I'm busy."

"When have you ever not been? When will you ever not be? The place didn't fall apart when you were ill, and that wasn't because I did such a wonderful job of filling your shoes. It won't fall apart if

you take a few weeks off. Play out a novel. Go off
to Lincoln incognito and perhaps you'll meet a
sweet-natured dairymaid to be your duchess."

The duke laughed, but something about the idea
caught his fancy.

Randal drained his glass and rose. "I must be off.
If you find yourself in the Shires, James," he added
with a twinkle, that showed he had read his brother
accurately, "and want some hunting, Ver keeps
open house. Hume House, near Melton."

James Ashby went out to see his brother and Sophie on their way, then returned thoughtfully to
his office. Escape. As long as his father had been
alive, he had not felt he could leave for any length
of time. If a crisis came up the duke would have
tried to handle matters, and he had not been a well
man. Now, however, things were different. He was
the duke, and his staff was excellent.

He'd do it. He'd take a plain coach and just a
coachman, groom, and valet and go to Lincoln to
see what Juno Rathbone and Chart were up to.

He suddenly felt amazingly youthful.

Juno decided to treat her escape from Hugh's
Grange and Chart Ashby as an exercise in self-
reliance.

Slipping out of the house was no trouble, as she
had brought little with her and chose to leave the
dresses Philo had lent her. She even abandoned
Lord Montboddo, as she had sworn off novels, which
were surely at the root of all her woes.

In the grey mists of dawn, she set out with just
one bag to walk into Lincoln, where she would hire
a conveyance. There was a creeping, frosty damp
that made the walk unpleasant, but then she had
the good fortune to be taken up by a farmer's wife
on her way into the town with eggs for her custom-

ers. Juno spun a tale of going into town to work as a companion and found it accepted.

In truth, she was enjoying her adventure, and if it were not for the miserable ache of cutting herself off from Chart Ashby her spirits would have been high when she arrived in Lincoln. Though she had been trained to self-reliance, she had never put it into action before and was pleased to discover she could cope. She had plenty of money well secreted about her person and a loaded pistol in her capacious reticule, a pistol she had been trained to use and care for.

She need be dependent on nobody. She remembered Katherine saying, "Some of us would like to be cossetted by the man of our dreams," but put the temptation firmly out of mind.

At the White Hart she had the innkeeper hire her a chaise and four for her journey. He was a little dubious and suggested she might be better advised to travel on the mail, but Juno looked him in the eye and produced the money, and soon it was arranged.

When she finally rolled out of the innyard in a clean equipage, drawn by four horses tended by two postilions, Juno was feeling very proud of herself indeed.

All went well the first day, though she felt very alone. They put up for the night in Nottingham, and she was careful to lock her door.

Nothing untowards occurred, and she told herself she was suffering from an overactive imagination brought on by too many novels. She took time before starting out for the second day of her journey to walk to a bookseller's and buy a very sensible book on the flora and fauna of the Caribbean islands. She settled to read it as the coach moved up into the hilly dale country.

* * *

Back at Hugh's Grange, Juno's disappearance threw Cressida into a panic. She must have mishandled the whole affair. Where would the poor girl have gone? She remembered as if it were yesterday how dreadful she had felt in a similar situation. Not that James Ashby had ever kissed her like that. . . . And certainly Mr. Trent hadn't.

She felt close to tears, which was ridiculous.

When she discovered Juno had carefully packed all she had brought with her, the panic subsided. That was an unlikely prelude to suicide. The girl had doubtless fled home, but Cressida wouldn't feel easy until she was sure.

When she was told Chart Ashby wanted to see her, she was relieved rather than annoyed.

He was unusually sober and looked a great deal more formidable. "Mrs. Trent," he said firmly, "I have considered your words yesterday and have decided that though your intentions are excellent, you are in error. My feelings for Juno may have taken me by surprise, but they are real." He suddenly smiled besottedly. "I think I've loved her ever since she snapped her fingers in my face. . . ." He dragged his mind back to the moment. "As for my family, ma'am, I keep my distance now, so if they try to freeze her out it will make little difference."

Cressida was aware of wishing the marquess had spoken like this to someone all those years ago. Who had given him the little "for your own good" lecture? It had been his aunt Susan who had spoken to Cressida, and with very little kindness. How had that cold, haughty woman given birth to Chart Ashby?

Was she being a sentimental fool? "She's gone," she told him.

He paled. "Gone? Where?"

"I'm not sure," Cressida confessed, becoming

fretful again. "She slipped away early. I'm sure she's gone home."

He picked up his hat and gloves. "I'll go after her. What in God's name did you say to her, ma'am?"

"Nothing unkind," Cressida defended. "I merely pointed out how unsuitable it all was. . . . How unlikely. . . ."

Just then Aquila knocked and came into the room. She was startled, then thoughtful to see Chart. "Cressida," she said, "I think you should see this." She handed over a heavy tome.

"Juno's book," said Cressida. "It was doubtless heavy to carry and she must know it by heart, so often has she read it."

"Open it," said Aquila.

Cressida did, and caught her breath. Chart moved closer to see what had so surprised her. From the middle she prised out another, slimmer volume. *"Desperate Love,"* she read blankly. "A novel? Juno?"

"She's been reading them all along while pretending to read that dull stuff," said Aquila, wide-eyed. "I don't understand it."

"I do," said Cressida with a little laugh. She looked at Chart. "I've been such a fool. Go to Oakham and find her, please. I'd love to have her come back here, but whatever happens, make her happy."

He smiled. "She likes novels?" he said with delight. "I'll be her perfect Lochinvar." With a perfect sweeping bow he hurried off to his horse.

" 'Oh, young Lochinvar is come out of the west,' " quoted Aquila dreamily, " 'In all the rough border his steed was the best . . .' Do you think she found his name in the water?" she asked wistfully.

In the hilly country the postilions occasionally asked Juno to get out and walk. She did not partic-

ularly like this pair of men but made no objection
to their reasonable request. She rather enjoyed the
exercise. She always took care to take her reticule
with her, for it contained her ready money. The rest
was in a secret pocket.

As she walked through the bleak, rough fell
country, she took stock of her life and decided it
was good, forcing down the pain of never seeing
Chart again. She would open a school, perhaps, or
some charity for indigent females. . . .

She was briskly climbing one slope when she became aware of something not quite right. She
looked round and saw that the coach had stopped;
one of the postilions was off his horse and approaching her stealthily. He had a long knife in his hand.

When she turned, he was startled, but after a moment he clearly decided whether she was aware or
not made little difference and he continued to approach. He even started to grin.

"What are you doing?" she asked, though it was
a very silly question. She just couldn't quite believe
such a wickedness.

He didn't answer, just grinned wider. Juno came
to her senses and backed away. She opened her bag
and pulled out her pistol. "It's loaded," she said,
struggling to keep her voice hard and calm. "Tone
of voice is most of the battle," Aunt Clarabel had
told her.

He stopped and looked at the pistol as if it were
a snake. "What yer doin' with that?" he demanded.

"Pointing it at you," she said. "And I'm going to
shoot you with it unless you put down that knife."

He eyed her. "I don't reckon as how it's loaded,"
he said at last. "Or as you know how to use it."

Juno forced herself to smile. "Drop the knife or
you'll find out." Inside, fear was taking a chilling
hold. She had only one shot, and there were two of

them. If they forced her to prove she could use the gun, she would be vulnerable to the remaining villain, and it was her *death* that was being discussed here.

Her hand began to tremble with fear and with the weight of the gun. She dropped her bag and put both hands around the butt. A movement forced her to flick her eyes sideways. The other man was coming over. At least, situated where she was on the side of the road, he couldn't sneak up behind her.

"Put down the knife!" she commanded loudly, and the man sullenly obeyed.

A victory, but a small one. If they had a trace of courage, they could take her. The other man was coming at her from the side.

"On your faces, both of you!" she barked, switching her eyes quickly between the two but trying to project confidence and the assurance that she would kill the one who hesitated. This was the crucial moment. She raised the gun slightly at first one man, then the other.

They fell to the ground.

Juno felt as if she would faint from relief. She was still a long way from safe, but the danger was lessened. She eyed the coach. If only she could get away in it and leave them there, but her straight skirt would make climbing onto the box very difficult even if she didn't have to hold the pistol, and managing the horses and vehicle on these hilly roads must be a difficult job.

She looked at the scrubby land sloping away from the road, occupied only by sheep, thinking to run and hide. Then she had a better idea. She made her way towards the coach and away from the edge of the road. "Up and walk," she said.

They looked up, then scrambled to their feet, puzzled and already scheming.

She didn't let her eyes waver. "Walk down there

away from the road and keep walking. I will be
able to see you and will be able to hit you if you
stop."

She saw them eye her and each other, but they
were cowards and didn't trust one another, and so
in the end they walked. Every step they took made
her feel safer.

She watched them as they grew smaller. Then
they stopped and turned. They had decided they
were out of range. Quite true. She wouldn't give a
ha'penny for her chances of hitting them at half the
distance. Now they were planning. If they had any
sense, they'd split and work round to come at her
from either side. Perhaps sending them away
hadn't been the cleverest idea after all.

Why didn't another vehicle come? Why should
one? This was the middle of nowhere, with no sign
of even a farmhouse. It was midwinter, and even
this early in the afternoon the first hints of darkness were gathering. She shivered with cold and
fear.

Should she walk for help? It could be miles, and
it would be more difficult to remain aware of the
men and their movements.

She started to pray as she tried to watch all sides at
once. She saw a sudden movement close by and almost
fired. A sheep bounded onto the road and across. Then
she saw one of the men climb up the slope onto the
road, still out of range. She knew the other would be
coming from the other direction.

And this time they would not be so easily awed.

She was going to die out here in the cold and
gloom, and no one would ever know what had happened.

Despite all her attempts to be brave, she swallowed tears and began to tremble.

At first she thought the rumble was part of her
fear.

Then she realised it was a vehicle.

The men realised it too, and disappeared just as a coach and four rose over a hill and then down and up towards her. She stepped forward and waved, and the horses were drawn up. A man stepped down from inside, looking in surprise at her, and warily at her pistol.

"You have some trouble here, ma'am?" he asked, and raised his beaver. "I'm James Ashby. May I be of assistance?"

Juno burst into tears and, to her everlasting shame, dropped the pistol. It went off, setting the coach horses plunging and her horses running wildly off down the road, empty coach rattling behind. Fortunately, the ball shot off across country and didn't even hit a sheep.

Juno soon found herself in the coach, wrapped in a rug and taking a sip of medicinal brandy. She managed to give a fairly coherent account of her ordeal.

"You appear to be both brave and resourceful, my dear," said her rescuer. He leaned out of the window. "Ah, good. Pudlow has asserted control over your conveyance. I think the best thing is for me to take you back to Nottingham, where this can be reported to the magistrates. In case you didn't catch my name, it's Ashby."

Ashby! She knew there was a connexion. She even fancied she saw a resemblance. "I would much rather go on," she said quickly.

He looked at her in surprise. "I'm sorry if your journey is urgent, but it is out of the question. For one thing, you no longer have postilions. You will be able to find more reliable ones to take you on tomorrow if you insist." The man gave the order, then sat back as the coach moved off. "You have not given me your name, ma'am."

Juno thought of lying, but was too exhausted to

contemplate maintaining an untruth. "Juno Rathbone," she said, and saw him blink with surprise,
then smile.

"Then we are by way of being connected, and
have an acquaintance in common, I think. My
cousin, Chart."

It was no surprise, but Juno knew she was blushing just at the name. "I do know him, yes," she
muttered. "But how do you know of me?"

"When Chart visited you on the old Duke of
Tyne's behalf, he wrote to report to me. I, you see,
am the new duke."

Juno swallowed. One of the people who would so
strongly disapprove of marriage between Chart and
her. He seemed pleasant enough, but he didn't yet
know the whole story.

"I had hoped to visit you either in Lincoln or
Oakham," he continued. "I remember your
mother—stepmother, I mean. She was great fun."

"Yes," said Juno wistfully. "I try to be like her,
but somehow it doesn't work."

"It's usually a mistake to try to be like someone
else," he offered.

"But she enjoyed adventures and hardships. She
would have thought this a merry jape. Mind," said
Juno morosely, "she would probably have had the
forethought to have brought a double-barrelled pistol."

The duke burst out laughing. "Would you have
shot them, then?"

"I might," Juno admitted. "At least, I hope I
would have. It would be rather foolish, wouldn't it,
to let them cut my throat for want of the resolution
to shoot?"

"How true." His humour subsided, and he looked
at her curiously. "Would you care to tell me why
you are travelling about the country alone? It is a
trifle unusual."

"*You* are travelling alone," she said.

"No, I'm not. I have my own coachman and groom, and a valet who has discreetly gone to travel in your vehicle so we can be private."

Juno felt some alarm at this, but he hastened to add, "I have no designs on you, Miss Rathbone. I merely thought we might be about to pull out some dirty family linen. Is Chart the reason you are traipsing across country?"

"No!" Juno protested, then sighed and said, "Yes. But it isn't really his fault."

He looked questioningly, and she added, "He wants to marry me. You won't approve, but you needn't worry. He doesn't really want to marry me."

He frowned over this. "Then why did he ask you?"

Juno blushed. "He didn't," she confessed. "He . . . he kissed me in the conservatory. And then he felt he had to. . . ."

"Ah. Chivalry."

"Well," Juno admitted. "Not just chivalry. Mrs. Trent discovered us."

The duke's eyes crinkled in a way that reminded Juno distressingly of Chart. "I see," he said. "But if you don't want to marry him, you have only to say no."

Juno imagined Chart asking her to marry him. Perhaps on his knees . . . "Women want a lover and protector; and behold him kneeling before them—bravery prostrate to beauty!" "He can be very persuasive," she said in despair.

"So you thought you'd leave before he did ask you, and you so far forgot yourself as to say yes."

"It isn't funny!" Juno protested, for he was laughing inside. She could tell.

There was the sound of hooves, and a horseman pounded by. The coach halted and the coachman opened the trap to say, "Beggin' your pardon, your grace, but that were young Master Chart kicking up the dust."

The duke burst into open laughter. "Give a blast on the horn, Waller. Otherwise, we'll have to turn and pursue."

The horn caught Chart's attention, however, that and the following postchaise. He came thundering back.

"James!" he gasped as he flung open the door. "Juno! Thank God. You must be mad!"

The duke rose and left the coach. "In you go," he said to his cousin. "I'll travel in the other vehicle and tie your horse behind. You love her. She loves you." He turned back to Juno with a friendly smile. "Delighted to welcome you to the family, my dear."

So Juno, speechless, found herself alone with Chart. "I could wring your neck," he said. "Even a middle-aged lady pugilist wouldn't set out on a four-day cross-country journey on her own! Anything could have happened."

Juno decided this wasn't the moment to tell him it almost had. So much for bravery prostrate to beauty. "I'm sorry," she said. "But did you chase after me just to berate me?"

"Of course not," he said, and kissed her hard and fast. "I came to ask you to marry me. And if you don't, I probably *will* wring your neck after the fright you've put me through! I went to Oakham first. Then I had to trace you from Lincoln. If you ever do anything so cork-brained again . . ."

Juno giggled. "I told the duke you'd be very persuasive," she said.

He relaxed and smiled at her, happiness beginning to glow in his eyes. "I love you, you little idiot, and I'm going to marry you. And I know your secret vice. I don't think I'm going to have to do a complete turnaround to make you happy. Will you be able to endure being cossetted a little, my sweet?"

"A little," she agreed.

"You won't throw a fit if I bring you roses every now and then?"

"I promise," she said, and found herself snuggled in his arms.

"You'll come with me sometimes to balls and parties, and let me dress you in silk and diamonds?"

She looked up, and he slipped her bonnet off. "If it's essential to your happiness," she admitted, "I suppose I can endure it."

He turned serious. "No, it's not," he said. "Promise me you'll do what you want, love."

"I promise," she said. "And this is what I want to do."

And she kissed him. And when she bethought herself of Mary Wollstonecraft's own amorous adventures, Juno rather thought that lady would approve.

An Afternoon Gardening

THERE WAS VERY little to do in the garden at this time of year, but Cressida felt the need to be outside and active. She was tidying the borders in front of the house. Philo had taken Toby for a walk. Katherine, accompanied by Juno and Chart, had gone to sketch the spring lambs. As Cressida moved round the garden, she could sometimes hear Aquila playing on the spinet. Cressida was glad to be alone. The sudden reappearance of Chelmly had upset her rather more than she liked to admit.

When two carriages had pulled up at the door of Hugh's Grange last week, she had hurried to the window to look out and been too relieved to see Chart helping Juno from the first to notice who was climbing from the second. She had opened the door herself, and found she was looking directly into Chelmly's eyes. Seventeen years had passed since she had last seen him, but she recognised him without difficulty, despite the streak of white over one temple.

And he had recognised her after all those years. "Miss Loop . . ."

"I am Mrs. Trent now," she had said, and then turned her attention to Juno.

Chelmly had been very much as she remembered him, retiring, self-effacing, and efficient. He had explained the situation while they were still in the hall, assuring her that Juno had come to no harm.

He then contrived to give the newly engaged couple a moment of privacy at one end of the drawing room by the simple expedient of having Cressida introduce him to Philo, Aquila, and Katherine, before taking himself and Chart off to the inn. Since then he had communicated with Cressida in a series of considerate, correct notes, but had never called, even to accompany Chart.

Cressida did not know if he kept his distance from a desire to avoid embarrassing both of them with memories of a foolish proposal, or from a distaste for her company. She remembered how, many years ago, this same trait of disliking to show his hand had annoyed her. Many had thought the young marquess was easy to please, or simply had no opinions of his own, but Cressida had known this to be untrue.

The spring Cressida was seventeen, Chelmly had returned to Lord William's country house, this time without his parents and in the middle of the Season. He entered fully into local society, and it was soon noticed that when he attended the Assemblies, he spent much time with the vicar's daughter. Cressida assumed that his attentions were prompted by a desire to keep the husband-hunting ladies away, and had no expectations. She recognised how foolish her passion of the previous year had been, and was able to convince herself that she felt nothing but friendship for the marquess.

And yet, and yet—she was never quite sure that he didn't hold some small regard for her. He would send her pink roses—and lilies to her mother. He would take her driving—with each of her brothers in turn. When they talked, he was open with her, explaining how he disliked people always trying to please him because he was heir to a dukedom. "I just want people to please themselves. I'm really very easygoing, but all they ever do is try to guess what I want. I hate to disappoint them."

She had been taken aback when he had asked if he could speak to her father about a betrothal, and had asked for time to consider. Had Chelmly been plain Mr. James Ashby and a tenth as rich as he was, she would have accepted at once. But she felt too young and inadequate. She was sure she could make him a good wife; she doubted she could be a satisfactory marchioness.

And then she had been summoned by Lady William. Cressida now felt rage, when once she'd felt shame, as she recalled that interview. Another woman might have used tact. Not Lady William. She blandly assumed that Cressida had no feelings towards Chelmly save a gross ambition to one day be a duchess. She viciously accused Cressida of trying to trap her nephew into marriage, and listed all the reasons why marriage to her would destroy him.

"But I realise that such arguments will carry no weight with you! However, my nephew now understands that if he were to marry you, his father would disown him. He has made his choice. His proposal is withdrawn. And since you gave your fish too much line and did not accept at first, you have no grounds for a lawsuit."

"I wish to see Chelmly," Cressida said, wanting to assure him she had never meant to trap him.

"He has left for London."

Over the next few weeks, Cressida had written many letters to him, and had sent none. Her grief turned to anger that he, who was so considerate when it came to others, had misunderstood the woman who loved him. Eventually, she came to a resigned knowledge that it was natural that a man would prefer his family to marriage with a woman from a very different station in life, even if there were no question of a title.

* * *

Cressida gave a harder than necessary tug at the hollyhock she was trying to uproot. She heard the front gate open, and turned to look without standing up. Chelmly was walking up the garden path.

"Don't get up, Mrs. Trent." He knelt to help her. "Don't you have a gardener? This reminds me of the first time I met you, and you were slaving over that mountain of invitations for my aunt."

"You remember!" cried Cressida. Feeling foolish, she added, "I have a gardener, John Barleyman. He won't be pleased when he sees the holes I've made in his borders." She stood, acutely conscious of the hand Chelmly slipped under her elbow. "Won't you come in, my lord. I should say, your grace. Pray accept my condolences on the death of your father. Is the duchess well?"

"Yes, thank you. May I?" He gestured towards the front door, and at Cressida's nod, opened it.

Cressida wondered if he referred to his grandmother or if he had married.

Once inside, Cressida took him to Mr. Trent's study, not wishing to have Aquila present, then she excused herself to go upstairs to remove her bonnet and pelisse.

When she returned, the duke came quickly to the point. "While it is obvious that Miss Rathbone has been happy here, I think she might wish to know the Ashbys better before her marriage. With her permission, I wrote to my brother, Randal, and his wife, Sophie, and asked if she could stay with them. I have just received a favourable reply. They are visiting—"

"I thought you approved of the match, or at least did not wish to prevent it."

"I am delighted by it, ma'am."

"Then why send her to stay with the family? I

would be very pleased if she were married from Hugh's Grange."

"Cre—Mrs. Trent. I know that I once offended you, but please accept that I do not wish to discomfort Miss Rathbone. If you feel she will not be happy, I will not insist. Only, can you tell me what you fear for her? My brother is in no way like me, I assure you, and Sophie will be a good friend to Miss Rathbone. They are only a few years apart in age."

"Your grace, even if you have no qualms about Mr. Ashby marrying Miss Rathbone, other members of his family might feel she is too far below even a cadet member of a ducal family."

"Ah, you are thinking of my aunt Susan. I remember how she treated you and Mrs. Loop."

"Your grace," said Cressida, "Lady William is Mr. Ashby's mother. But if Lord Randal shares her sentiments and—well, to be blunt—uses the time Miss Rathbone spends with the family to warn her off, it would be very unpleasant for her."

"If I were to travel with them, Mrs. Trent, and escort Miss Rathbone back to you if she were unhappy . . . ?"

Cressida felt safe in accepting his offer. "If she wishes to go, and you are certain she will be welcome, I will not object to that arrangement."

"Then I shall intrude no longer, Mrs. Trent."

Cressida showed him to the door, and kept it open a moment longer than necessary, watching Chelmly walk down the path. She must learn to think of him as the Duke of Tyne. It would make him seem less like the man she had loved. He had walked to the house from the inn, unattended by anyone. He seemed as unaffected as ever, unchanged in so many ways.

A Maid at Your Window

Tomorrow is Saint Valentine's day,
All in the morning betime,
And I a maid at your window,
To be your Valentine.
—Shakespeare, Hamlet

"I CANNOT GO with you." Philomena delved into the wardrobe for her warmest cloak. "I promised to take Toby to see the wizard."

"Wizard?" Seated at the dressing table in her elegant green velvet wrapper, her sister seemed more interested in the exact placement of one blond curl.

"Mrs. Barleyman says village rumour has it that a wizard has rented Marsh Cottage."

"Really, Philo, you cannot persuade me that you believe in witches and warlocks," murmured Aquila, "when you are forever prating about scientific methods of canary breeding. And you spoil that brat abominably." She studied her face in the mirror and sighed. "I suppose the vicar's wife will be shocked if I darken my eyebrows. How I miss Vienna!"

As Philomena stuffed her fur-lined mittens into the pocket of her cloak, she admired her half sister's aristocratic profile and English fairness. She herself had inherited her Italian mother's dark hair, delicate features, and fragile appearance.

"Of course I don't believe in wizards. I daresay it is some inoffensive old eccentric. But I had rather take Toby for a walk than help with the pageant. All the ladies in the village will be there."

"Cousin Cressida is no gossip. You need not fear that everyone will be staring at you, waiting for you to betray your origins, as did my wretched aunt. Admittedly, a morning spent making paper flowers for the St. Valentine's Day pageant and taking tea with the vicar is not the acme of excitement, yet what else is there to do, buried as we are in the depths of the country?"

"We should have stayed with your aunt," said Philo guiltily. "At least there was more society there, even though we were still in full mourning."

"Out of the question," Aquila responded with unwonted vigour. "Papa might not have been the most conscientious of parents, but he would never have allowed you to be insulted as you were in that household."

A violent thumping on the door of the chamber the girls shared announced five-year-old Toby's arrival. "Philo, I'm ready. Mama putted on my boots and my coat and said be good. Come on, 'fore the wizard flies away on his broomstick."

With a laugh that transformed her rather solemn face, Philo kissed her sister's cheek and obeyed the summons.

"We must feed the birds before we leave," she said to the boy as they went downstairs.

"We already did, right after breakfast, 'member?"

"Not the canaries; the robins and bluetits in the garden. When the weather is so cold, they need feeding as much as the canaries do."

A burst of liquid song greeted them as they crossed the drawing room and opened the French door into the small conservatory with its wide, south-facing windows. Only a withered palm and several pots of dormant begonias showed its original use. In a pair of spacious cages on a shelf to one side, the female canaries hopped and fluttered, while Metternich and Talleyrand puffed out their yellow chests as they warbled a serenade.

Philomena paused on the step to listen. As always, her heart filled with delight at the joyful sound. Daughter of an opera singer and named for the nightingale, she was sadly mortified by her inability to carry a tune. Breeding canaries was some slight consolation.

Toby was already opening the sack of canary seed that stood in one corner of the room, spilling grain on the slate floor. He had learned to be gentle and quiet around the birds and could usually be trusted to fill their water dishes without spilling a drop. Today he was impatient.

"Come *on*, Philo. The wizard will fly away."

He filled a tin cup with the grain, and they took it outside to replenish the supply on the bird table. Beneath their feet the frosted grass crackled, glittering in the rays of the morning sun.

"Mrs. Barleyman says we can get to Marsh Cottage through the back gate, across the field and down the lane," Philo said.

"I know the way," Toby told her importantly. "I'll show you."

Philomena's modish grey, fur-collared cloak was more suited to strolling in the Prater in Vienna than to climbing stiles and tramping down a Lincolnshire lane. Fortunately, the overnight freeze had hardened the muddy ruts and even glazed the puddles with a thin layer of ice. Though Marsh Cottage was isolated from the village, they were soon close enough to see a trickle of smoke rising from the chimney.

Between leafless hawthorn hedges, the lane ran

down a slope to ford a small stream, with a narrow wooden bridge for foot passengers. On the other side, in a dank, overgrown hollow, stood the wattle-and-lath cottage.

"Its situation does look aguish, as Mrs. Barleyman said, but it's not really tumbledown," Philo commented as they stopped, by silent mutual consent, to observe their goal. "Just dilapidated."

"What's lapidated mean?" Toby held her hand tightly, his round cheeks pink with cold and anticipation.

"Badly cared for. It needs a coat of whitewash, and the tiles are covered with moss though there don't seem to be any holes in the roof, nor broken windows. But the fence has fallen down, and it looks as if the garden has grown wild for years."

"That's good, 'cos there's lots of bushes for us to hide behind when we look through the windows."

Philo was struck by the impropriety of their expedition. She had not really intended to do more than view the place from a distance. *I don't care*, she thought rebelliously. It was all very well for Aquila to be a model of decorum; *her* mother had been their father's lawful wife. As Aquila's aunt and cousins had made plain, the offspring of an unmarried Italian opera diva was beyond the pale no matter how well behaved.

"Come on," she said. "We'll climb through that gap where the fence has fallen down."

Philomena's cloak caught in a tangle of bare rose stems, and Toby reached the diamond-paned window first. He peeped over the sill, then ducked and made hurry-up gestures, mouthing silent words, his eyes sparkling with excitement. She joined him, crouching.

"It's a *real* wizard," he whispered. "Look!"

Cautiously she straightened until she could see into the room. Amid a clutter of glass tubes and vessels burned a lilac flame. By its ghostly light a dim figure was visible, moving in the background. A hand reached out, holding a beaker, and poured something over the flame.

A flash of brilliant white and an earsplitting *crack* made Philo jump and blink. In the afterglow of the explosion, she saw a black face, oddly distorted, that slowly sank from view.

"Stay here!" Philomena cried to the open-mouthed Toby. "I must see if he's hurt."

The cottage's front door opened directly into the room. After a momentary hesitation on the threshold, Philo hurried round the equipment-laden table. The wizard was sitting on the floor, his soot-masked expression somewhat dazed.

"Are you all right?" she demanded sharply.

"I think so." His speech sounded educated. Struggling to his feet, he added, "Only, I don't seem to be able to see very well."

She pulled off a glove, reached up, and removed the blackened spectacles from his nose. He grinned, his teeth startlingly white.

"Thank you, Miss . . . ?"

"I am Philomena Ware."

Despite his filthy blue smock, his bow was gentlemanly. "Thank you, Miss Ware. Allow me to present myself: my name is Robert Mayhew." Centred in pale circles that had been protected by the glasses, his hazel eyes smiled at her.

"How do you do, Mr. Mayhew." She curtseyed, feeling foolish and wondering how to explain her presence.

Toby's voice piped up behind her. "What went wrong with your spell, sir?"

Mr. Mayhew turned to the small boy. "Nothing," he said courteously. "It worked very well, but rather more vigorously than I had expected. Are you Miss Ware's brother?"

"No!" said Toby, outraged. "I haven't got any sisters. Girls are silly. 'Cept Philo, most of the time, and she's not Miss Ware 'cos Aquila is. Aquila is silly," he added.

"Toby is a sort of cousin," Philomena explained hurriedly. "I beg your pardon for intruding, sir. We must go."

"I want to see the magic stuff," Toby objected.

"It's not magic. Mr. Mayhew is not a wizard, he is a chemist, are you not, sir?"

"I am indeed, Miss Philo, though I'm surprised that you recognised it. You hoped to see a wizard, did you, Master Toby?"

To Philo's relief, his voice was full of laughter. It was hard to tell with his features obscured, but she thought he was quite young. He was tall and lean; his hands, with their long, chemical-stained fingers, gave an impression of capable strength.

"What's a chemist?" Toby asked. "If that big bang wasn't a spell, what was it?"

"An experimental investigation of the properties of chlorate of potash."

"Oh. Can you make that purple fire again?"

"Easily. I simply put a bit of potassium in water." He busied himself among the glassware.

"Pray do not blow yourself up again!" Philo backed towards the wall, pulling Toby with her.

"It's quite all right. That happened when I added spirits of salt." The lilac light flared again.

"What's potass . . . what you said?" Toby pulled away from Philo, and she followed him to the table, fascinated.

"It's a new metal, discovered just a few years ago by Sir Humphry Davy. I am doing some experiments for him."

"You know Sir Humphry Davy?" Philo queried eagerly, then flushed as he looked at her in surprise.

"Yes. I worked with him developing the miner's safety lamp. It is not a subject that usually engages the attention of young ladies."

"I read about it because I breed canaries. They are used in mines, too," she excused herself, "to detect dangerous gases."

"And Davy's lamp protects against explosion of those same gases," he agreed. "So you breed canaries, do you?"

He actually sounded interested!

"I have two pair," she said shyly. "I did have more, but I had to leave them in Vienna, so most of my breeding charts are useless."

"Charts, eh? You are going about the matter scientifically, then. Good for you. I should like to see how you keep your records."

"Really?" She could not be sure whether he meant it; the soot on his face made him inscrutable. As she tried to read his eyes, her gaze locked with his and she was oddly breathless when she went on. "But I ought not . . . Toby! Don't touch! We really must be off."

Mr. Mayhew swung round. "No, don't touch! Potassium can be dangerous all on its own if it's not handled carefully. I'll tell you what, Master Toby, I shall prepare an experiment you can do by yourself next time you come to visit me."

"But we cannot—" Philo started to protest.

"Cor, a real 'speriment?" Toby interrupted, awed. Then he remembered his manners and bowed. "Thank you, sir. When can we come?"

"Any time. Mornings are best."

"We ought not." Philo frowned worriedly, then seeing the child's disappointment, she capitulated with an unexpected giggle. "Oh, very well. I confess I should like to see what Mr. Mayhew looks like with a clean face."

He touched his face with his finger and inspected

the result, grinning and shaking his head. "Of course, I should have guessed from the state of my spectacles. Just my luck to meet a lady who is both beautiful and intelligent when I'm not fit to be seen."

Dragging Toby with her, Philo fled in confusion.

She should not have made that impertinent remark about his face, she scolded herself as they trudged up the lane. It would have served her right to receive a thorough set-down. Impertinence was foreign to her nature, and she could not think what had come over her. She had to put it down to the fact that Mr. Robert Mayhew was unlike any gentleman she had ever met.

Toby's persistent tugging at her sleeve interrupted this intriguing train of thought.

"When can we go back, Philo? The day after today?"

"Perhaps."

"Praps always means no. I'll go by myself, or ask Mama to take me."

"No, Toby, you must not tell your mama about Mr. Mayhew. I daresay she would not like it."

"Why not?"

"Because we were not properly introduced. Promise you will not tell."

"If you promise you'll take me back."

"I'll take you!" she said in exasperation, then resorted to a little blackmail of her own. "And if you tell, then I'll tell that you said 'Cor.' You know your mama dislikes it excessively."

"Girls!" said Toby disgustedly.

Robin Mayhew's opinion of the female sex had always been similar to Toby's. Unlike Toby, he had an excessive number of sisters, none of whom had the slightest respect for his life's work, which they frequently described as a childish interest in bangs and stinks. It was refreshing, he thought as he washed his face, to meet a young lady who showed signs of appreciating the fascination of science.

Especially, he admitted to himself, since she was a most attractive young lady. He sat down at his desk, picturing her delicate cheeks abloom from the cold, a hint of black curls under her hood, and those dark, long-lashed, expressive eyes. He was glad Theo's bailiff had recommended this place to him.

He caught himself writing "Philomena" in place of "Potassium" in his report of the experiment.

This was ridiculous! Robin knew better than to believe in love at first sight. Besides, there was no room for females in the life of a dedicated natural philosopher. He put the visitors firmly out of his mind and went back to work.

Some time later, a noise in the kitchen informed him that his servant had returned from the village. He realised he was hungry.

"Bodiham?" he called.

The man appeared in the doorway. "Got a nice bit of 'am for your dinner, sir," he said cheerfully. "Do it with taties in their jackets and it's a meal fit for a king."

Or would be with anyone else cooking it, Robin thought gloomily. None of the village women could be persuaded to cook for a wizard. Still, the fellow was loyal, a good groom, and an adequate valet—it was unfair to expect him to excel in the culinary arts also, and how far wrong could even Bodiham go with a baked potato? "Fine," he said. "What do you have that I can eat now?"

"Bit o'bread and cheese? Tell you what, sir, I'll 'ave a go at a Welsh rabbit."

"Bread and cheese will be fine."

"You needs something 'ot in your stummick this time o' year," Bodiham said firmly, and disappeared into the kitchen.

A few minutes later, the odour of burning toast overwhelmed the chemical smells of the laboratory. A more complex aroma Robin ascribed to burning cheese. He sighed. Combustion was a subject worthy of study, but the kitchen was the wrong place for it.

It was incomplete combustion of a residue of carbon from the mixture he used to make the potassium that had blackened his face, he deduced. Most young ladies would have fled screaming at the sight of him, but not Miss Philomena Ware. *She* had rushed to the rescue. Would she return? He must think up some harmless but engrossing experiment for the boy, something that would make young Toby insist on coming back again and again.

He found himself wondering whether Miss Philo could cook.

Being early risers, Philo and Toby often breakfasted in the kitchen. Seated at the kitchen table next morning, Philo watched Mrs. Barleyman flip a pancake with a neat twist of her dimpled wrist.

"Will you teach me to do that?" she asked.

"Lor', miss, it's not fitting for a young lady to be messing about in the kitchen."

Philo was silenced. She did not think it wise to explain that Cousin Sarah had advised her to learn to cook since she had no hope of making a brilliant match.

"I'm *tired* of pancakes," said Toby mutinously.

"Mrs. Barleyman is practising for the Shrove Tuesday race." Philo spooned a generous dollop of raspberry jam onto the brown-speckled pancake on his plate and rolled it up. "That's only two weeks away. Think what fun it will be to watch her win."

"I s'pose." He heaved a deep sigh and attacked his breakfast with spoon and fork.

Philomena squeezed lemon juice on her own pancake and added a sprinkle of sugar. Her delicate appearance concealed a healthy appetite.

"Can we go *today*?" Toby asked through a sticky mouthful. "Can we go for a *walk*?"

She smiled at his cautious roundaboutation. "Yes, Toby, we shall go, if you will drink your milk and help me feed and water the canaries first."

The milk rapidly disappeared, and Toby submitted with no more than a token protest to the dishcloth that removed the white moustache and red smear of jam from his face.

"I'm ready," he announced, watching with disfavour as Philo gulped her hot tea. "You don't want another cup, do you? Do we *got* to feed the canaries first?"

"Yes," she said firmly.

She had not reckoned with everyone rising early because of St. Valentine's Day. Poor Toby had to wait through what he called "a lot of fuss and bother" over the flowers found on the doorstep, but at last they escaped.

While Cousin Cressida felt it incumbent upon her as widow of a clergyman to be present at the special service, she did not feel it necessary for the rest of the household to attend unless they chose to. Aquila would go because she had nothing better to do, and Katherine seemed quite enthusiastic. Philo would not be missed.

As they walked along the lane, Philo tried to convince herself that the St. Valentine's Day game they had played was only a game—not an oracle. Toby, trotting by her side, interrupted her thoughts.

"Mama says St. Valentine's Day is the day all the birds choose their mates. That means they decide who they want to marry. Will the canaries choose their mates today?"

The days were still too short for canaries to think of nest building, and the bare hedgerows suggested that wild birds with any common sense would wait a few weeks.

Philo did not want to disillusion Toby, though. "The canaries were married in Vienna," she told him.

The breeding charts in her cloak pocket were in a sense their marriage lines. She touched the roll of papers. She would not show them to Mr. Mayhew unless he asked again. Everyone else laughed at her; it did not seem possible that he was serious.

Suddenly she wished she had not come. Mr. Mayhew's invitation had seemed sincere, but perhaps he was only being polite. He would think her forward, especially on this day of all days, a day for lovers. If Toby had not been with her she would have turned back, but he was running ahead down the hill, nearly at the bridge with its rickety handrail. She hurried after.

This time they entered the garden between the posts where the front gate had once hung. Walking up the path, Philo glanced at the window. No odd-coloured light, no explosion. She almost hoped he was not at home. Almost.

The door swung open as they reached it. Mr. Mayhew himself stood there, a smile of welcome on his thin, clever face. He looked to be in his mid-twenties, about what Philo had guessed, with brown hair, somewhat longer than was fashionable, brushed back from his high forehead.

Philo realised she was staring, flushed, and looked down. The chemist was dressed today in the everyday clothes of a county gentleman: a plain brown coat, buckskins, and top boots. He made her feel shy, as he had not with his stained smock and besmirched visage.

He chuckled, and her gaze flew back to his eyes. "Well? I believe I succeeded in removing all the carbon from my person."

Before she was forced to answer, Toby interrupted.

"Good morning, sir. Did you 'member my 'speriment?"

"Certainly, Master Toby. Pray step inside, Miss Philomena. You know what to expect, so I shall not apologise for my humble abode. To tell the truth, it was not easy to find a landlord willing to allow my experiments within his desirable residence."

"Where is it?" Toby demanded eagerly. He darted past the adults into the room, scanned the worktable, and pointed at a row of glass bottles. The crystals inside were yellow and blue and green and violet, enough to tempt any child. "Is those it?"

"Ladies first," said Mr. Mayhew firmly. "You will not mind sitting at my desk, ma'am?"

Philo shook her head. Her voice had gone astray. How she wished for Aquila's well-bred ease in company!

After Aquila's mother's death when the girls were nine, Cousin Sarah had impressed upon Philomena that it behooved her to be self-effacing. For years Philo had thought it was because she was the younger, if only by a few months. That was before she learned the dreadful truth about her own mother.

Mr. Mayhew had pulled out a battered but sturdy wooden chair from the desk by the front window and he was waiting, an enquiring look on his face. Dismissing her memories, she hastened to seat herself.

"Did you bring your charts?" he asked.

She nodded, filled with gratitude that he had remembered. It did not matter whether he was truly interested or only being kind.

If he was puzzled by her silence, he politely ignored it. "Then excuse me, pray, while I give young Master Toby something to keep him occupied."

"Do you *got* to call me 'young Master Toby'?" the child asked in a long-suffering voice. "That's what Mama calls me when I be naughty."

"What would you like me to call you?"

"Just Toby."

"Then you must call me just Robin. Now let's put this smock on you and then you watch while I show you what to do."

Philo hoped he realised a five-year-old's limitations. Surely he would not give Toby anything dangerous?

As if he read her mind, his first words when he returned to her side were reassuring. "Bicarbonate of soda, acetic acid, and an indicator. That's baking soda, vinegar, and red-cabbage water to you, but don't tell Toby. They fizz nicely and change colour, besides being cheap. May I see your papers?"

She spread them on the desk where, to her embarrassment, they refused to stay flat after being rolled in her pocket. Robin Mayhew collected some empty beakers to hold down the corners. Though his hands were stained they were well scrubbed, she noted, and the nails were neatly trimmed. She liked his hands.

"Explain." He pulled up a stool.

Somehow it was easy to talk about her work. She showed him the family trees she had drawn up in Vienna. "That is where I started keeping records," she told him. "I had a parrot in Brazil, but Cousin Sarah made me leave it behind when Papa was posted to Lisbon."

"Your father was a diplomat?"

"Yes. We stopped in the Canary Islands, and to make up for losing my parrot he bought me a wild canary in a cage. It was a little green finch, very different from the tame canaries they had in Portugal. Papa said the Spaniards had deliberately bred one from the other. That seemed to me very clever and exciting. I did not try breeding my own, though, until we went to Vienna in 1813. In 1814 I raised two broods, eleven nestlings, then last year when the new clutches were hatching, Papa died."

"I'm sorry."

"There was a dreadful scandal." Philo realised she was departing from the subject. Besides, Mr. Mayhew would hardly be interested in Sir William Ware's dramatic demise in the arms of his latest mistress. "Anyway, we had to leave Vienna just when the baby canaries were testing their wings. I had to give away all of that generation, but I managed to bring two older pairs with me."

"Right across Europe? In the middle of the Hundred Days?" He sounded incredulous.

"Waterloo was already over when we reached Brussels. It was not easy, though, and Aquila—my sister—complained a good deal. The birds make her sneeze, so you cannot blame her. But I was determined, and it was worth the trouble because otherwise I'd have had to start all over again. The birds I brought have proved themselves as breeders, and the males are good singers. These are their charts."

He pored over the papers, leaning disturbingly close to her, his hair flopping over his forehead. "Very clear and neat," he said with approval. "I fear, though, that you will not find it easy to continue with family trees like these as the generations grow larger. Have you considered just keeping a written record, say a page for each bird? You could list its parents and offspring and still have room for information about its characteristics."

"It would certainly be quicker," she agreed, frowning in thought. "Yes, I see how it could be done. I shall try it. By the third generation it was already difficult to fit all the offspring onto a family tree, even though my writing is small."

"As is mine. I daresay it is a necessity for us scientific experimenters." His smile was full of complicity, counting her a part of the group of enquiring minds to which he belonged.

A passionate desire to be worthy of Robin Mayhew's regard swept over Philomena. Was it possible that with her dedication to science she might somehow make up for the shame of her birth?

The door to the kitchen swung open and a short, wiry man appeared, bearing before him a tin tray with a teapot and three saucerless cups.

"I made a spot o' tea for the lady, sir," he announced.

"Thank you, Bodiham." Mr. Mayhew looked a trifle harassed.

"Is there biscuits?" Toby started to struggle his way out of Robin Mayhew's smock.

"Leave be, young gentleman, afore you does yourself an injury." The servant set the tray on the corner of the table and helped Toby take off the all-enveloping garment. "Biscuits, eh? No, there ain't no biscuits, more's the pity."

"Thank you, Bodiham," Mr. Mayhew said again. "We shall do very well without."

"Biscuits!" There was a gleam in Bodiham's eye. "Won't be no trouble at all, sir. Flour an' sugar an' butter," he muttered as he headed for the kitchen. "Eggs, now, do we want eggs in biscuits? Have to do a bit of experimenting." The door closed behind him.

Philo heard a distinct groan from her host. She thought of offering a receipt for a particularly delicious Viennese biscuit, but she did not want to offend. "Shall I pour?" she enquired. Cousin Sarah had always had a kind word for the elegant way she served tea, though the service before her was like nothing she had ever seen.

For a start, there was neither milk nor sugar. She picked up the pot. It was an earthenware monstrosity, an odd contrast with the fine china cups and much heavier than she expected. Despite her care it dribbled as she poured, leaving a puddle on the tray.

"Good gracious!" Philo failed to restrain a startled exclamation at the pale, muddy colour of the liquid in the cups. "Your servant seems to have put milk in the pot with the tea."

Mr. Mayhew flushed. "Sugar too, I fear. He says it saves unnecessary washing up."

"I like lots of milk and sugar in my tea," Toby assured him. "This is good."

Philo sipped at the syrupy stuff, trying not to show her distaste. In this she was unsuccessful.

"Pray do not feel obliged to drink it, Miss Philomena. Bodiham will not take offence. I frequently leave the greater part of what he cooks."

"It is rather horrid," she admitted, looking at him worriedly. He was thin, to be sure, but not excessively so, and he did not look unhealthy. Still, he had been at Marsh Cottage only a short time, so perhaps he had not been subjected to the servant's cookery for very long.

It would be an act of charity to keep an eye on the situation, to make sure Robin Mayhew did not fade away. Frequent visits to the cottage were obviously called for.

Afraid of wearing out her welcome, Philomena resolved to stay away from Marsh Cottage for two days. Torrential rain helped her abide by this resolution. She occupied herself in transferring the information on her breeding charts to individual notes for each canary, taking pride in the small, neat handwriting Mr. Mayhew had praised.

After their valentine's offering, Juno's cousin, Mr. Ashby, and his friend, Mr. Cornwallis, had stayed in the village and were frequent visitors at the Grange. Philo found their presence helpful in passing the time but useless in distracting her mind from Robin Mayhew.

As the downpour continued, Philo became concerned that the hollow by the stream might flood. She wandered restlessly about the house, irritating Aquila to the point of snapping.

Though Aquila had cultivated a languid air even in the brilliant society of Vienna, the double confinement of their half-mourning and country living introduced her to true tedium. Even in the best weather she could not ride, as Cressida kept no horses. She practised halfheartedly on the spinet in the drawing room, complaining that she could not hear herself because of the canaries' warbling, though she played only because it was expected of a young lady. Philo understood her crotchets and forgave them. Nonetheless, it was a relief when a watery sun broke through the clouds on Saturday morning and she could escape from the house.

Toby was occupied with his mother, and Philo had no intention of telling Aquila or the other girls about her wizard, so she set off alone. The grassy field path was easy going, but the lane was deep in mud. Undaunted, she squelched down the hill, only to find that the stream had risen and was washing the underside of the footbridge. She eyed it uneasily.

If she had been superstitious, she might have thought it was a warning that to call alone upon a young gentleman was the height of impropriety.

"Miss Philomena!" Robin Mayhew's voice hailed her.

She looked up to see his lanky, hatless figure approaching the ford from the other side. His smile made her heart turn over.

"Good day, sir. I was wondering whether the bridge is safe."

"Pray do not attempt it until I have tested it. Dare I hope you were coming to see me?"

Flushing, she nodded. He seemed oblivious of her want of conduct. Perhaps a gentleman dedicated to the study of the natural sciences had no time for the conventions, or perhaps he simply considered her a vulgar, forward hussy.

"I feared you might have been flooded out," she hurried to explain.

"No worse than half a dozen leaks in the roof and a lake around the back door," he said cheerfully. He set foot on the bridge. It creaked but held, and he crossed to her side. "I was going to go for a walk. I promised my mother to exercise daily for my health. Will you go with me? Or we can go back to the cottage and have Bodiham make us a cup of tea."

"Oh no, I had much rather walk!"

He laughed at her vehemence. "I'm sorry, I was teasing you. It is a bad habit one falls into when one has half a dozen sisters. I promise you need not drink tea."

She regarded him dubiously, uncertain how to react. "I should like to walk, only it is shockingly muddy."

"I know a way across the meadows that should not be too bad, if you will allow me to help you climb that stile over there."

His hand at her elbow supported her, and to her relief he did not take advantage of her unsteadiness on the slippery wood to attempt any familiarity. Relief, yes—but she recognised with horror that there was disappointment too. She would have quite liked to stumble into his arms.

Was Aquila's aunt right? Did Philo indeed take after the dead mother she had never known?

Aghast at the thought, she walked in silence across the sodden, straw-coloured grass, keeping a good yard between herself and her alarming companion. Of the dashing hussars and silver-tongued attachés who had pursued both sisters with equal enthusiasm in Vienna, even when they were in mourning for Cousin Sarah, not one had made Philo feel like this.

She glanced at him sideways, careful not to meet his eyes. He was not especially handsome; rather, his clear-cut features and high forehead gave him a look of intelligence. His voice was a pleasant light tenor. She forced herself to concentrate on what he was saying.

"I was thinking about what you said of the little green finch that was the ancestor of the canary. I wonder if they can be bred with our native British finches."

It was the one subject guaranteed to put her at her ease. "Oh yes, they have been crossed with linnets and chaffinches and any number of others. Most of the offspring are infertile, but I have read that a hundred years ago there were already twenty-five varieties of canary in England. The English mostly breed for colour and size, and the Germans for song."

"And you?"

"For song. That is why I have the Harz Rollers. They are not the most beautiful, but they are the best singers."

"Perhaps you should try crossing them with nightingales."

"Nightingales are not finches. Oh, are you teasing me again? About my name?"

"As a matter of fact, I was. I do apologise, Miss Philo. I shall try to break the habit."

"No, it's all right. I think I shall like it when I am used to it. The thing is," she confided hesitantly, "I cannot sing a note."

She expected him to laugh, but he said in a commiserating tone, "What a shocking irony! I suppose your parents could not tell when they christened you, but it just goes to show how careful one ought to be in naming a child. Never mind, it is a pretty name."

Philo was tempted to confess the other half of the irony, that her mother had been an opera singer. She restrained herself. She dreaded the possibility that Robin Mayhew might turn from her in disgust.

When they reached the far side of the meadow, she hurried over the stile without his help, then stepped back, startled, as a large bird scurried away from almost under her feet.

"Oh, what was that? It's beautiful!"

"A pheasant. A splendid fellow, is he not, with his red wattles and green neck? Look, he has left you a tail feather." He handed her a narrow, eighteen-inch feather, glossy brown barred with black. "I suppose you have been too much abroad to know our English birds well."

"Cousin Cressida has taught me some of the garden birds. Blackbirds and thrushes, and the different kinds of tits, and we saw a nuthatch one day, running headfirst down a tree trunk."

"And robins, no doubt." He grinned but did not comment on the coincidence of their both being named for birds. As they walked on he pointed out a busy flock of fieldfares, a pair of wrens chattering in a hedge, a kestrel hovering high overhead. "I once wanted to be a naturalist," he said, "before I was introduced to the joys of what my sisters refer to as the stinking science."

Philo had never guessed that a ramble through the winter countryside could be so enjoyable.

Climbing the stile once again on their return towards the village, she heard the church clock chiming noon. "I did not mean to be gone so long," she said in alarm. "They will wonder where I am. Thank you, sir, for a delightful walk."

"I hope you will go with me again one day. There are many more birds to be found. And bring young Toby to visit again."

"I shall," she promised, then added, greatly daring, "if you will let me make the tea."

His laughter followed her up the hill.

What an odd little creature she was, Robin mused, watching her slight figure hurrying away. One moment shy as bedamned, the next full of earnest questions and artless confidences. She had obviously been bred a lady. What emboldened her to defy convention by visiting him?

Robin was not a vain young man. He concluded that Miss Philomena's interest in science was sufficient explanation for her behaviour. She trusted him to be a gentleman, and he had no intention of betraying that trust, however much her soft lips tempted him. Her presence would render his temporary exile in this dreary spot more agreeable by far, until his home laboratory was completed. How fortunate that he had thought to display his knowledge of birds! That would keep her interest if chemistry palled.

He quite forgot that scarce a fortnight since he had pulled a wry face when his mother insisted on his interrupting his studies with exercise.

In the week that followed, Philomena walked with Mr. Mayhew once more, adding four more birds to her list, and took Toby to Marsh Cottage twice.

Although Mr. Cornwallis had left to pursue foxes as soon as the weather improved, Juno's cousin had remained in Valentine Parva. Since Katherine's noble rescuer, Sir Anthony, was also a regular visitor and was even teaching Katherine to ride, Philo's frequent walks seemed to go unnoticed.

The first visit to Marsh Cottage was brief, a detour on the way home from the village shop where she had bought Toby a pennyworth of peppermint bull's-eyes and butterscotch drops.

"I helped Philo clean the floor," Toby explained. "The canaries like flying around free, but they make a *terrible* mess. Do wizards like sweeties?"

"They do indeed," said Mr. Mayhew gravely.

"Philo doesn't, but I did think you do. Which do you like best? No," he changed his mind in a burst of generosity, "you can have one of each."

They left Mr. Mayhew with one cheek bulging and a sticky confection held gingerly between thumb and forefinger.

"Come for elevenses on Monday," he called after them in a glutinous voice. "Bodiham has been experimenting."

After that warning, Philo set out for Marsh Cottage on Monday with a degree of caution, Toby with enthusiasm.

Bodiham's experiment turned out to be some oddly lumpy biscuits that he aptly described as rock buns.

"These are pebbles," said Robin, pointing out a raisin. "I believe a geologist would call them aggregate rocks."

Philo ventured a nibble. "Interesting," she pronounced, then caught Robin's eye and giggled.

Toby thought they were delicious.

Philo busied herself with the tea tray. This time it bore an empty teapot, a steaming kettle, a canister of tea, a milk jug, and a sugar bowl. The cups even had saucers.

"I'd forgotten tea could taste so good," said Robin with a sigh, draining his cup.

"I like Bodiman's better," Toby disagreed. "You didn't put enough sugar in mine, Philo."

Philo regarded Toby's continuing interest in 'speriments as a mixed blessing. On the one hand, having the child with her added a touch of respectability to her visits. On the other, it was only a matter of time before he gave their secret away. Cousin Cressida, always busy, was grateful to Philo for taking care of her son so often. Looking after the canaries was teaching him a sense of responsibility, but sneaking off to call on Mr. Mayhew was the reverse. It made Philo feel guilty, yet she could not bear to give up seeing him.

Fortunately, neither Aquila nor Katherine nor Juno had the least desire to join her in tramping, as they thought, across endless muddy fields.

A few days after the elevenses party, Philo went alone to Marsh Cottage. When Mr. Mayhew, wearing his smock and protective spectacles, opened the front door in answer to her knock, a wave of malodorous gases assailed her nostrils.

Involuntarily she stepped back, raising her hand to her nose. "Good day, sir," she choked out, her eyes beginning to water.

"Oh dear, is it that bad? One grows accustomed to it and does not notice." He came out to join her on the doorstep.

"What is it?"

He sniffed cautiously. "You are right, it is horrible. The stench of rotten eggs is sulfuretted hydrogen. The hint of sweetness is laughing gas. Then there is spirits of ammonia, the chief ingredient in smelling salts."

"The combination is enough to wake the dead. It cannot be good for you. You ought to have a canary to warn you when it is dangerous."

"That is a famous notion," he exclaimed, much

struck. "I cannot imagine why I never thought of it myself. I shall write and suggest it to Sir Humphry. In the meantime, I hesitate to invite you into my humble abode, unless you wouldn't mind taking tea in the kitchen? The inglenook is passably comfortable."

"I daresay the kitchen is as elegantly appointed as your drawing room," she pointed out.

He grinned. "I have an apt pupil. I shall cease to refrain from teasing you, now that you are ready to respond in kind. I shan't ask you to go through my 'drawing room.' Let us go round to the back door. I'll leave this open to air the place out a bit."

He led the way, courteously holding back one or two overgrown branches that barred the path. As they reached the kitchen door, a Dutch door, the upper half swung open and Bodiham's head appeared in a cloud of smoke, coughing and wheezing.

"Be damned if I can get the hang o' flipping them pancakes, sir," he gasped. "Begging your pardon, miss, I didn't see you there."

"Another one in the fire, eh?" Mr. Mayhew asked with a sigh. "Bodiham has a fancy to beat the village women in the race next Tuesday," he explained to Philo. "You may well laugh. I have been living on singed pancakes for days."

"So have we, though not singed. Mrs. Barleyman is in the contest. I persuaded her to teach me the trick of it, but I do not believe I ought to give away secrets to her competitors."

"Have mercy, Miss Philo! Show him how to do it before I starve to death."

He was joking, but she remembered her concern that he was not eating enough. With a mental apology to Mrs. Barleyman, she agreed.

"Just wait half a tick while I scrape off the one as stuck to the ceiling," Bodiham requested.

When Philo saw the cooking facilities the servant

had to contend with, she suddenly sympathised with his incompetence. There was no range, merely an open grate with a griddle balanced across it, on which he set the frying pan for the pancakes. A hinged hook in the chimney allowed a kettle to hang over the fire. The rock buns must have been a triumph of ingenuity, and she was sorry she had scorned them.

Bodiham quickly picked up the art of tossing a pancake.

"Let me try," demanded his master, stirring the batter. "Miss Philo, have you any other tricks of the trade to teach him?"

"I'd take it right kindly, miss," Bodiham admitted.

Philo had never expected to bless Cousin Sarah for making her learn to cook.

With this added excuse, she went daily to the cottage for the next few days. Mr. Mayhew was generally busy in the laboratory, but he always popped into the kitchen at frequent intervals to see what was going on.

"After all, cookery is a form of chemistry," he said. "You heat certain substances together, and the result is something quite different. Take baking soda, for instance." He explained how heating bicarbonate of soda releases carbonic acid gas, which forms bubbles in the dough and makes it rise.

Philo regarded her ingredients with a new respect.

Busy with his new receipts, Bodiham forgot about the pancake race.

"I haven't reminded him," Mr. Mayhew said as he walked with Philo and Toby as far as the bridge on the Saturday before Shrove Tuesday. "If, under your tutelage, he won, he would probably be accused of witchcraft. You have no idea, Miss Philo, how my life has changed since you have been sharing your knowledge. The stew he made last night was delicious."

"You like stew, sir?" Toby asked in astonishment. "I hate it. You can't tell what's in it."

"That was a sort of goulash," Philo said, "a Hungarian dish, but it should have had paprika in it."

"We are going into Lincoln on Monday. Perhaps I can find some there. Shall I see you on Tuesday?"

"I doubt it. I promised Mrs. Barleyman to watch the race."

"Mama says I can go too." Toby screwed up his face in a horrid grimace. "I hope Mrs. Barleyman wins, or she might go on practising *all year* for the next race."

Philo and Mr. Mayhew laughed, their eyes meeting over the child's head. She found it impossible not to wonder what it would be like to be married to him, to have their own child skipping between them.

Shrove Tuesday was a beautiful day for the end of February, sunny and clear, with a promise that March meant to come in like a lamb. Even Aquila condescended to stroll to the village green to watch Mrs. Barleyman compete. A number of peddlers had spread their packs on the grass, or even set up stalls. Villagers and farm folk wore their holiday clothes, giving the place a festive air.

Cousin Cressida kept Toby beside her in the crowd. Under the escort of Mr. Ashby and Sir Anthony, Philo wandered with her sister and Katherine and Juno, examining the peddlers' wares. Mr. Ashby bought them all some gilt gingerbread. Aquila, despite her world-weary air, found a set of buttons she liked. Katherine was trying to decide between two blue satin ribbons in slightly different shades when Philo saw Robin Mayhew.

Her breath caught in her throat. How would she explain it to the others if he spoke to her?

It was a miracle that the secret had lasted so long—except that looking back she realised it was only two weeks. She felt as if she had known Robin forever. Their first encounter had been unconventional by sheer chance, but the longer she went on meeting him clandestinely, the more impossible it was to confess. If anyone found out, she would never be allowed to see him again.

Meeting his gaze, she tried to convey a desperate appeal with her eyes.

Robin read her meaning easily. Not that he had had any intention of accosting her while she was with those elegant young ladies. She was alarmingly elegant herself, with a charming hat topped by a curling feather and a high-waisted, pale-grey garment that accentuated her slender figure in a way that made him frown. It did not surprise him that she wanted to conceal her acquaintance with so peculiar a gentleman as himself, though he thought he looked quite respectable today. He was even wearing a hat, which he hated.

All the same, he wanted to talk to her. Catching her eye again, he began to drift towards the row of huge old elms that lined one side of the green. A Punch and Judy show surrounded by a noisy crowd of children would provide cover for the exchange of a few words.

A few minutes later she stood near him at the back of the audience.

"How clever of you to guess that a puppet show is far beneath Aquila's dignity," she said in a low voice, slightly breathless. "Though for a moment I thought Katherine would come." Then she blushed, looking enchantingly uncertain. "You did want to speak to me?"

"Yes." He forced himself to tear his eyes from

her face, turning back towards the booth where
Punch had just whacked a scarlet-clad devil over
the head to a great outcry from the children. What
was it he had wanted so urgently to tell her? "Ah,
yes. I bought a canary in Lincoln yesterday. Will
you come tomorrow and tell me how to care for it?"

"I'll try. Oh dear, Cousin Cressida is bringing
Toby to see the show."

Robin glanced round and saw his young friend
tugging on the hand of a reluctant matron.

"Oh lord, do you think he has recognised me?"
he groaned.

"In a hat? Never!" Philomena's voice was teasing, but he caught an anxious undertone.

"I'll be off. Until tomorrow." Hoping his departure looked casual, he moved away.

Philo watched Toby's approach. He did not seem
to have noticed even her presence, his wondering
gaze fixed on the puppets. Cousin Cressida had seen
her, of course, but had no reason to connect her with
the tall gentleman who happened to have been
standing nearby.

"Philomena, be a dear and take charge of Toby.
Mrs. Barleyman is in her altitudes over something
or other and I must see if I can calm her down."

"Of course, ma'am." Philo took Toby's hand.

"Angel!" Cousin Cressida hurried off, leaving
Philo feeling guilty.

Toby could not be dragged away from Punch and
Judy to watch the race, so she did not discover till
later that Mrs. Barleyman had come in third, and
promptly taken to her bed. Philo cooked dinner that
night. She hoped it would compensate to some degree for her deception.

Guilt or no, as soon as Philo had fed and watered
her canaries next morning, she headed for Marsh
Cottage.

Toby was thrilled to hear that his friend Robin had bought a canary of his own. In fact, he took it upon himself to instruct the gentleman in the care and feeding of the little bird, the importance of fresh drinking water and a bath two or three times a week.

Robin listened with sober attention, while Philo did her best not to laugh as her own oft-repeated words emerged from the child's mouth.

"What's his name?" Toby asked at last.

"Faraday, after a scientific friend of mine."

After a moment's thought, Toby nodded his approval. "That's a good name for a canary."

The next few times they called, Toby catechised Robin to make sure he was treating Faraday properly. A week passed, however, before he thought of one point he had not mentioned.

"Did you let Faraday out of his cage to fly around?" he enquired. "He will like to stretch his wings, you know."

"No, I didn't," he replied, with a questioning look at Philo.

She was about to tell him that Faraday's cage was large enough to make free flight unnecessary, when Bodiham stuck his head round the door to ask her advice. Robin followed her into the kitchen. She was tasting a fair approximation of what Bodiham described as a "betchermell sarce" when the crash of breaking glass startled her.

Robin leaped for the door to the laboratory. Philo thrust the wooden spoon into the servant's hand and dashed after him as another crash resounded.

"Don't move," shouted Robin.

Toby, standing in the middle of the table surrounded by shards of glass, turned towards him and more equipment went flying.

"Don't move, Toby," said Philo, tying to keep her

voice steady. "You will cut yourself. Robin will help you down."

"But I got to catch Faraday. I can't reach him from the floor," Toby said tearfully, his mouth quivering. "He'll get hurt. I thought he would sit on my shoulder like Metternich does, but he flied up there and he won't come down."

Faraday was perched on a curtain rail, surveying the catastrophe below with a smug look in his beady eye. He whistled a gay trill.

Robin gave a shout of laughter. "Little devil," he said, admiring. "Two little devils. Bodiham!"

Bodiham was already there, dustpan and brush in hand, to clear a path through the glass on the tabletop. Robin lifted Toby down, and he ran to bury his face in Philo's skirts.

"I didn't mean to be naughty," he sobbed.

"Of course you didn't, love," she said helplessly, stroking his dark head, "but I'm afraid it will cost a fortune to replace all Mr. Mayhew's equipment."

"Not quite a fortune," Robin said, still grinning. "And I can well afford it. You are not to worry; it was my fault. I should have known better than to leave the child alone in the laboratory. But first things first. Tell me, Miss Philo, how am I to recapture that cheeky bird without smashing what little is left?"

With Bodiham's assistance, a hair sieve was fastened to the end of a broomstick. Makeshift bird net in hand, Philo stalked Faraday, breaking only one more retort as she turned incautiously. Soon the canary was back in his cage, gobbling seed as if he had been starved for a month.

"I believe I shall turn my mind to devising the perfect canary food while I am waiting for the new glassware," said Robin, eying Faraday thoughtfully.

He had succeeded in soothing Toby while Philo

recaptured the bird. She decided they had best make themselves scarce before he started totting up the damage. Searching his face as she said good-bye and apologised once more, she could detect no sign of anger. It was hard to believe that would not change once he realised the extent of his loss.

It took considerable courage to call at Marsh Cottage the next day, and in fact Philo was too craven to take Toby with her. In her reticule was the pin money she had saved since they came to the village. Though there had been little to spend it on, it was a small sum, but she was sure he would refuse it anyway.

Bodiham answered the door. He did not look like a servant whose master is in a towering rage.

"Morning, miss," he greeted her with his usual cheerful demeanour. "Mr. Mayhew's gone to see a farmer 'bout some different kinds o' seeds for the bird. He won't be long. Come on along in and I'll make a *proper* pot o'tea while you wait." He grinned.

"Is Mr. Mayhew very angry about yesterday?" Philo hesitated on the doorstep.

"Lor' bless you, miss, the master reckons it's a waste of energy getting in a miff. It's unscientific's what he says. Here he comes now, he can tell you hisself."

Robin did not tell her anything of the sort, simply because he was too busy showing her the variety of grains he had obtained for Faraday and asking her opinion as to how best to test them. Philo indulged him, though she suspected that, like her own birds, Faraday would eat the seeds he fancied and ignore the rest. A canary's preference was no more susceptible to scientific analysis than a human's.

At least, she doubted that her own preference for Mr. Robin Mayhew could be weighed in the balance, as he was now weighing small amounts of seed. She looked fondly down at his bent head, his too-long hair curling over his collar.

"I suppose you will want to weigh him too, to see how he thrives on different diets," she said.

He glanced up eagerly. "Do you think we can persuade him to sit on the scale? Dash it, Philo—Miss Philomena, I believe you are teasing me! It is a good idea, all the same."

Whether because of or in spite of his experimental diet, Faraday throve. The same was not true of Robin.

He had gained weight since Philo taught Bodiham to cook. Now he was losing it again, and his face was pale, with an unhealthy cast. She noted that when they walked together he was ready to turn back sooner than usual. Anxiously she interrogated the servant about his menus, tasted leftovers, suggested new receipts to tempt Robin's appetite.

Philo felt guiltily sure she would have noticed the seriousness of the problem sooner if it hadn't been for all the excitement over Juno. Who would ever have imagined that such a serious person would be caught in the conservatory in a passionate embrace? In truth, Philo had been aware of a pang of envy, of a longing that a certain gentleman of her acquaintance would forget himself as Charteris Ashby had. It was her confusion over this, as much as her concern over Juno's whereabouts, that had blinded her to Robin's ill health.

He was not exactly ill, but he was far from well, and it hurt her because she loved him. She had even dared to wonder whether the illegitimate daughter of an opera singer was truly an ineligible bride for plain Mr. Robert Mayhew of Marsh Cottage. Her father had left her a dowry, nothing to compare with Aquila's splendid fortune but enough to help make Robin's life more comfortable. That was all she wanted.

One warm, sunny day towards the end of March, she stepped into the cottage through the open door to find him clutching dizzily at the edge of the table, his face deathly white.

"Philo . . ." His voice trailed off.

"What is it? What is wrong?" Rushing to his side, she guided his stumbling steps to a seat. His skin was clammy. He sagged against her, then jerked forward and cast up his accounts on the floor.

"Bodiham!" she cried. "Bodiham, come quick!"

Robin leaned back, eyes closed. She loosened his cravat as the servant rushed in.

"Gawd, he's been and gone and pizened hisself."

"Poisoned? What do you mean?" Philo glanced at the table, where a sparse array of glass dishes and jars were all that was left of the onetime tangle of equipment. "Robin, what have you been doing?"

"Tasting chemicals," he said shakily. "It's a common way to identify them."

"Tasting chemicals! How could you be so foolish? Come on, Bodiham, we must get him into his bed. Really, Robin, you've less sense than a five-year-old. If you kill yourself, what good will that do anyone?" Scolding, half crying, she helped Bodiham support him up the narrow stair to a tiny chamber under the eaves.

He collapsed across the bed, breathing stertorously.

"I'll get him into his nightshirt, miss, but what'll I do then?"

"I don't know. Keep him warm and make him drink strong tea." She had no experience of illness, let alone poisoning, but that felt right and could do little harm—she hoped. "I must go for help. Robin, listen to me." She dropped to her knees on the bare plank floor by the bed. With immense effort he turned his head towards her. "Promise me, *promise* you will never do that again."

There was a glimmer of a smile in his eyes as he whispered, "I promise."

Much as Philo wanted to stay, she jumped up and ran from the room, down the stairs, out of the cottage. Surely Cousin Cressida would know what to do.

The tears were falling faster now, making it hard to see her way. She brushed them away, then stopped, blew her nose, and took a deep breath before picking up her skirts again and hurrying on. Never had the mile to the house seemed so long.

She entered through the conservatory, ignoring Talleyrand's welcoming warble. Katherine was reading in the drawing room.

"Where is Cousin Cressida?"

"In her sitting room, I think, giving Toby a lesson. You have been crying, Philo. What's wrong?"

The question made a lump rise in her throat. She shook her head and went on.

After one look at her face, Cressida sent Toby to play and took the weeping girl in her arms.

"Come and sit down and tell me all about it."

"It's Mr. Mayhew—the wizard—down at Marsh Cottage. Only he's not a wizard, he's a chemist, and he has poisoned himself."

"What with?" asked Cressida sharply. Rising, she went to a locked cabinet and opened it with a key from her pocket.

"I don't know. Lots of different things, I think. He was tasting chemicals to identify them. I didn't know what to do except keep him warm. And I told his servant to give him tea."

Cressida took a small leather case from the cupboard. "A good start. We shall just have to try a bit of everything, but tell me the symptoms while I fetch my bonnet. Bring this with you."

Clutching the case, Philo trotted after her, describing Robin's condition. Cressida was relieved to hear that he had vomited and that he was not in a total stupor. Philo's hopes revived, only to plummet again when Cressida ordered John Barleyman to run to the inn in the village and send an ostler to Lincoln for the doctor.

Bodiham was overjoyed to see them. He propped Robin, pallid and inanimate, against a couple of pillows and then scurried to do Cressida's bidding. Down Robin's uncomplaining throat poured a stream of warm water mixed with chalk and charcoal, egg white, olive oil, and calomel. Milk followed, then more hot, sweet tea.

At last Cressida began to pack up her little case of medicines. "I have done all I can," she told Bodiham. "Continue to give him as much liquid as he will take: milk, tea, and beef tea."

Philo, whose gaze never left Robin's face, saw him raise heavy-seeming eyelids. "Trying to drown me, ma'am?" he murmured.

Involuntarily Philo took a step towards him, stopping when Cressida frowned at her.

"It is the least you deserve, young man." Cressida eyed him sternly. "Are you by any chance a connexion of Baron Mayhew of Aisby?"

"Brother." Exhausted, he closed his eyes again.

"Hmm. I believe he had best be informed. I have sent for the doctor, and I shall write down for him what I have given you."

"There's paper and pen below, ma'am," Bodiham told her.

"Thank you. Come, Philomena."

"Oh, but I must stay and take care of him."

"Out of the question. His man seems competent enough." Cressida swept from the room.

Philo followed, with a miserable backward glance

at the bed. She could not be sure, but she thought Robin winked at her.

While Cressida wrote a note for the doctor, Philo explained to Bodiham how to make beef tea. She knew Cressida noted this further indication of her intimacy with the household, and she was prepared for interrogation as they set out for home.

"Well?"

The story tumbled out. Beyond ascertaining that Mr. Mayhew had never attempted any physical familiarities, Cressida made no comment.

When they reached the house Aquila appeared at once, with questions obviously hovering on her lips. Cressida sent Philo straight to bed, saying only, "You will be the better for a rest, and I must think what is to be done."

Dragging her suddenly weary feet up the stairs, Philo hoped she did not imagine the kindness in her voice. She went to bed in her shift and fell asleep before she could consider the implications of the day's events.

Aquila woke her in the late afternoon. She bore a tray with tea and biscuits, which she set on the bedside table before pulling up a chair. Not for Aquila the inelegance of sprawling on her sister's bed.

She looked at Philo consideringly. "Toby asked me to tell you that Metternich is trying to feed his feet. I gather this is a matter of some moment?"

"Yes, it's the first sign that he is ready for mating." Sitting up, Philo rubbed her eyes. Suddenly everything came flooding back into her mind. "Does Cressida know you are here? Am I in disgrace?"

"Should you be?"

"I have made such a mess of everything, Aquila," she wailed. She told her sister the tale of her developing relationship with Robin Mayhew, concluding despairingly, "And the worst of it is that he turns out to be brother to a baron!"

Aquila raised skilfully darkened eyebrows. "I cannot see why that should throw you in the dismals. He is a gentleman; he will do the right thing by you."

"Not when he finds out that Papa was not married to my mother. Besides, I do not want him to 'do the right thing' by me."

"I am not surprised. He sounds to me quite mad, and I am certain you can do better for yourself, if only you will not be so shy. Do you not recognise his name?"

"Mayhew? No." Philo was puzzled.

"When we were in Brazil we knew a gentleman by that name."

"A diplomat? No, I do not remember. Cousin Cressida said she meant to send a message to Lord Mayhew at once. Even if Robin does not mind about my birth, his brother will never countenance his offering for me."

"Then you need not worry about Mr. Mayhew 'doing the right thing,'" Aquila pointed out, uncomprehending.

Philo realised that her sister, expecting to make a marriage suitable to the wealthy granddaughter of an earl, had no understanding of love. Despite her own misery, she pitied her.

Cressida accepted Philomena's heartfelt penitence for her deception and, to her surprise, did not absolutely forbid visits to Marsh Cottage.

"You may go if you can persuade Aquila or Katherine to go with you; or take Toby, who tells me, incidentally, that Mr. Mayhew is his best friend. While Mr. Mayhew is ill, you are only to call to ask after him. Once he is recovered you are not to stay longer than half an hour, and if you walk with him it must be in company."

"You are sure he will recover?" Joyful, she was ready to accept any restrictions.

"The doctor called on his way back to Lincoln. He doubts there is any permanent damage to the organs. Philo, I am not sure I am acting rightly in this. I trust you to show me that I am."

Philo promised fervently that she would.

Despite Aquila's lack of understanding, she actually offered to accompany her sister to Marsh Cottage next day, claiming that she was curious to see a wizard's lair. Bodiham assured the ladies that his master was much improved, sitting up and demanding food. Philo had to be content with that, though she longed to run up the stairs to the little chamber to see for herself.

Toby went with her the day after. She nobly allowed him to go up to Robin while she waited below, mindful of her promise. When they reached home, after stopping by the stream to see if there were any tadpoles yet, they entered through the back door as usual and found Aquila at the spinet.

She greeted Philo with the news that Lord Mayhew was closeted with Cousin Cressida.

"What are they saying? What is he like?" Philo was cast into high fidgets.

Vulgar inquisitiveness was beneath Aquila, but she had happened to be coming down the stairs when his lordship entered the hall. "Unless I am much mistaken, it is the gentleman we knew in Brazil, when we were children. He was not then a baron; I should remember that." As she spoke she continued to play, competing in a desultory way with Metternich and Talleyrand. "We called him Theo."

"I meant, does he look amiable?"

Aquila shrugged.

"I *wish* I knew what they are saying!" Philo moaned.

* * *

At that precise moment, after an exchange of the
amenities, and expressions of gratitude on the baron's part, he was saying to Cressida, "I imagine
you had some particular reason for asking me to
call before I see Robin?"

"I did. I do." Cressida hesitated.

"I am very anxious to see my brother."

"Of course, but I promise you he is in no immediate danger."

Looking relieved, Lord Mayhew accepted a seat.
"You were saying?"

"I fear you will think me very remiss. I must
warn you that a young lady who is in my charge
has been visiting your brother unbeknownst to me."
She flushed at his look, at once astonished, unbe-
lieving, and amused, and hurried to add, "I do not
believe that anything of a . . . an *indecent* nature
has occurred."

"I trust not!" His lordship now sounded grim.
"Robin has always been too busy with his experiments to run after the petticoats—if you will excuse
the expression, ma'am—but you may be sure that
if he has in any way compromised your ward he
shall do the gentlemanly thing by her. I will not
permit a member of my family to ruin a respectable
young lady."

Cressida's face grew still hotter. Gamely she
struggled on. "As for that, my lord, I fear that Philomena Ware's antecedents are not . . ."

"Philomena Ware! Good lord, are we speaking of
little Philo? Sir William's daughter? My dear
ma'am, I was intimately acquainted with the family some eight or nine years since. I am well aware
of Philomena's history."

"I expect you will change your mind, then, about
your brother." Cressida sighed, with relief that

awkward explanations were unnecessary, and with pity for Philo.

"You mean I think Robin above her touch?" Lord Mayhew's grin was charming. "On the contrary, ma'am. Because of his peculiar activities, the stuffier members of my family already consider him a black sheep. If he has compromised Miss Philomena he shall wed her."

"I would not go so far as to say she is compromised. However, I suspect she has fallen in love."

"Little Philo in love with Robin?" The chemist's bother was torn between amusement and dismay. "I am sorry to hear it, for he is wedded to his profession and I doubt he has noticed her existence. Shall I go and beat some sense into his thick head?" He paused. "You know, come to think of it, I had been wondering why he lingered here. His place was completed a good month since."

"His place?"

"He recently inherited a house in Staffordshire; no estate, but enough money in the funds to keep him—and raise a family—comfortably. My sisters object to his experimenting at Aisby, so he rented the cottage here while he was having the stables at the new place converted into a laboratory. The work was finished weeks ago. Hmm, I shall have to have a chat with young Robin."

Cressida was beginning to like the baron. "I need not ask you not to reveal what I said of Philo's feelings."

Again the charming grin. "No, of course not, yet I feel we need not despair. Tell me, is Philomena's half sister also with you? What was her name— Madame de Cressy called her an unfledged eaglet— Aquila, is it?"

"Yes, she is here."

"I should like to meet her again, and Philo, of course."

"Doubtless the girls will be delighted to renew the acquaintance." Cressida rose with a smile—good-looking young noblemen were in short supply in the village, and she was aware of Aquila's boredom. "Pray come this way, my lord."

Philo retained only a confused impression of a gentleman who bore an astonishing likeness to Robin, though slightly shorter and more compactly built. All that mattered, to her mind, was that, far from frowning upon her, he had smiled. He had even teased her gently about not remembering him from Brazil.

"Of course, I was only one of the young men prostrate at your feet," he reminisced, "and you skipped blithely over us to go and chase the birds and butterflies."

Tongue-tied, Philo was grateful when Aquila, at her most languid, came to the rescue and told him about her continued interest in birds.

She was afraid the baron's cordiality stemmed from ignorance of her behaviour or of her illegitimacy, but Cousin Cressida assured her that he knew everything. She dared to dream again.

Toby went with her again the next day to see Robin. He was downstairs, well wrapped up and ensconced in the inglenook in the kitchen. His brother was there too. Lord Mayhew had taken rooms at the village inn and announced his intention of staying until the invalid was fully recovered.

Robin looked much better, and his welcoming smile was all she could have hoped for. However, between Toby's chatter and the baron's inhibiting presence, Philo was unable to return to their accustomed easy camaraderie. After a stiff enquiry about his health she spoke only when directly addressed. Sitting silent at the kitchen table, she was miserably aware of Robin's puzzled glances.

Matters did not improve. She never saw Robin without his brother or Aquila or Katherine or Cressida. Sometimes she felt the whole village was there. He was not well enough to walk far, so they did not even have the privacy that falling behind a group in the fields might have allowed.

Lord Mayhew brought him to the house in his carriage one rainy afternoon. Tea was served in the drawing room, to the accompaniment of energetic trills and warbles from the conservatory. Philo remembered the first time she had taken tea at Marsh Cottage. She caught Robin's eye, and he grinned. Certain that he was remembering the same event, she was oddly reassured.

"I should like to see the canaries," he said, setting down his cup. "Will you introduce me, Miss Philomena?"

She looked at Cousin Cressida, who nodded permission. Robin followed her through the French doors.

Philo was shy. They were alone, but the knowledge that everyone in the next room was aware of their once-secret friendship oppressed her. She showed him her birds. The females were busily constructing nests, while Talleyrand and Metternich sang as if they had not a care in the world.

"That's right, fellows, let the women do the work," Robin told them. "You can scarcely hope to improve their voices," he observed to Philo. "Poor Faraday cannot compete with such splendid singing. He will come into his own when I begin my experiments again. The new equipment arrived this morning, and I left Bodiham unpacking it."

"I meant to offer to help pay for it, but somehow the right moment never came. Will you take . . . ?"

"I certainly will not! Broken glass is a hazard of the profession."

"So is poisoning. You will remember you promised not to taste the chemicals?" Anxiously she searched his face.

"An extorted promise, when I was in extremis," he teased, but his eyes were warm. "No, I shall not forget." He reached for her hand just as Katherine stepped into the conservatory.

"The canaries are curious, are they not, Mr. Mayhew?" Katherine said. Robin looked blank. "The females do the useful work while the males are expected merely to be decorative," she explained.

The momentary intimacy was lost. By the time Philo retired that night, she wondered whether she had imagined it.

Afraid that she had misread Robin's intentions, Philo let several days pass without visiting Marsh Cottage. She could not bear him, or anyone else, to think she was pursuing him. Their friendship was changed by the unvoiced conjectures and expectations of those who knew of it.

In the end, she gave in to Toby's incessant demands and they walked down to the cottage. It was a grey, chilly day, the hedgerows still showing no signs of breaking into leaf, but like the canaries, optimistic birds were nesting anyway.

Bodiham answered the door. Robin was in the middle of an experiment involving numerous bubbling retorts linked by yards of glass tubing.

He looked up, smiling but preoccupied. "I'll be with you in a moment. I can't leave this just now."

Toby rushed to his side. "What are you doing?"

Philo hesitated, then went to join them as Robin explained the process of distillation. His kindness to the little boy, his animated enthusiasm for his profession, his deft movements as he made a precise adjustment to a spirit lamp, all filled her with admiration and a vague longing.

Bodiham brought tea a quarter of an hour later,

just as Robin straightened with a sigh, saying,
"There, it will take care of itself for a while."

Philo poured, very much aware that only fifteen
minutes remained of the half hour Cousin Cressida
had limited her to. Stupidly, she could not think of
anything to say, and Robin, too, had fallen silent.

Toby was under no such constraint. "Wilhelmina
and Dorothea have laid some eggs," he announced
importantly.

"Wilhelmina?" asked Robin.

"Mrs. Metternich," Toby explained, "and Dorothea is Mrs. Talleyrand."

Robin shouted with laughter, and Philo knew her
face was scarlet. She had never mentioned her female canaries' names to him, for the very good reason that they were not those of the famous
statesmen's wives but of their mistresses. She had
correctly guessed that even a gentleman as engrossed in his experiments as Robin must have
heard some of the scandal from Vienna.

"They are funny names," Toby agreed indulgently. "Philo says I can give the babies their
names when they get hatched. Look!" He pointed
at the window. "There's Aquila and sir my lord riding horses into your garden!" He jumped down from
his stool and ran outside.

" 'Sir my lord' has a poor sense of timing." Robin
sighed, and regarded Philo with a quizzical look. "I
suppose we must go and speak to them."

Though Robin had regained most of his strength,
Lord Mayhew showed no sign of leaving the village. He had sent for a couple of hacks so that he
and his brother could ride together, and he often
lent one to Aquila, presuming on old acquaintance.
Philo was grateful to him for giving her sister an
occupation, but she wished the two of them had not
arrived just now. Suddenly there were a thousand

things she wanted to say to Robin, and by the time they left her half hour would be over.

Aquila went riding again the next morning with Lord Mayhew. Toby was doing his lessons. Katherine had suggested Philo sit with her and sketch some dried oak leaves, but Philo found it impossible to settle to any occupation. She decided to walk down to the stream.

She would not go to the cottage, but if Robin happened to look out and see her, surely no one could object if he came out to exchange a few words.

Climbing the stile from the field into the lane, she saw Bodiham tramping towards the village. He waved and called a greeting but continued on his way, turned a corner, and disappeared. Robin was alone, then.

When she reached the point in the lane where she and Toby had stopped, the day before Valentine's Day, to look down at the wizard's house, she paused. To the outward eye the view was unchanged: the dilapidated cottage, the overgrown garden, a thin spiral of smoke from the chimney. Yet all was different now, because she knew the wizard. Without taking the trouble to cast a spell, he had enchanted her heart.

Philo smiled as she recalled her first sight of Robin, his face black with soot.

For an instant the explosion seemed a part of her memories. Then a second thunderous boom split the air and the cottage's tile roof sagged.

Horror rose in her throat, stifling a scream. The brick chimney toppled with agonising slowness.

Her skirts gathered in both hands, Philo raced down the hill, pounded across the bridge, darted between the clutching branches in the garden. The window glass lay in shards on the ground; even the leading was torn and twisted.

Inside, an orange-yellow light danced.

Fire!

A blast of heat met her as she sped up to the gaping hole. The paint on the flame blistered.

"Robin!"

He must be in there. A dry sob shook her. She ripped off her pelisse and flung it across the sill. Taking a deep breath, she nerved herself to climb in.

"Philo . . . Philomena . . ." It was little more than a croak, behind her. She swung round.

A black tatterdemalion stumbled towards her. She ran into Robin's arms.

"Philo, don't cry, my darling." His tender words were cut short by a spasm of coughing. "I'm all right, honestly, but I think I had better sit down."

Pulling her with him he sank to the ground, his back against a tree trunk. She leaned against his chest, oblivious of the filth, unable to stop weeping, conscious only of his strong arms holding her close.

A crash followed by a crackling roar made her look up.

Flames leapt from the roof. The heat dried the tears on her face.

"We must move farther away." She scrambled to her feet and reached for his hands. "I'll help you. Put your arm around me. That's it. Just a little farther. There, I think that will do. You can lean against the gatepost." She knelt beside him, took his soot-blackened face in both hands, and gazed lovingly into his bloodshot eyes. "You are really not hurt?"

"Just a little shaky. Come here." He pulled her to him and kissed her. His kiss was anything but shaky. It left her breathless.

Another crash from the blazing cottage drew their attention. One wall was gone, and another fell inward as they looked.

"What were you doing?" asked Philo, awed.

"Kissing you. A most successful experiment. Would you like another demonstration?"

"Yes, please."

Robin obliged. After he had once again robbed Philo of breath, he dropped gentle little kisses all over her face. Then he held her away from him and studied the effect.

"Black measles," he said with a satisfied grin. "Adorable. I think I can fit another one in there." He aimed at the center of her forehead.

She pushed him away. One more kiss and she would dissolve altogether. "That's all very well," she said, trying to sound prim, "but I meant the experiment that caused that." She waved at the remains of the cottage, now little more than a pile of glowing embers. "You cannot call that successful."

"I certainly can. I learned a great deal from it. I learned always to have a back door. I learned the advisability of a reinforced roof. And, most important, I learned that you love me. You do, don't you?"

"Oh yes. I fell in love on St. Valentine's Day."

"Me too." He laughed, and filled in the space on her forehead with another sooty smudge. "Considering our names, I daresay it was inevitable. You know what the next experiment is, don't you?"

"No, what?"

There was a wickedly teasing twinkle in his eye. "Why, we get married and then, my darling, we shall try a little scientific breeding!"

A Gentleman Calls

TO HER INTENSE ANNOYANCE, Cressida found herself counting the days of the duke's absence. He had written once, promising to return and give her a full report of Juno's state. The excitement of Philo and her wizard, and Cressida's worry over Aquila's boredom, made her wish for someone to discuss things with. One night, as she lay in bed, she was amazed to find herself in the middle of an imaginary conversation, not with Mr. Trent, but with the duke.

When the duke did return, he was still travelling incognito. He came into the Grange long enough to tell Cressida that all was well with Juno and that he would be breaking his journey in Valentine Parva for a few days. He called a day later to see if he could do anything to entertain the young ladies, and after that he came often to Hugh's Grange with Chart and seemed less uneasy in her company. Cressida wanted to be sure he no longer thought she had once pursued him with mercenary motives. She asked him to call at a time when she knew the others would be out. She did not want to make a point of deliberately excluding them from his visit, but she wished to speak with him alone.

After an exchange of pleasantries, Cressida said, "I gathered from something you said that you feel you have in some way wounded me. I wish, your grace, to assure you that I in no way feel your behaviour reprehensible. I also wish to assure you that I am fully aware that the easy footing of our youth is a thing of the past. Indeed, I never looked for anything but friendship between us." There was no need to speak of her hopes.

"Indeed, Mrs. Trent," he replied.

Only one who knew him as well as Cressida had would recognise the impatience in his tone. She felt a rush of tenderness towards him, and tried to mask it by replying, "I do not wish to presume."

"You are the least presumptuous woman I have never known. Could you call me Tyne? I remember I was finally able to persuade you to call me Chelmly."

"That was years ago," Cressida said, wishing she had never embarked upon so intimate a conversation.

"I was given to understand that you had confided to someone that my attentions made you uncomfortable, and you did not wish to tell me directly for fear of hurting my feelings. I was told that if I wished to avoid giving you further pain, I should leave without contacting you.

"Since the lady who told me this was not always considerate of others' sensibilities, I confess I did wonder why you had chosen to confide in her. Your manner and kindness to me, since our reacquaintance, have left me uncertain as to whether you made such a confession."

Cressida's heart soared. Lady William meddling again! She had told him the one thing certain to make him, a man desperate not to presume on the good nature of others, leave. Cressida realised that his courtship of her had taken some courage. It had required him to put himself forward when he could have arranged a marriage with a member of the aristocracy without having to show his feelings.

There was a silence. Cressida wished she knew

what to say. Feelings she thought long dead, buried when she married Mr. Trent, were coming alive in her again. Like a tree, blighted by a long winter then warmed to life by the coming spring, her love for Chelmly was still alive. It was an altered love, matured by the years of separation, her time as Mr. Trent's wife and Toby's mother. And Chelmly, too, had changed. He was more certain, less diffident. She could not imagine him today, climbing out of a window to avoid a party of young ladies.

But he seemed to be saying that he no longer loved her. Cressida wondered if he remembered that once he had all but proposed. Finally, she said, "Well, as you say, that is all past now. I hope you understand that I never found your friendship unwelcome."

The duke rose from his chair and came to stand before her. Taking her hand, he said, "I hope it is welcome now."

April When They Woo

You ask whether Theo shows an interest in Miss Woodley. Not a particle, my dear sister. Hopeless. He will not Bite, though she has cast the Lure. Almost I resign myself to the odious Ophelia. To *her* Theo is kindness itself.

Scratch. Splot. Ink spattered the paper.

"Drat," said Venetia Mayhew.

"Shall I mend your pen for you?"

"Thank you." Venetia covered the letter with the pen-wiper as her brother strolled to the rosewood secretary.

Theo had been standing by the drawing-room window gazing out at the rain-drenched park. Venetia wondered what he had found worth looking at. Though it was nearly April, only a few crocuses showed. The trees had not yet begun to bud.

"Letter to Calla?" He took a silver penknife from the pocket of his breeches and began to repair the nib. "There. Give her my love and tell her I shan't take Miss Woodley to my bosom."

Venetia said with dignity. "I cannot conceive what interest our sister might have in Marianna Woodley."

Theo cocked a satirical eyebrow but said nothing further. He drifted to the fire and gave the coals a stir with the poker.

Venetia uncovered the paper, dipped her pen in

the inkwell, and cast her brother a cautious glance. He was staring into the fire, one foot on the fender. She scribbled:

I believe he encourages Ophelia's delusions. He sits with her whenever she calls on Mama and listens to her with every sign of sympathy.

Ophelia continues the pretence that she and Frank were betrothed. Sighs like a bellows and dresses in black, though even Mama is wearing half-mourning. Only last week O. produced a locket she claims contains Frank's miniature. I cannot see the likeness, and besides dear Frank would never have sat still long enough to be limned. If her posturing did not disturb Mama, I should laugh at the absurdity. Ophelia Bliss was Frank's latest flirt, no more, and we all know he flirted with every unattached lady in Lincolnshire.

It is past bearing, Calla. If O. gulls *Theo* into marrying her, I shall come to you and live out my life as an Aunt!

The pen splattered again, and a blot formed on the hand-pressed paper. Venetia dabbed at it fiercely.

"Shall I frank your letter for you?"

She sniffed. "Not yet, Theo, thank you. I daresay I should go up and dress for dinner, but I'm nearly done and I mean to finish." She scrawled a few lines more, the usual kisses for the babies and greetings to her sister's husband. She was sanding the last blotched line when the Mayhew butler entered.

Theo straightened. "What is it, Davis?"

"A young fellow rode up with this just now, my lord. He says he will await your answer." Davis extended his salver and Theo took the note. He opened it and began to read.

Venetia watched, speculating. It might be an invitation from one of their neighbours, though the household was still officially in mourning for her eldest brother, Francis, who had been killed at Waterloo the previous summer. Still, a small dinner party or a musical evening would be unexceptionable. . . .

Theo went pale. "Good God!"

She rose. "What is it?"

He glanced at her, then at Davis. "The messenger is waiting?"

"Yes, my lord."

"Tell him to inform his mistress that I shall come at once."

"Very good, my lord." Davis bowed and retired from the room at his usual measured pace. Venetia wondered whether he would move faster if the house caught fire.

"Is it Gussie?" Their eldest married sister was increasing again. Venetia expected to attend her in her confinement.

"No, no." Theo ran a hand through his brown hair. He cleared his throat. "I beg your pardon, Vee. I don't mean to alarm you. A Mrs. Trent has writ me from Valentine Parva."

"Valentine . . . but that's Robin!"

"Yes. She says Robin has made himself ill tasting chemicals, and she has sent to Lincoln for a doctor to examine him. I daresay it's just another of Robin's beastly experiments gone wrong, nothing serious."

Venetia felt her heart lurch and beat faster. "But you said you would come at once!"

"I don't know Mrs. Trent's circumstances, and I don't like the idea of Robin being cared for by strangers—or that clunch Bodiham." Theo's voice was matter-of-fact.

"Oh, dear, no. Shall I go with you? I'll just pack a—"

"No, Vee. I mean to ride, not order up the carriage, and in any case I don't wish to alarm Mama. If you were to fly to Robin's side, she would be certain he was at death's door."

Venetia's heart sank. Though Lady Mayhew was a firm-minded woman, she had not yet recovered from the shock of her eldest son's death. "How can Robin be so thoughtless?"

Theo rubbed his brow as if a headache were forming. "Not thoughtless. Absentminded. When he pursues one of his famous theories, Robin forgets everything, including his own safety. You know that as well as I."

"Indeed." Brother and sister fell silent. Venetia was remembering their childhood. She was two years younger than Theo. Robin, the youngest of the three boys and her junior by two years, had had a genius for getting into scrapes from which Theo was always rescuing him. More often than not, Robin's scrapes had sprung from his boundless curiosity. "But I just wanted to know!" he would explain, sure that his inquisitiveness was a kind of Moral Imperative.

And here he was in another scrape. Theo would dash to his rescue, as usual, and Robin would thank him charmingly, vow to reform, and plunge headlong into the next scrape, also as usual.

"You cannot spend your life rescuing your brother," she said gently.

Theo regarded her for an unsmiling moment, then shrugged. "Probably not, but I shall do my possible now. Your part is to prevent Mama and the girls from imagining horrors. I know I can count on you, Vee." He kissed her on the cheek and left the room without further ado.

Venetia sank onto her chair, but several minutes passed before she took up her pen. Before she ap-

plied the seal, she hesitated again. Ought she to
add this latest crisis to the letter? On the whole,
she thought not. The idea of Robin ingesting poi-
sonous substances in the name of Natural Philosophy would cause Calla unnecessary anxiety. Surely
anxiety was not called for. Theo would make everything right. He always did, even at the expense of
his own needs. She wondered why that was a mel-
ancholy idea.

Sighing, Venetia affixed a wafer of pale-blue wax
to the folded sheets and sealed the letter. She would
go up and have Theo frank it before he left. It was
raining. She hoped he might not catch his death.
The phrase sent a shiver up her spine. Whatever
was Robin thinking of?

Theo set off for Valentine Parva with every intention of covering the distance that evening. By the
time he had gone ten miles, his riding cloak was
wet through and his hat dripped an icy stream of
water down the back of his neck. Unwillingly, he
decided to rack up at the coaching inn in Hughsdon. He saw to his horse, made a hasty meal in the
ordinary, and retired to a private bedchamber, having cajoled the promise of hot shaving water from
the landlord at an hour of morning when sensible
travellers would still be abed. The inn was noisy
and his mind unquiet. Despite his weariness, he did
not fall asleep at once.

He had not shown Mrs. Trent's letter to Venetia,
because it roused in him the gravest apprehen-
sions. The phrases stuck in his mind—Robin disori-
ented, pulse thready, fallen into a stupor. Mrs.
Trent had induced Robin to vomit, but she could
not be sure how long a time the unknown poisons
had had to act on his body. She had sent for Dr.
Stark. Every confidence but . . .

What if Robin were to die? Theo shifted on the

lumpy bed. His mind shied from the possibility, circled, returned to it. Frank was dead, after all. Why not Robin, too?

As a boy, Theo had hero-worshipped Frank. Maturity had taught him that his splendid elder brother was a nodcock, but the knowledge had not diminished Theo's affection. Who could have foreseen that Frank's sluggish and ornamental regiment would be called upon to fight Napoleon? In a decade of war, it had never once left London.

Headlong and heedless, Frank had ridden off to battle as to a race-meeting, and died in a Belgian ditch, over-ridden by the hooves of a hundred French cavalry horses. Theo, by then in Brussels with a diplomatic mission to the Bourbon court, had seen his brother buried in the field, sailed home to console the family, and taken up Frank's title and Frank's obligations. Theo had given up his own promising career with the Foreign Office. Baron Mayhew of Aisby was tied to his Lincolnshire demesne with bonds as unrelenting as those of any medieval serf.

In the past months Theo had told a great many diplomatic lies about glory, but he had not stopped dreaming of his brother's mangled corpse. He devoutly hoped that Robin would not supply him with fresh nightmares.

Tossing on the mattress—was it stuffed with acorns?—Theo realised he had been counting on Robin. Robin was his heir, as he had been Frank's. If he couldn't stay the course himself, if he threw over the traces and ran off to Trebizond or Serendip, the family could fall back on Robin—but not if Robin were dead.

I shall have to marry, Theo reflected. His sisters' efforts to strew his path with eligible damsels took on a new, cold clarity. However incomprehensible their choices, his sisters were right. He must take a wife and get an heir and let Robin go his own way. Theo fell into uneasy sleep on the realisation.

When he woke next morning to the chamber-maid's knock, the dreary conviction had not left him. He sighed and called for her to enter. He must find a wife. Not Marianna Woodley, who giggled, nor the melodramatic Ophelia Bliss. He shaved and dressed, found the landlord, and paid the shot. It had stopped raining, but the sky still lowered as he set off for Valentine Parva.

The village consisted of a church, a handsome green, and a few street shops and cottages with several outlying houses. It had a faint ecclesiastical air, as if it were home to any number of retired prebendaries, choirmasters, and vicars' relicts. The church was in notably good repair, and several large houses, set back from the street amid graceful elms, suggested a muted prosperity. Theo had formed the vague idea that the village belonged to the bishop of Lincoln. Not an auspicious site for the conduct of chemical experiments.

The only inn was a half-timbered structure with handsome pargetting. There Theo asked for Mrs. Trent's house. The host replied amiably, but an enquiry about Marsh Cottage lowered the social temperature. The man scowled and muttered direly about strange goings-on.

Time for the heavy guns. "The tenant of Marsh Cottage," Theo said with a fair assumption of hauteur, "is my brother, Robert. I am Mayhew. My groom and valet will arrive shortly with my carriage. Be good enough to direct them to the cottage when they come."

A great deal of flustered my-lording ensued. Theo left his horse with the ostler and his saddlebags with the host. He had the feeling the amenities of Marsh Cottage would not rise to Goucher's standards. His valet was accustomed to move in the highest circles. Theo himself was less toplofty.

"But I love Robin." Philomena Ware sat up in bed, nightcap askew on her dark curls. Her eyes brimmed with tears that glittered in the flickering light of the candle. "I want to spend my life with him."

Her sister, Aquila, reached over, snuffed the candle, and lay back on the heaped pillows. The room plunged into darkness, except for the faint rosy glow of coals on the hearth.

"I see," said Aquila in carefully neutral tones. In fact, she didn't see at all. Philo's sudden passion for her mad chemist had boiled up out of nowhere, like a Brazilian thunderstorm. Given Juno's amazing exploit and Katherine's growing attachment to her handsome rescuer, Aquila wondered if a form of madness hadn't infected the Grange. She thought of the Valentine's Eve ceremony. If she were superstitious, she might imagine they had tampered with the Fates. But that was nonsense.

"Tell me about him, Philo," Aquila murmured.

Philo slid down onto her side of the bed and began a poetic and rather incoherent description of Robert Mayhew's unique charms. He was brilliant, he was kind, he had beautiful hands, he liked birds, even canaries, he knew exactly how to deal with children. Shy little Philo, who sometimes spent whole evenings in company without saying a word, was babbling like a brook, transformed by the magical power of love. It was very strange. Also, because Aquila didn't know the gentleman, a trifle boring.

Aquila had not heard of Mr. Mayhew's existence until that day. That Philo had met him on her own, without introduction, was shocking and interesting. One did not meet eligible gentlemen while roaming the countryside with a five-year-old child. One was introduced at a ball or at the theatre or in the home of some fashionable friend. Juliet had met Romeo at a ball. True, he was not supposed to be there . . .

"Do you think . . ." Aquila began, but a soft snore told her her sister had fallen asleep in mid-paean.

"Do you think he would make you a good husband?" she had meant to ask.

Since their father's death the previous spring, Aquila had felt as if she were responsible for Philo's well-being. Aquila was only half a year older than her sister and they had two respectable guardians, so the feeling was not entirely reasonable, but the thing was, no one else understood about Philo.

Certainly Aquila's relatives, her mother's people, had not understood about Philo. Aquila squirmed, remembering the taunts and disapproving sniffs and outright insults her cousins had dealt out. Even after the scandal-mongering the Ware sisters had endured in Vienna, neither she nor Philo had been prepared for the cruelty of the Lincolnshire gentry. The sisters had lived all their lives in a world in which a love child was the accepted consequence of dalliance, and dalliance the order of the day.

Aquila's mother had raised Philo, treating her husband's by-blow with the same remote kindness she had extended to her own daughter, nursing both children through illnesses, supervising their governesses, receiving their nightly homage with mild, approving kisses. No one, least of all Aquila, knew what her mother felt about Philo. Lady Ware had never offered an opinion.

To Aquila, Philo had simply been her little sister, Papa's other daughter. It was not until after Lady Ware's death, when their father's cousin Sarah came all the way to Brazil to oversee their education, that Aquila was brought to realise the oddity of Philo's presence in their household.

Cousin Sarah was a good Christian. She took Aquila aside and charged her particularly. Aquila was to lend Philo the cloak of her own respectability. The world was not kind to bastards. Cousin Sarah was a plainspoken woman. It was the first time Aquila, then eleven, had heard the word in English.

Rain gusted, rattling the windowpane. Aquila burrowed deeper in the feather bed. Since their father's death in Vienna the previous spring, she had appointed herself Philo's protector, a useful and even interesting role. Nothing but real affection would have prompted Aquila to sneeze her way across half of Europe in the same carriage with Philo's canaries, nor had it been easy, afterwards, to contrive their escape from the Lincolnshire relatives. But if Philo were to marry suitably, her husband would become her lawful protector, and where would that leave Aquila? Of course, there was no saying Mr. Mayhew would offer. If he did not, Philo would be broken-hearted. Aquila imagined herself consoling her sister, diverting her with gifts, travel . . .

She fell asleep on the thought. Next morning she woke determined to find out Robert Mayhew's circumstances and, if possible, his intentions. Cousin Cressida had very properly put a stop to Philo's unescorted visits to Marsh Cottage. At breakfast, Aquila volunteered to chaperone her sister.

Cressida eyed her doubtfully.

"I have a great curiosity to see the wizard's lair," Aquila murmured, buttering a bit of toast.

Philo's eyes shone. "May we go, ma'am?"

Cressida sighed. "Very well, but no more than half an hour, Aquila, and she is not to enter the sickroom."

Philo promised to conduct herself with the utmost decorum, and presently the sisters were pick-

ing their way across a muddy field. The stile gave
Aquila pause.

"Are you sure this is the place?"

"Yes, yes. Do hurry." Philo was already scram-
bling over the stile. Aquila followed her down a
muddy lane to Marsh Cottage in a spirit of enquiry.

And returned not much the wiser. While Mr.
Mayhew was reported to be much improved, he did
not come down. The servant, though well-
intentioned and respectful of Philo, was remarkably inarticulate. A jumble of beakers and retorts
and glass piping in the main room baffled Aquila.
There was a canary.

Regaining the lane, she sneezed thoughtfully.
"You cannot wish to live in such squalid surround-
ings, Philo."

Philo scowled at her from the top step of the stile.
"I should live happily in a hovel if Robin were with
me."

"Tut," Aquila murmured. "Tut, tut." Of all
things, she abhorred fustian. However, Philo was
visibly sincere. Sighing, Aquila gave her sister her
hand and Philo stepped down.

The word "squalid," though appropriate, had put
Philo on the defensive, and she spent the rest of
their walk explaining how her dowry would make
it possible for Mr. Mayhew to let a more suitable
cottage and build a separate structure in which to
poison himself. Aquila listened. When they reached
home, Philo thanked her sister a trifle stiffly for her
company and went off towards the kitchen. She had
lately taken up cookery.

Aquila hung her pelisse and bonnet on the coat
tree and wandered into the drawing room. She sat
at the spinet and played dutiful scales, read a little
from a French novel she kept hidden among the
music, drifted upstairs to mend a torn flounce on
her lilac dinner gown—all the while puzzling over

her sister's conduct and her own inability to enter
Philo's feelings.

When the members of the household had eaten a
light nuncheon, Philo retreated to their bedchamber to rest. To brood, Aquila fancied. She returned
to the spinet, playing a Mozart minuet until she
had mastered the proper pace. When she was certain Cressida had retired to the study, she even took
out the valse she had brought from Vienna. She
played it—very softly—and dreamt of dancing again.

Next morning at breakfast, Philo announced that
she wanted to take Cressida's little boy Toby for a
walk. It was clear to Aquila that her sister meant
to call on the invalid.

"How kind," Cressida murmured.

Toby gave an approving bounce. Under the ladies' combined stares, Philo blushed, but she didr't
invite Aquila to join her.

Later, Philo whisked from the house with Toby
hopping about her like a flea. Aquila watched from
the drawing-room window until they disappeared
from view.

"Aquila?"

She started. Katherine was sketching a vase of
immortelles and ignored the interruption.

Cressida stood in the doorway. "May I speak with
you privately?"

"Of course." Aquila followed her cousin to the
small study.

"Do sit, my dear."

Aquila perched on the edge of one of the leather-
covered chairs. Perhaps Cressida's late husband
had written his sermons in the very masculine
room.

"I daresay you are wondering why I give your
sister so much liberty."

"Isn't Toby rather young to act the duenna?"

Cressida sighed. "I hope I am doing the right

thing. Philo is not a wilful girl, and I think she truly regrets her deception, but, my dear, she is in love."

"Yes. So she said."

"I prefer not to drive her to do something desperate."

Aquila meditated. "Like running off to Gretna Green?"

"Precisely." Cressida ran a hand over her smooth brown hair. Her eyes were tired, as if she had not slept well.

"Is Mr. Mayhew apt to suggest such a course?" Aquila kept distaste for the ramshackle idea of elopement from her voice.

"I trust not. I cannot be sure, however."

"Love," said Aquila, "is a very strange thing."

Cressida smiled at her.

"I should not like to see my sister reduced to living in Marsh Cottage."

"My dear, I think that most unlikely. I have heard from Lord Mayhew. John Barleyman brought the message last evening."

"Then there is a connexion?"

"Oh, yes. They are brothers. Mayhew is coming soon. In the next day or so, I collect."

Aquila permitted herself a sigh of relief. Lord Mayhew would remove his brother from the neighbourhood and Philo would mope, but surely absence would cool her fervour.

Aquila had mounted the stairs and reached the first-floor landing when the door knocker sounded. She paused, wondering whether she ought to admit the caller herself. She was unused to living without a butler. Just as she had taken up the hem of her skirt to descend to the foyer, Eliza, one of the housemaids, entered the hall, sniffing. Eliza had a cold.

She opened the door and bobbed a curtsey. Aquila

heard the murmur of voices, then Eliza stood back
and a man entered. He had removed his curly-
brimmed beaver, so Aquila could see his brown hair
and clean-cut profile, but she had very little idea of
his stature. As she took a step downward, the better to see his face, he looked up and met her eyes.
He gave her a polite smile and handed Eliza his
hat and cloak. Then he and Eliza disappeared from
Aquila's view in the direction of the study.

Aquila stood very still. Lord Mayhew? But that
was not right. The gentleman she had known in
Brazil . . . Memories, not all of them happy, washed
over her. Her mother had died in Brazil. Slowly,
hand on the mahogany bannister, Aquila made her
way back downstairs. Mayhew.

She wandered into the drawing room, deep in reflection. Katherine looked up from her sketching
and when Aquila didn't reply, she gathered her papers and slipped from the room.

Oh dear, I've snubbed her, Aquila thought. She
wondered if she ought to apologise, hesitated,
drifted to the spinet, and stood leafing through the
stack of sheet music without seeing it. Presently
she sat and began playing softly from memory. She
was still at the instrument half an hour later when
Philo returned and found her there.

Philo was saying something about tadpoles.

Aquila turned on the stool. "Lord Mayhew is
here. He and Cousin Cressida have been talking
this half hour."

Philo twisted her hands. She was still rosy from
her walk, but her dark eyes were huge with appre-
hension. "What are they saying? What is he like?"

Aquila ran her fingers over the keys, playing for
time. She could hear the canaries trilling in the
conservatory. She supposed they had been singing
all along. Ordinarily the sound annoyed her, but
today she hadn't noticed them. She picked out the

melody of "Robin Adair," one-handed. "Unless I am much mistaken, Lord Mayhew is the gentleman we met in Brazil when we were children. He was not then a baron. I'd remember that. We called him Theo."

"I meant, does he look amiable? I wish I knew what they're saying," Philo moaned.

Aquila's hand slipped on a dissonance. She lifted it from the keys. "I daresay we'll know soon enough. Compose yourself, Philo. And tidy your hair. He cannot eat you."

Philo flitted to the oval mirror by the window. "There. Is that better?"

"Much. You look very handsome."

"Tell me what to say."

"Everything that's proper, of course!" Aquila bit her lip. There was no use feeling impatient. Philo was shy of strangers with good reason. "It's his first visit. He won't stay long."

Philo took a deep breath and shut her eyes.

Aquila was trying to think of something heartening to say when the door opened and Cressida entered with Lord Mayhew close behind her.

Aquila rose. Philo had gone quite pale.

"My dears, here is Lord Mayhew. He says he is an old friend and wishes to renew his acquaintance with you both."

Aquila curtseyed. So did Philo, after a brief hesitation.

Mayhew—who was unmistakably the young man they had known, though less gangling now—took their hands in turn and said graceful things. He was smiling. He had always had a pleasant smile, Aquila remembered.

More to the point, he seemed bent on putting Philo at her ease. It was clear that Philo had no recollection of him, though he mentioned Brazil. He had lived for a month or so in their father's house-

hold and must know of Philo's antecedents, so there
would be no awkward explanations about Sir William's fondness for opera singers. With a mixture
of relief and embarrassment that made her cheeks
hot, Aquila realised that Lord Mayhew would also
have heard of the manner of their father's death.

Sir William had perished of a heart attack in the
arms of his last and most pneumatical opera singer.
The scandal had rocked the Congress of Vienna,
until Buonaparte's escape from Elba gave Gossip
fresh grist for the mill. For three months afterwards, Aquila and Philo had lived in social isolation, attended only by servants and one of Sir
Charles Stuart's elderly female cousins.

By the time Mr. Browne, Sir. William's man of
business, made his way to Vienna, Aquila had come
to an understanding of their need to behave discreetly. If another breath of scandal were to touch
them, their social isolation might well become permanent. Living cut off from the World suited Philo.
She had always been shy. After the first shock of
loss, she had been happy enough breeding German
canaries. Aquila had been miserable.

Lord Mayhew was extending his condolences, polite and blessedly uneffusive. "I never knew a man
with as much charm as your father."

Aquila felt the sting of tears. Sir William *had*
been charming. To his fellow diplomats on all sides
of the conference table, to his daughters, to his mistresses. She thanked Mayhew in colourless tones,
hoping he would leave, then added, almost at random, "But you are in mourning, too, my lord, are
you not? Is it a recent bereavement?" He wore a
black neckcloth.

"My eldest brother Francis was killed at Waterloo."

Her hand flew to her throat. What a gaffe! She
and Philo had passed through Brussels within a

week of the battle. "I beg your pardon. I should
have known. . . ."

"How should you? Frank was a mere captain of
cavalry, Miss Ware. There were so many other
deaths—"

"But *I* should have known," Cressida interjected.
"Mayhew is an important name in the county, and
I ought to have drawn the connexion. What a sad
chance, my lord. Your mother . . ."

"Won't forgive me if I neglect the health of her
other son." Mayhew smiled. "I really ought to look
in on Robin, Mrs. Trent. I daresay he's on the mend,
but I want to be sure."

"For your mother's sake," Cressida murmured,
approving.

"Oh, no. For Robin's sake. I mean to comb his
hair with a joint stool, you see. When he's quite
well. I did consider strangulation. . . ."

Cressida laughed. "I see why you came so
quickly."

Mayhew left almost at once, promising to call on
the ladies when he had settled in and seen to his
brother's most urgent needs. Cressida ushered him
to the door.

Theo had decided to nurse Robin round the clock or
read him the Riot Act, whichever seemed called for.
He did neither. Though languid and pale, Robin was
clearly in no immediate danger of sticking his spoon
in the wall. Indeed, Theo found him propped in bed
scribbling the symptoms of his poisoning into a
notebook.

"For the College of Physicians," he explained
when Theo raised his eyebrows. Robin tapped the
paper with the stub of his lead pencil. "I daresay
they'll find it very enlightening."

"Unlike your nearest kin, who think of you as a
rune wrapped in a riddle tied up in a conundrum."

Robin grinned. He never took offence at personal criticism—just ignored it.

"I have met Mrs. Trent," Theo said abruptly.

Robin's grin faded. "How is Philo . . . Miss Philomena? Is she not the daintiest creature imaginable?"

"She was a charming little girl, like a Reynolds painting, and she has fulfilled the promise of her childhood." Theo explained his Brazilian encounter with Sir William Ware's daughters, adding, "Is young Philo always tongue-tied?"

Robin stared. After a moment he said stiffly, "I find her particularly lucid. She is a woman of rare discernment."

"That is praise indeed."

"She perceived the importance of my experiments at once." Spots of colour burnt on Robin's cheeks. "Only consider, Theo, she actually understands Evidence! She keeps the most meticulous breeding charts."

Theo stared.

"For her canaries," Robin said impatiently. "And she has observed thirteen distinct species of birds in the short time she has been in Lincolnshire . . ."

Bemused, Theo let his brother ramble on unchecked. Could Mrs. Trent be right? Theo had thought it possible, from the girl's blushes and the depth of her silence, that Philomena had developed a *tendre* for Robin. Did Robin return her feelings?

"Shall I never see a bachelor of threescore?" Benedick's lament popped into Theo's head, and he suppressed a laugh. Well, well. Robin in love. Would wonders never cease?

". . . and when she found I was ill she acted with the greatest presence of mind," Robin was saying. "Bodiham told me so. She is the most redoubtable lady!"

"I'm sure Mama will be grateful to her."

Robin shifted on the pillows, eyes wary. "Do you have to mention this to the Family?"

"If by 'this' you mean your latest venture in self-destruction, it's too late to prevent Mama knowing. Venetia was in the room when Mrs. Trent's message arrived."

Robin groaned.

"I daresay I can forestall a visit from Vee. Unless you'd prefer her ministrations to mine."

"No, but I'm not a dashed infant. Why must everyone make such a fuss?" The hectic spots burnt on Robin's cheeks, and his forelock was dark with sweat. "I'm perfectly well now."

"So I see," Theo said peaceably. "Rest, Robin. I'll come back at dinnertime."

The dark eyelashes fluttered. "Oh, very well. If you must." His voice slurred and his eyes closed.

Theo went over to the tiny window, bending his head to avoid bumping it on a protruding beam. Robin's Staffordshire manor house was surely ready for occupancy—even for chemical experimentation. Had Robin been staying on in Valentine Parva only to further his acquaintance with Philomena? Possible, even likely.

It was raining. When he was sure Robin had fallen asleep, Theo tiptoed down the narrow stairs, left directions with Bodiham for his brother's comfort, and stepped out into the drizzle.

Theo did remember Philo as a child. She had had the kind of prettiness that is the same at nineteen as at ten. He also remembered Aquila. The older child had been less attractive than Philo, and rather more interesting to him.

At eleven Aquila had had a sharp little beak of a nose and a frizz of lint-white hair that defied brush and comb. "She looks like an unfledged eaglet," Madame de Cressy had murmured—in Aqui-

la's hearing. Everyone laughed, for the remark was
apt, given the child's name. Besides, the languorous
Madame de Cressy, Sir William's latest mistress,
ruled the roost.

Then nineteen, abroad on his first minor diplomatic assignment, and homesick for his six sisters,
Theo had spent some time devising amusements for
the little girls. Philo he had found charming. For
Aquila, by turns sullen and demanding, he had felt
something else. Compassion? Or anxiety? He could
recall wondering what sort of woman she would become.

That day his brief encounter with her had revived the old interest. Her manners had improved
and she had grown into her nose. It was still aqui-
line, a noble nose, but it now fit her face. The linty
hair had darkened to ash blond. She wore it piled
at the crown of her head, escaped tendrils softening
the strict line of cheekbone and chin. He thought
she probably darkened her brows and lashes. If so,
she had a subtle hand. Grey eyes, luminous but
rather cool, regarded the world enigmatically, as if
she had questions she wasn't sure anyone, least of
all Theo, could answer.

He reached the inn as his groom drove the light
travelling carriage up the street. The landlord and
assorted ostlers and stableboys swarmed out, eas-
ing the vehicle through the archway and into the
cobbled yard of the inn.

Theo opened the carriage door, and his man,
Goucher, stepped down.

"Pleasant journey?"

"Passable, my lord." Goucher's lip curled. "The
Valentine Arms? What arms, pray, does St. Valentine bear?"

"Why, Cupid's bow, of course," Theo said blandly.

* * *

What with a duke and ducal relations, a baronet, and now a baron, Valentine Parva was in a great twitter. The cut of Lord Mayhew's coats was admired, as was the crest emblazoned on the door of his carriage. His groom was soon a popular figure in the ordinary, though everyone gave the valet, Goucher, a wide berth. Goucher kept to himself and was said to be death on bootblacks. As for his lordship, he was an affable man, according to all reports, not at all high in the instep, not above being pleased. Top of the trees. A regular out-and-outer.

Aquila, naturally, kept aloof from this kind of gossip. It passed to her from Toby and the servants. She told herself she listened only from the most disinterested of motives, concern for Philo's happiness. Twice she accompanied her sister to Marsh Cottage, and the second time he—Mayhew, that is—was there.

Philo's chemist had finally come downstairs. He was personable, Aquila decided, even handsome. They sat at the kitchen table and chatted and drank tea. The two brothers shared a strong family resemblance, but Mr. Robin was not so well-knit as Lord Mayhew. Taller, perhaps, but less graceful. Definitely less animated, or perhaps that was an effect of his illness. His hair was darker than Mayhew's and wanted trimming.

"What do you do to amuse yourself, Miss Ware?" Mayhew smiled at her over his teacup.

What did she do for amusement? "Ah. Well, we must live retired until our mourning is over."

"Of course." He had hazel eyes. They smiled into hers.

"Cousin Cressida has a spinet. There are books."

"But no circulating library?"

"She belongs to one in Lincoln. We read *Ivanhoe* in January. Juno, that is, Miss Rathbone, brought several improving works of Moral Philosophy with her. And of course there are pleasant walks when the weather allows."

"Sounds a bit dull. Do you ride?"

"Aquila is a splendid horsewoman," Philo offered, and blushed when the others looked at her.

Aquila lowered her eyes modestly, though she knew herself to be a superior equestrienne. "Papa's horses were sold up when we left Vienna. My cousins had a nice little mare I was used to ride, but Cousin Cressida does not keep a stable."

Mayhew nodded. "I have sent for a hack for Robin. He'll have to confine himself to very short rides until he's feeling more the thing, though. Should you like to explore the countryside with me, Miss Ware? I feel the want of exercise, but I dislike riding alone. I'm sure you can master Robin's hack, our sister Vee often rides it. I'll ask the landlord to find a sidesaddle."

To ride again, to escape from the village and the houseful of ladies, to explore the countryside with Lord Mayhew. Aquila's heart thumped, but she kept her voice cool. "If Cousin Cressida does not object, my lord."

Next morning, Mayhew called on Cressida. When he told her his groom would accompany the rides, she offered no impediment.

Aquila dug her best habit from the large trunk in the lumber room and asked Cousin Cressida's maid, Maudie Brick, to steam out the creases. It was cut in Prussian blue broadcloth, fortunately with black frogs clasping the front of the jacket and heavy black braiding suitable for half-mourning. Aquila knew the jacket emphasised her slim waist, and the colour set off her hair to perfection. The hat was a rakish kepi with a daring plume of feather curling down over her brow. The habit had been a singularly modish garment when it was made up

in Vienna, but Aquila had worn it only twice before
Papa died.

The next fortnight passed in a blur. Aquila rode
with Mayhew daily, and she could not have said
how Philo's romance went, for she and Mayhew
rode to the cottage only once. Robin was nearly
well. Mayhew brought him to tea in the carriage,
and Robin and Philo brooded, as it were, over the
canaries.

It occurred to Aquila to wonder why Mayhew
stayed on in the village when there was no longer
an urgent need for him to remain at his brother's
side. She was careful not to ask his reasons.

Theo could not have said why he stayed. Early in
April he rode home to Aisby to deal with estate
matters. When his sisters and mother cross-
examined him, he fobbed them off with the tale of
Robin's avian romance. That diverted all four of
them sufficiently to permit Theo to escape them
with his own feelings unexamined.

He left for Valentine Parva very early and called
on Mrs. Trent the same afternoon. The ladies were
taking tea in the drawing room. Two of the damsels
living in Mrs. Trent's household, Miss Tilbury and
Philomena, were shy as bedamned. Philo continued
to regard him as a fawn about to take flight watches
a gamekeeper. Theo answered Mrs. Trent's polite
enquiries after his family suppressed impatience,
then turned to Aquila. "Shall you ride with me tomorrow?"

The fugitive dimple appeared at the corner of her
mouth and the luminous grey eyes lifted to his, but
her tone was as calm as usual. "If you wish, Mayhew. Eleven o'clock?" The cat had not got *her*
tongue. He liked her composure.

"I'll come for you at half past ten, if Mrs. Trent

doesn't object. We can ride to Hughsdon and be back before one."

Aquila nodded. Theo wondered what it would take to break through her admirable self-possession.

The ride went well. He had wanted to show Aquila the Saxon church. They admired it and the village well with its odd kerbing, and rode back to Valentine Parva, taking their time. They spoke of his mother's feelings about Robin and Philo, which were favorable, of the Trent household, of Aquila's plans for her come-out in the Little Season, of Theo's mangel-wurzels, which hadn't yet sprouted. Riggs, Theo's groom, kept well behind.

They rode back to the village along a lane that led past the field above Marsh Cottage and had almost reached a copse that hid it from view when an explosion shook the air.

Theo steadied his mount and reached out to take the hack's bridle, but Aquila had already brought her horse under control. It danced on the grassy verge, wild-eyed.

"What was that?" She patted the horse's sweating neck.

"My brother . . . another damned experiment." Theo gathered the reins and dug his heels into his gelding's sides.

Aquila was beside him. "Philo—" she cried, but he didn't need to hear the rest of her words. Philomena was used to calling on Robin at that hour.

They covered a mile at a breakneck gallop and slowed as they reached the stream, splashing across it. A wall blocked their way, but Aquila's horse cleared it ahead of Theo's. He thought he had heard a second *krump-krump* as they rode, but he wasn't sure. As they neared the overgrown orchard behind the cottage, heat shoved at them. The air reeked of smoke.

Theo slid to the ground and looped his reins over a low branch, his eyes on the rear of the cottage. The chimney had collapsed into the kitchen where Robin received his guests. Fire crackled along the tiles of the roof. Robin . . . oh, God, I'll have to enter . . . "No, Aquila! Stay back!"

She was running towards the cottage. Theo reached her as she was about to plunge through what remained of the Dutch door. It was smouldering.

He yanked Aquila back and pulled her to him. Her fists pounded on his chest. She was screaming something. Smuts rained from the crackling air. He could feel the skin of his face tightening. No one could live in that inferno.

A blast of heat forced them away. Stumbling on the rough ground, he half dragged, half carried Aquila to the tree where he had left his horse. Hers had run off.

She had stopped struggling, but she trembled in his arms like a wild thing. Absently he stroked her back, murmuring nonsense that had to be inaudible below the roar of the fire. He kept his eyes on the blazing cottage. With a thud the entire roof collapsed inward.

"Aquila . . ."

She shivered in his arms.

"Listen, there's a chance . . . I'm going to walk round to the gate. Robin's workroom was in front. He may have got out . . ."

"Philo . . ."

"We don't know she was there. She's probably safe with Mrs. Trent, safe as houses." He bit his lip at the unfortunate choice of words.

Aquila seemed not to hear. "If she isn't . . ."

"Come with me." The noise had abated, though the pall of smoke made Theo's eyes water. Aquila coughed and straightened.

Hand in hand, they picked their way at the extreme edge of the overgrown dooryard, stumbling in the murk of smoke on weeds and small bushes. Theo's eyes were on the wreck of the cottage, and he was just wondering whether there was any point in trying to go closer when a voice, practically at his feet, froze him where he stood. Aquila squeaked.

"I say, it's Theo." Robin was sitting on the ground, leaning against the gatepost, with Philomena clasped in his arms. They were covered in soot, both of them, and twining like ivy.

Theo drew a long breath. "Where is Bodiham?"

Robin's wide, white-toothed grin faded. "In the village. By Jove, Theo . . ."

"And young Toby?"

"Home with his mama." Robin disentangled from his lady and scrambled to his feet. He pulled Philo up, too, and Aquila swooped on her sister like an eagle on a mouse.

Robin beamed at him through the masque of soot. "It's the most famous thing, Theo. Philomena loves me. She has promised to marry me."

"I congratulate you," said Theo, and planted his brother a facer.

It was a solid left hook. Robin went down hard. He sat in the sooty grass, rubbing his jaw and staring up at his brother.

Philomena gave a gasp, broke from her sister, and flung herself at Theo, pummelling his arm until Aquila pulled her away. She dropped to her knees beside Robin, who put a protective arm around her. She was crying.

Theo was too angry to apologise or explain. He turned to Aquila. "She's all right? Not burnt?"

Aquila nodded, wide-eyed. A smear of ash darkened one cheek, and her dashing kepi had fallen off. Blond curls straggled. Theo wanted to kiss her. He wondered if he were giddy with relief, or something else. "Then let's go. . . . " He was about to point out that the entire village would be converging on them at any moment, when it did.

A frantic Bodiham and Theo's man, Goucher, who was carrying a horse blanket, led the rescue party. Young Toby ran up, whooping, and made straight for Philo. She covered him with sooty kisses. They were followed by all the men and boys in Valentine Parva, and, trailing the pack and out of breath, Mrs. Barleyman and Cressida Trent.

It took a good half hour to sort everyone out. Cressida and Mrs. Barleyman soon cut Toby and the Ware sisters from the herd and escorted them homeward, scolding. Bodiham lent Robin his shoulder. Theo directed the villagers to beat out the few secondary fires that had started from flaming debris, though the thickening drizzle probably made their labour unnecessary.

Theo was calming Farmer Braithwaite, the owner of the cottage, when Riggs rode up leading Aquila's hack. Wearily Theo handed Riggs his own reins and directed the groom to attend to both horses. They not only wanted soothing, they had probably suffered spot burns from flying sparks. He promised Braithwaite full compensation for the loss of property. Then he plodded back along the line towards the inn, Goucher at his side.

"Quite a contretemps, my lord."

Theo gave short laugh. "You might say so. I thought it was all up with brother Robin."

Goucher prudently said nothing.

Theo took a long, uneven breath. "Tell me, Goucher, why the horse blanket?"

"For smothering the flames, my lord. You will recall that wet sacking was reported to be efficacious in the siege of Zaragoza. I intended to sluice the blanket in the stream."

"Always prepared, Goucher."

Goucher smiled a tight smile. "I surmise that Mr. Robert and the young lady intend to wed."

"True. A flaming passion, you might say."

Goucher ignored the feeble joke.

The next morning Theo, Goucher, and Robin set out for Aisby in the travelling carriage, Robin with his wrists and ankles sticking out of a suit of Theo's clothes. Goucher had salvaged Robin's boots and little else.

Fortunately, the blow to Robin's chin had not brushed his self-esteem or shadowed his delight. He called on Mrs. Trent the evening of the explosion, gave notice of his intentions, and was received as Philomena's affianced husband.

Theo accompanied him to the house, hoping for a word with Aquila, but Mrs. Trent had already sent the young ladies upstairs for a hot bath and a supper of milk toast. They were exhausted, she said. Probably asleep. She would convey Robin's love and Theo's farewells and good wishes. Miss Tilbury and Miss Rathbone bore mute witness in the drawing room. The canaries were silent in their shrouded cages. It was all very unsatisfactory.

Robin grumbled and yawned his way back to the inn, and was soon asleep on the truckle bed the landlord had obligingly supplied. Theo lay on his own couch, hands clasped behind his head, and stared at the shadowed ceiling.

His anger had burnt itself out. Robin was Robin. He would continue to regard the odd episode of poisoning, the occasional explosion, as ordinary risks in his personal voyage into the Unknown. He was fortunate indeed to have found a woman who would sail with him.

Theo's mind was not on Robin. Theo was thinking of Aquila. How brave she had been and how frantic. How small her shoulders had felt beneath his hand. How he had longed to kiss her.

More than once in the past weeks, Theo had considered making Aquila an offer of marriage. Her horsemanship was impeccable, he admired her self-possession and elegant appearance, he enjoyed her quick intelligence. He liked her, but he had not thought of himself as being in love. Robin was in love. Theo was merely seeking a suitable wife. He had hesitated because he was not sure what lay beneath the polished surface of Aquila's manners.

Now he knew, and knew he loved her, but he was not at all sure she could return his feelings. Perhaps she could learn to love him. No, that was not enough. He wanted her to feel for him what he felt for her—freely, without cajolery.

He lay awake for a long time as night deepened and the inn fell silent, wondering what he ought to do.

They drove off early the next morning in the carriage. Theo would have to remain at home. He had been putting off his bailiff far too long, and his man of business was set to arrive from London soon after Easter. Robin meant to return almost at once. He would stay at the inn and court his lady in proper style. Theo envied Robin with all his heart.

My dear Miss Ware,
Mama has writ your sister a letter welcoming her to the Family with Sentiments we all share, and suggesting that you and Miss Philomena make an extended Visit to Mayhew Hall as soon as may be. I add my own ramshackle note in the hope that you will feel as welcome as our new Sister—there ought to be a word for sister of sister-in-law—honorary Sister? Theo says he wishes to show you his mangel-wurzels. What a Dullard. Do come. I shall lend you my roan mare Fancy and show you all kinds of wonders that have nothing to do with Turnips.

Your obt. servt.
Venetia Mayhew

P.S. My younger sisters, China and India, send their love.

Aquila lowered the single sheet of elegant paper and peered over her shoulder. Robin and Philo were in the conservatory clucking over the canaries again.

"What think you, Aquila?"

She turned to face Cressida. "I think my sister won't leave her birds until both clutches have hatched." She kept her voice cool with an effort.

"I meant, do you wish to go, too? You need not, my dear, though Lady Mayhew's invitation included you most particularly."

Aquila tucked the note into her reticule. "Do you think I should go?"

"By all means. You've had a dull time of it here the past sennight. You want diversion."

Aquila sank back on the sofa. "Heavens, yes. One cannot expect chemical explosions every day."

A smile tugged at Cressida's mouth. "You have been missing your rides, though."

And Theo Mayhew. The name hung between them, unsaid. Cressida was inviting her confidence, but Aquila's feelings were too confused to admit to anyone, even Cousin Cressida.

"Shall you go?" Cressida repeated, gently insistent.

"I should like it of all things," she heard herself saying in tones of sedate propriety that gave no hint of her inner turbulence. She avoided meeting Cressida's eyes.

". . . but China is younger than India," Robin explained. The carriage swayed.

Aquila was sitting with her back to the horses.

Robin had protested gallantly when she volunteered to do so, but he did not seem displeased when
she insisted. It had occurred to her that Philo would
be less likely to brood over the coming ordeal if
Robin were beside her, and so it had proved. Facing
the newly betrothed pair, Aquila had an excellent
view of her sister and soon-to-be brother. Philo
looked faintly green. Mayhew's carriage was well-
sprung, but as a child Philo had been known to suffer from motion sickness when she did not want to
travel. She definitely did not want to visit Mayhew
Hall. They had just passed through the village of
Aisby.

"Do all of your sisters have unusual names?" Aquila ventured by way of distraction.

Robin smiled at her. "Lord, yes, and Theo was
named for a great-uncle who died and left his money
to a home for aged thespians. Frank and I escaped
lightly."

"Aged thespians? You must be bamming me."

" 'Strewth. He aspired to tread the boards, but
his papa insisted that he take holy orders instead.
Great-uncle held the living at Wanley. He had a
handsome fortune from his mother, too, and he
never married. Everyone thought he'd forgot about
the theatre. You may imagine the consternation
when the will was read. And there was my brother
stuck with Theobald. What a time he had of it at
Eton."

"Poor boy," Philo murmured. She looked as if she
might cry, though probably not from sympathy for
Mayhew.

"And your sisters . . ." Aquila was eying Philo
uneasily.

"Mama wanted her daughters to marry diplomats," Robin went on. "The eldest, Augusta, wed
a naval man. Portia married an MP. Calla's husband is a tulip of the *ton*, does nothing and does it

handsomely. Not an attaché or ambassador in the lot."

Aquila digested that. "Calla . . ."

He grinned. "Calpurnia. Caesar's wife, you know."

"Above reproach?"

"Exactly. The ideal wife for a diplomat. Mama was reading Plutarch at the time."

"Will all of them be there?" Beneath the rim of her modish bonnet, Philo's eyes were huge and dark.

"Heavens, no." He patted her hand. "A small house party, I promise you. Mama and Theo and the girls. And Vee, who isn't a girl, exactly. She's two years older than me."

"Are they very fashionable?"

"Plain country mice. You mustn't worry, my darling. They'll love you. *I* do."

Philo gave a small sigh and leaned against him. "I'm being foolish, I know, but I do dread meeting strangers."

"Goose," said Robin fondly, gazing into her eyes.

Aquila began to feel ill.

Beside her Maudie Brick gave a sentimental and approving sniff. Cressida had lent Philo and Aquila the maid's services, partly in an effort to ease Philo's ordeal and partly, Aquila suspected, because Maudie was wild to see Mayhew Hall.

Aquila had mixed feelings. She had wanted time to reflect before she met Mayhew's family. On the other hand, she missed the daily rides with Mayhew, and there would be horses. . . .

Robin gestured at the window. "You can just see the gatehouse beyond those trees. I used to conduct my experiments in it until Frank decided my bangs and stinks might frighten his horses. He banished me to a shed in the kitchen garden."

Indignation flushed Philo's pale cheeks. "How cruel!"

"*I* thought so," Robin said cheerfully. "I was thirteen at the time and set on my dignity. But Frank lent me the estate carpenter. Withers built a snug set of cabinets and a handsome shelf for my gear. Frank was a great gun." He fell silent.

"Do you miss him dreadfully?" Philo asked after a moment.

He sighed. "We all do, of course. The odd thing is, Theo misses him most, and Theo was hardly ever at home after he left Oxford. He hadn't seen Frank above half a dozen times in ten years." He peered out the window. "Ah, here we are. Gatehouse first, then the drive. It's only half a mile to the Hall as the crow flies, but my grandfather laid out a meandering carriageway when he remade the park."

Philo uttered polite exclamations about the beauty of the grounds as Robin pointed out his grandfather's innovations. Aquila wished he would offer to change places with her again. She could see the gatehouse, a pleasant-enough brick building. The shrubbery was beginning to leaf out. The beeches were well-grown and graceful. Still, she had no prospect of the house itself until she stepped down from the carriage.

And then, of course, there were people. She saw a blur of mellow brick and a pleasant neoclassic facade, but her appreciation of the house was diluted in the rush of greetings.

Besides the butler, Davis—Aquila was always careful to note the names of important servants—and assorted footmen, the carriage was met by Lady Mayhew and her daughters. The ladies made much of Philo, which was perfectly natural, and Venetia, a trim woman no longer in the blush of youth, welcomed Aquila warmly.

Mayhew himself came out as the greetings subsided and said friendly things to Philo. He took Aquila by the hand and suggested a ride on the morrow. She was not averse to the idea. As she met Mayhew's smiling hazel eyes and felt the warmth of his touch, she found herself suddenly breathless. An effect of the journey, she told herself.

Venetia's maid poked her head in the door. "It's Mr. Theo . . . I mean his lordship, wanting a word with you."

Venetia was dressing for dinner the second evening of the Ware Sisters' visit. She gave her nose a dusting of rice powder. "Very well, Annie. I shan't need you. See if the girls want help." The Mayhew ladies shared Annie's services.

Annie slipped out, and Theo entered in full evening rig.

"You look very fine," Venetia murmured to her brother's reflection in the pier glass. She wondered if her cheeks required a touch of rouge. When one approached eight-and-twenty, one had to consider these small adjustments to Nature.

"You look like the rose of summer yourself," Theo said absently. He *was* a diplomatist. "What think you, Vee?"

Venetia turned her head and smiled up at him. "She has an excellent seat on a horse."

He stopped in the middle of the carpet. Brother and sister locked eyes. Theo made a rueful face. "I might well have been asking your opinion of Miss Philomena. How did you know?"

She returned her attention to the mirror, hiding a smile. "That you are in love with Aquila Ware? It occurred to me halfway through your prolonged stay in Valentine Parva that Robin was in direr straits than you had let on, or that you had found some Object in the vicinity to fix you to the spot. When I saw Miss Ware, I understood at once. Or rather, I understood when I saw you looking at her."

He pulled a chair to the dressing table and straddled it backwards, chin on his fist. "Are my feelings so transparent?"

She picked up her silver-backed brush and touched a curl. "Only to me, brother dear." She laid the brush down, reached for her jewel case, and withdrew a pair of pearl and sapphire earbobs.

Theo watched her as she screwed them in place. "When I first caught sight of you, Vee, you were swathed in your christening robes and looked like a lace bolster. I recall wondering what would happen if I put the pillow over your face, but Nurse came in and sent me away before I found out."

Venetia grinned. She fluffed her side curls so they softened the blue glitter of the sapphires.

"What do think of her, Venetia?"

She felt her smile fade. "My dear, I like her very well. Elegant bearing, polished manners, and, of course, the right connexions for a baroness. She would do very well."

After a moment, he said quietly, "But?"

She drew a breath. "But I find her reserved, unusually so for a girl of nineteen. Can she love you? I should dislike it very much if you married only for the Family's sake."

"I thought you were doing your best to shackle me to half the unwed ladies in the county."

She heard a defensive note in his voice and lightened her own tone. "Nonsense. I was merely trying to prevent your marriage to Ophelia Bliss—" She broke off.

His face, reflected in the glass, showed the liveliest astonishment. "Ophelia Bliss? Good God, credit me with a dram of common sense. The woman's a menace."

"But you listened to her with every appearance of interest!"

"I had to deflect her from pouring her vulgar imaginings over Mama." He rose and began pacing the carpet.

So much for the odious Ophelia, Venetia reflected. All those unnecessary heart-burnings. She rose, too, tossed her dressing gown on the floor, and yanked the dinner frock over her head. "Drat, I've mussed my hair."

"What's that?"

"Do up my buttons, Theo, there's a dear. I shall have to put my hair in order again."

Obediently he began buttoning the tiny pearls that fastened the gown up the back—they were a modish touch, but nuisances to fasten. Venetia stood still and thought about Aquila Ware.

Theo hooked the top button and brushed the back of her skirt straight. "There. All correct and accounted for." His voice deepened. "When you say 'reserved,' what do you mean?"

Venetia returned to the dressing table and reached for her comb. The silence extended a beat too long. She looked up and met his eyes. He was frowning painfully. "Does she have a heart, Theo? I don't like these tales of her father."

"Sir William was the most self-absorbed man I have ever met—and one of the most charming." He rubbed his brow, as if to erase the frown. "I did wonder when I met her again if Aquila had inherited the old rip's callous disregard for anything but his own feelings. I was wrong." He began to tell her of the explosion and of Aquila's response to it. He was pacing again.

Venetia listened with complete attention.

"And I thought I should have to pull her bodily from the flames," he finished, his voice rough. "She had no regard for her own danger at all, Vee."

Venetia smoothed her curls into place with absent fingers. "She is courageous and loves her sister. I agree that she can feel deeply. But with such a father, will she be able to trust you sufficiently to love you? For a woman, trust is paramount."

He bowed his head. "I know it."

She rose, laying the comb aside, and gave him a hug. "Have patience, Theo. If she can't love you, she has very bad taste."

He laughed at that. "What a crass partisan you are."

"Aren't you glad you didn't smother me in my cradle?" She hooked her arm in his and turned him to face the pier glass. "We're a handsome pair. Are you ready to go down?"

"If you are."

She moved towards the door. "This guardian, the one you and Robin were closeted with this afternoon, shall I like him?"

Theo made a face.

Aquila would have remained happily at Mayhew Hall for a month but for two considerations. The first was her sister's fixed intention of going back to Valentine Parva at the end of a mere week. Her hatchling canaries needed her. The second consideration stemmed from Aquila's confusion of feeling.

That Mr. Browne had come to Mayhew Hall to see to Philo's marriage settlement deepened Aquila's unease. She could not ask his advice. He looked at her as if she were a ledger. Nor could she confide in Philo. What was there to confide?

Aquila had looked forward to riding again with Mayhew. Unfortunately, their excursions were now accompanied by his sisters, excepting Miss India, who was nursing a spring cold. India kept Philo and Robin company, and Venetia or China, frequently both, chaperoned Aquila and Mayhew. Aquila liked the ladies very well, but she longed for the old comradeship with Mayhew, Riggs trailing them at a comfortable distance.

What troubled Aquila most was that Mayhew made no attempt to take her off by herself. He might have easily enough, by lagging behind with her or challenging her to a cross-country gallop. The roan mare was more than equal to that. Instead, they explored the manor and the rolling countryside around Aisby in a clump. The conversation was lively—Aquila enjoyed Mayhew's bantering exchanges with Venetia—but it was not private.

It *was* proper, however, Aquila realised the depth of her own slackness. She had come to expect Mayhew's sole company. She had been reading more into their daily excursions from Valentine Parva than he had intended. Mayhew would be Philo's brother-in-law, no more. Aquila tried to be glad, but her spirits sank as the week wore on.

The evenings were the most difficult. Apart from Mr. Browne, no strangers sat at the dinner table. Lady Mayhew kept Philo at her right hand, in the place of honour, and exerted herself to make Philo welcome. The well-meant attention reduced Philo to silence. Only Robin could draw spontaneous remarks from her, and Robin sat halfway down the table, between his sisters.

Philo's excruciating shyness placed a burden on Aquila that made each dinner a minor social ordeal. She hoped Lady Mayhew and Robin's sisters understood. They seemed to.

The last evening before their departure, the party expanded to include the vicar, Mr. Bliss, and his wife and daughter. Philo dressed in a state of near-mutiny. Only Robin's promise to sit beside her at dinner kept her from pleading a headache. She looked very pretty in a gown of soft grey, with the pearls she had worn during their brief season in

Vienna clasping her slender neck, but she was quiet as a mouse in the drawing room while they waited to go in to dinner, and her smile was visibly strained.

Aquila, correct in lilac and her own pearls, kept at Philo's side, parrying the curiosity of the female Blisses. When dinner was announced, she gave her sister over to Robin's care with a sigh of relief.

Aquila could have arranged the table, ordered up the dinner, and seen to the conversation of fifty guests. In the brief months she had acted as her father's hostess in Vienna, she had discovered in herself an aptitude for social arrangements. Tonight they were only twelve at table, and she wondered at Lady Mayhew's seating chart.

Propriety put Mr. Bliss at the dowager's right and Mrs. Bliss at Mayhew's, and kindness placed Philo at her ladyship's left with Robin beside her. Aquila herself sat at Mayhew's left, though the honour ought to have gone to Miss Bliss. Not that Aquila objected, but there were too many ladies for a comfort. Aquila knew from their casual remarks that all three Mayhew daughters had suitors, so the imbalance of the sexes was a concession to Philo's shyness. Still Aquila wished propriety had not seated Miss Bliss at her left whilst Mayhew's attention was monopolised by Miss Bliss's loquacious mother.

Through the soup and the fish, Miss Bliss showed Aquila her shoulder. The vicar's daughter was a dramatic brunette with huge sunken eyes and a costume that suggested mourning, though neither of her parents wore black. She had seemed courteous enough in the drawing room. Perhaps she was being kind to Mr. Browne.

Three times, as sole succeeded the vegetable madrilène, did Mayhew direct pleasantries to Aquila. Three times did the vicar's wife recall his attention with imperious questions having to do with the well-being of the parish. Aquila was accustomed to suave give-and-take over dinner, a graceful alteration between dinner partners that could be timed almost to the second. Mrs. and Miss Bliss's manners were quite outside Aquila's experience. She took a bit of sole and surveyed the table.

Excellent crystal, gleaming linen, delicate china, and handsome people. The Mayhew sisters, far from being the country mice Robin had promised, dressed in what Aquila supposed was the latest crack of London fashion. True, they did not display the insouciance of Paris or the opulence of Vienna, but they looked charming and confident. Robin's dinner coat had probably been tailored for him when he was at Cambridge—he had broken the family pattern of Eton and Oxford—but he seemed comfortable in company, and so, for once, did Philo. She was smiling at something he had said and the dreadful stiffness had vanished. Aquila breathed a small sigh of relief.

Lady Mayhew was deep in conversation with the vague, scholarly looking vicar. Venetia and India chattered cheerfully, as Davis and a well-drilled footman replenished the wineglasses. Venetia caught Aquila's eye and raised her brows. Aquila smiled at her. She liked Venetia.

"You were not acquainted with Frank, Miss Ware." Miss Bliss had decided to honour her with speech. "Lord Mayhew, that was."

"No." Aquila took a sip of wine.

"I pity you."

Aquila cut another bite of fish and sought a neutral comment. "His lordship was a cavalry officer?"

Miss Bliss heaved a sigh. She wore a shawl with a long silk fringe that dipped perilously near the lemon sauce. "Frank was so Dashing. I adore a uniform. Do not you, Miss Ware?"

"Er . . ."

"A man in uniform," Miss Bliss went on, fixing her dramatic eyes on Aquila's, "is a Presence." She had a trick of pausing before some nouns so that she seemed to speak in capital letters. She sounded as German looked—Significant. "In uniform, a man seems above the run of ordinary Mortals."

It occurred to Aquila that, uniform or no, the late Frank had proven his ordinary mortality. She repressed the thought.

"On horseback he looked a veritable Centaur."

"I daresay." Aquila tried to visualise a centaur in the uniform of the Life Guards.

"Uniforms make men seem . . . how shall I say it . . . Masterful."

"But the hangers are a nuisance."

Miss Bliss blinked.

"The swords men wear with dress uniforms," Aquila explained. "I was once at a ball in Vienna, quite a formal affair. One of the archdukes stumbled on his hanger and fell at the Princess Sakhanov's feet. Of course, he was very young."

Miss Bliss's mouth opened and shut like a fish.

"Her royal highness was in a good mood, or he might have caused an incident, for Russians, you know, are not fond of Austrians in spite of the alliance. I believe the emperor sent him back to Salzburg."

Miss Bliss's magnificent eyes flashed.

"But I daresay Lord Mayhew looked very well in uniform," Aquila added in a spirit of conciliation.

"Frank and I," Miss Bliss's voice throbbed, "had an Understanding." She turned her shoulder.

Aquila addressed the fish.

"Masterful."

She looked up to find Mayhew watching her, eyes sparkling with amusement.

She felt her cheeks flush. "I oughtn't. It isn't fair."

"No, but it's satisfying. Did you make that up?"

"No, truly, it did happen. I didn't see it myself, but everyone talked about Fritz's clumsiness for weeks."

"Poor devil."

"He was only fifteen and very fat."

Mayhew chuckled. "Fritz? That would be Ferdinand's youngest, or do you mean one of the Esterhazys. . . ."

"Mayhew," said the imperious voice on his right, "the lych-gate wants mending again."

He gave Aquila a fleeting smile and a shrug, and turned back to Mrs. Bliss.

Aquila and Mayhew exchanged phrases over the roast lamb and several whole sentences over the savoury. Neither said anything very remarkable, but as the ladies withdrew, Aquila found her spirits had risen.

The gentlemen joined them almost at once, forestalling further revelations from Miss Bliss. China and India sang a duet, Aquila played a sedate Mozart piece on the pianoforte, and Miss Bliss sang one of Mr. Moore's airs, accompanying herself on the harp. She looked very handsome, but she would not be persuaded to sing again. The Blisses left shortly thereafter.

In the flurry of good-nights, it was not possible for Aquila to speak with Mayhew privately. She thanked him for his hospitality, and he did press her hand as she and Philo retired to oversee Maudie's packing. The warmth of his touch lingered.

Their departure next morning was delayed by Mr. Browne, who requested the favour of an interview with Aquila.

He awaited her in the bookroom, a handsome apartment with a distinguished collection of works in the classical and modern languages. Aquila presented herself in her travelling dress.

She coveted the calf-bound volumes of French essays and the memoirs of the Princess de Clèves in the bookcases. Aquila spoke three foreign languages well—Portuguese, French, and Italian—and German passably, but French was the only language besides English that she read with ease. A month would not have sufficed for her to explore the bookroom.

"Hah-hmm. I have been meaning to call on you in your new establishment at . . . hah-hmm, Miss Aquila."

"Valentine Parva."

"Yes, yes. You are comfortable in Mrs. Trent's care?"

"Certainly."

"I ask because I do not quite understand how this relationship between Miss Philomena and Mr. Mayhew arose."

"Very properly," Aquila lied. She didn't even blink.

"Well, hah-hmm, I am relieved to hear it. I believe I have concluded a comfortable settlement for your half sister."

"I'm sure my sister will be grateful to you."

His sharp little eyes narrowed at the correction. "Your own case will be far more complex. You do realise that?"

"I realise that I inherited Papa's fortune. That reminds me. I should like to make my sister a bride-gift."

"Some silver, perhaps, from Rundle and Bridge? I shall—"

Aquila interrupted him. "Five thousand in Consols."

His nearly invisible eyebrows shot up. "Five

thousand . . . no, no, indeed, Miss Aquila, I cannot advise . . ."

"Can I not spare the sum?"

"Well, yes."

"Then five thousand to be settled on her children. And a silver tea set from Rundle and Bridge." She made to rise.

He cleared his throat again. "I shall discuss the matter with Sir Henry Goodnight." Sir Henry was their other guardian.

"If you must. Now, if there's nothing further . . ."

"Have a care, Miss Aquila. You are altogether too independent-minded for a young lady in your circumstances."

"I have always conducted myself with propriety, sir."

"No doubt," he said testily, "but you must understand that your wealth makes you vulnerable to the unscrupulous as your . . . hah-hmm sister is not. Be wary of the importunate, Miss Ware, most especially be wary of importunate young men. I should not like to see you prey to a fortune hunter."

"Cousin Cressida will advise me." She stood up and straightened her skirts. "Should the need arise."

He had risen, too, of course. "I daresay. A worthy woman. Means to go to London in the autumn, eh? Very appropriate, but 'keep you in the rear of your . . . hah-hmm affections,' Miss Aquila."

"Good day, Mr. Browne." She left, hoping her agitation was not writ on her face.

She had had some experience of elderly gentlemen who made suggestive comments. Mr. Browne was not of that ilk. He was a dry stick, an impossible old curmudgeon, but not a lecher. His advice had made him at least as uncomfortable as it made her. She thought his concern was real, and she won-

dered whom he had been warning her against.
Mayhew?

It was an ugly thought. Mr. Browne and Mayhew's man of business had been in conference together for four days. Surely by now Mayhew knew
that she was an heiress. Had he known all along?
He had lived in her father's household.

With Robin's escort, they reached Cressida's
rambling house in time for tea. By then Aquila was
feeling calmer.

Philo's canaries were well. The little birds looked
repellant to Aquila, who took one peek at them and
left the conservatory sneezing. At dinner Philo
spoke happily of her visit as if she had not spent
half the time paralysed with shyness. Aquila ate
little. Her throat tickled and she thought gloomy
thoughts about canaries. She did not sleep well that
night.

The next morning Mayhew called as they lingered at the breakfast table. He had ridden over
early from Aisby. The cold wind had stung colour
across his cheekbones, and his hair was tousled. He
looked, in a word, magnificent, and he was asking
Cressida's permission to take Aquila for a ride. He
said Robin's hack wanted exercise. Aquila ought to
have refused the invitation, but she could not.

They headed out along the overgrown lane that
led past the ruin of Robin's cottage. Mayhew kept
up a cheerful flow of comment. There was much to
be said for a diplomat's training. Aquila brooded.
Her throat hurt. So did her heart.

He pointed his crop at an odd hillock they had
explored earlier, an ancient tomb. "Up there?"

"If you like." Her voice scratched her throat.

The path meandered across Farmer Braithwaite's pasture and up a rough hillside. By the time
they reached the slope, it was drizzling and wind
gusted from the east. What was the point?

"I'm going back," Aquila called.

He turned in the saddle. "I beg your pardon?"

"It's too wet."

"Aquila . . ."

She wheeled her horse and set off down the slope at a fast walk. Wind chilled her hot cheeks and stung tears from her eyes. She jumped the hack over the wall into the pasture and began to canter, no longer attending to the path. As she reached the patch of mud halfway across the lea, the hack slipped and stumbled, tossing her into the mire.

Aquila kept hold of the reins and her dignity. She had struggled to her feet by the time Mayhew reached her. He slid from the saddle, eyes alight with amusement.

"If you laugh at me . . ."

"Believe me, nothing could be further from my mind." He took a step closer. "You've mud on your cheek."

"And on my habit. May I trouble you for a hand up?"

"Oh, Lord, Aquila, take my hand and my heart."

Ice shot through her veins. "I beg your pardon?"

He looked rather pale. "Not the happiest choice of settings, my dear. I asked you to marry me."

She clenched her eyes shut, opened them, and willed her voice to be civil. "I'm sensible of the honour you do me, my lord, but we should not suit."

For some reason her words amused him. His eyes danced. "My dear fool . . ."

"I am in earnest, sir. Do not press me."

"Well, I won't now, but . . ."

"Ever," she gritted. "Love? I wonder at your gall. Cream-pot love, Mayhew. Mr. Browne warned me . . ."

He was staring at her as if she had fetched him a hard blow to the head. "Aquila!"

"Kindly assist me to my saddle." The lump in her throat had swollen so she could scarcely speak.

He helped her up and remounted, face blank. They rode back to the house in silence. Aquila thought she might fall off. She felt remarkably unwell—and thoroughly miserable.

He parted with her at the door. She thought he wanted to say something, but she gave him no opportunity. She had almost reached the first-floor landing when she fell down in a faint.

Theo escorted Aquila as far as the house in a state of numb disbelief. By the time he saw to the horses and entered the inn he was in a fury with her, and with himself.

When he entered their private parlour, Robin looked up from his book. "Did you take a header? You're covered with muck."

Theo said between clenched teeth, "I'm riding home now."

"You'll ruin your mount. Stop over tonight, at least."

"I am leaving. Now." Theo drew a breath. "I'll have to hire a nag. See to the horses, will you, Robin? I'll send Riggs for mine tomorrow." He stumped out, leaving Robin gaping.

Cream-pot love, indeed. Theo wondered what novels Mrs. Trent had supplied the ladies of her household from the circulating library. He was no seedy confidence man, no down-at-heels subaltern. He was Mayhew of Aisby, lord of all he surveyed. Any respectable woman ought to be honoured by his attentions. That was his mood at Hughsdon.

At Purleigh the rain sheeted down and his anger turned inward. How could he have been such a fool as to propose marriage to Aquila in a sheep pasture? She was no hurly-burly miss. She was a lady of the most impeccable standards. Because he re-

membered their unescorted rides fondly he had had
no right to assume she would entertain the same
feelings of nostalgia. He ought to have done the
thing in form in Cressida Trent's drawing room.

By the time he reached home he was too cold,
wet, and miserable to feel anything but the black-
est despair.

Two days later Riggs returned with Robin, Bodiham, and the spare horse. Robin brought Theo a letter
from Mrs. Trent.

"No point in my staying on in the village," he
explained. "I can't see Philo. Her sister's dashed ill
and Philo spends her time in the sickroom." He
sounded faintly aggrieved.

"Ill?" Theo tore the letter open.

"Fever." Robin drifted off in search of suste-
nance.

Theo sank back in his chair. He had been dealing
with estate business in the bookroom. He shoved
the mass of papers back and laid the letter on the
blotter.

My Lord,
As your brother will have told you, Aquila
Ware is ill of a serious fever. She seems to have
taken a chill when she fell from her horse during
that ill-advised ride in the rain. She was unwell,
indeed she fainted, before you had left for Aisby,
and she is now quite delirious. She keeps calling
your name. Her mind seems troubled over some
unresolved question that lies between you. I
should hesitate to write you so frankly, but the
connexion Philomena will soon enjoy with your
Family emboldens me to beg this favour of you.
Please come to Aquila, my lord, and set her mind
at rest.
Yours in haste, Cressida Trent.

Theo's impulse was to saddle his horse at once and ride to Valentine Parva, fling himself down at Aquila's bedside, and not move until she had agreed to marry him. It was already dark, however, and he thought he would do her very little good with a broken neck, so he gritted his teeth and ordered up the travelling carriage at first light the next morning. He spent the night tossing and turning.

Venetia, sleepy-eyed and still in her robe, saw him off. "Give her my love, Theo."

He said grimly, "If she knows my voice, I shall give her *my* love. Yours can wait until later."

She kissed his cheek, her eyes troubled. Behind her, Goucher cleared his throat.

"I'm off," Theo said. "Tell Robin I couldn't wait."

"Here I am," Robin grumbled from the foyer.

At Valentine Parva Theo left coach, groom, valet, and brother at the inn and strode to Cressida's house without waiting for refreshment. A wide-eyed maid took his dripping cloak and ushered him up to the sickroom.

Both Mrs. Trent and Philomena were in attendance, but Theo had eyes only for Aquila, her blond curls tumbled on the pillow and her cheeks flushed with fever.

Mrs. Trent was saying something cautious.

"Leave us, if you please." He took the girl's slender hand. It was hot to his touch.

Philo had followed him to the bedside. "Did Robin—"

"My brother is at the inn," Theo said impatiently. "He'll call on you shortly. If you please, Philo . . ."

Both ladies left the room.

"Now, Aquila." He cleared his throat. Her hand stirred in his. He gripped it tightly. "I've come for an apology, and I'm going to stand here until you're ready to give me one."

"Th-theo?"

"That's right."

"Oh . . ." Her eyes fluttered.

"What do you need, water?" He took the carafe from the bedside table and poured half a glassful. She drank thirstily when he held it to her lips. It seemed to hurt her to swallow, and he had appalling visions of putrid sore throat or cholera.

He set the glass down and let her head rest on the pillows.

She frowned. "Where's Theo?" Her voice was blurred, and her half-open eyes glittered. "Th-theo . . ."

"Yes, I'm here."

"S-something to tell him . . ." Her voice trailed and she slept. He watched for a long time. It was a heavy, restless sleep, and when he touched her brow her skin burnt. He was in for a long watch.

Aquila woke clearheaded and refreshed but quite weak. It was dark out. That was odd. "Why . . ."

Cressida was at her side almost at once. "Ah, so you've decided to join the living." She looked very tired.

Aquila frowned. "I've been ill? How long?"

"Five days—and nights."

Memory returned, and Aquila winced.

"What is it?"

Weak tears filled her eyes. "I've been such a fool . . ."

"If you're referring to Mayhew, he's here in the village."

"I don't want to see him," Aquila moaned.

"It's too late for you to shrink from his sight, my dear. He has been at your bedside constantly for the past three days."

"Oh, no!"

"You called for him, Aquila, and you would not rest until he came. He stayed until your fever broke this afternoon. I sent him off for some well-earned sleep. He'll visit you tomorrow."

Aquila burst into mortified tears. Cressida gave her a handkerchief and a drink of water, but no sympathy.

As Philo was resting in Juno's old room, there was no one to confide in. It seemed to Aquila, staring at the reflected firelight that flickered from the ceiling, that she might well die of embarrassment. Instead, she fell asleep.

Next morning Philo brought in a tray of tea, buttered eggs, toast and jam, and watched sternly as Aquila devoured her handiwork. "Are you going to marry Mayhew?" she asked as Aquila washed down the last bite of toast.

Aquila swallowed. "Do you want me to?"

Philo removed the tray. "You have my permission. Shall I bring you your dressing gown and a fresh nightdress? He'll be here soon."

Aquila refused to receive Mayhew in her bedchamber. Over Philo's and Cressida's protests, she dressed in a morning gown and a shawl, and went down to the drawing room to await her doom.

Theo was met at the door by the little maid, Eliza, who beamed at him and bobbed a curtsey. She had just taken his hat and driving coat when Cressida Trent emerged from the bookroom.

Mrs. Trent gave him her hand. "Ah, Mayhew, how wise of you to wait until Aquila was in command of herself."

"Is she . . . ?" He nodded at the stairwell.

"She came downstairs half an hour ago. Philomena is with her." She stuck her head in the drawing-room door, said, "Lord Mayhew, ladies," and ushered him in, effacing herself at once.

Aquila looked like a startled dove, but Philo rose, swept him a curtsey, and said, with great aplomb,

"Ah, Mayhew, how kind of you to call. I know you will both excuse me. It's past time I saw to my birds," and she disappeared with a twinkling of skirts through the French door to the conservatory.

Theo felt like a boat borne on a strong tide. He cleared his throat. "I have several things to say to you, Aquila."

"I didn't mean it," she blurted, blushing painfully.

He sat beside her on the sofa and took her hand. It was no longer hot, but it wasn't cold either. She did not try to pull away. "At first I had no idea what you meant by cream-pot love. I'm still not sure."

"I inherited Papa's fortune. Mr. Browne was at Mayhew Hall. I thought he must have spoken to you of my . . . circumstances."

Theo sighed. "I scarcely saw him, Aquila. I supposed you were comfortably dowered, as your sister is. Sir William was a wealthy man, but such fortunes are often entailed on heirs male. You live simply here. I had no reason to think you an heiress."

She nodded, avoiding his eyes.

"Shall I tell you about my brother Frank?"

Her eyes flew to his. "He was killed last summer," she said timidly, "and you had to come home."

That was perceptive. "I was not meant to raise turnips," he said slowly, "but you mustn't underrate turnips. Mayhew and the manor of Aisby produce a handsome income. Frank inherited land that was well managed. My father and my grandfather were members of the Royal Agricultural Society and correspondents of 'Turnip' Townsend. They understood farming. Frank didn't." He cleared his throat again. It was hard to talk about Frank.

Aquila pressed his hand.

"But my brother did understand himself. He knew he would muddle things if he tried to fill my father's shoes, so he found an excellent land agent and handed the estate over to him."

"Then the mangel-wurzels . . ."

"I don't know a mangel-wurzel from a left-handed seed drill," he confessed. "My agent . . . Frank's agent deals with the turnips for me." He paused, trying to order his thoughts. Her luminous grey eyes distracted him. "Frank enjoyed his life. He cut a swath through Society, he swanked about his regiment, he rode to hounds." He felt a smile forming. "And he flirted with every lady who showed an inclination to return the favour."

"Miss Bliss?"

Theo saw an answering amusement in her grey eyes, and his heart lightened. "Exactly so. Miss Bliss. I never knew a better man than my brother. When he died the estate was in good order, my sisters were provided for, and there was the house in Staffordshire for Robin. So you see, Aquila, I had no reason to hang about looking for an heiress."

She flushed. "I think I knew that. It was Mr. Browne . . ."

"I daresay he confused you, but he was right to warn you." Now for the hard part. He stroked her palm. "I wasn't looking for a wealthy wife, but I was looking for a suitable one. You had birth and breeding to recommend you, and I liked you very well. I came close to asking you to make a suitable marriage, Aquila. I hope you will forgive me."

Her eyes widened. "But . . ."

"Hush. Let me speak my piece. I knew your father . . ."

She looked away.

"He was an admirable man in many ways, but where women were concerned he had no scruples. Philo has suffered for that and so have you. I am going to ask you to marry me, Aquila, but if you cannot love me, if you cannot trust me with your whole heart, I beg you to say no."

She had turned back to him. Her eyes were wide, the pupils dilated. Her mouth formed an *O* of surprise.

"I fell in love with you." He smiled. "I think the feeling came over me with a bang. It is not a cautious, proper feeling. I don't want a suitable wife any longer, Aquila. I want you."

"Oh," she said tremulously. "Oh, yes."

Theo found he had been holding his breath. He let it out slowly. "Are you sure?"

Aquila bit her lip. "I've loved you a long time, Mayhew."

"Theo," he corrected gently.

"Th-theo. I've loved you since I was eleven years old."

Theo felt his cheeks go hot with pleased embarrassment.

"It's true." The dimple hovered at the edge of her mouth. "Though you mustn't fancy I was brooding about you all those years. But when I met you again I realised I had been measuring other men against you." She reached up and touched his face. "I never met your equal."

"Aquila!"

"Shall I show you what I feel?" She leaned towards him and kissed him on the mouth. It was a proper, ladylike kiss to begin with, but it warmed to something else in no time.

They drew apart at last, breathless and giddy, as a knock sounded at the drawing-room door. Aquila's cheeks were flushed and her eyes bright.

Cressida Trent was smiling across the room at them. "Do I take it you've reached an agreement?"

Aquila touched Theo's lips with the tips of her fingers. "Oh, yes," she said, eyes locked on his. "We've decided to run off to Gretna Green."

On the Church Porch

CRESSIDA WAS BEGINNING to think that Mrs. Warren was right: the girls were too much for her. She had expected her visitors to enjoy a quiet stay in the country. Instead there had been illness, near murder, and explosions. At least she expected no more alarms. Three of the girls were engaged, and so engrossed in planning their weddings that they had no time to fall into trouble. And Aquila seemed much too well bred to cause any sort of excitement.

Cressida wished she had some of that young lady's sangfroid. She was spending far too much time daydreaming about Tyne. It did not seem to help that she knew it was hopeless. Even if he still felt any love for her, she had the same doubts Lady William had played on so cruelly. Was a canon's widow any better suited to be a duchess than a vicar's daughter a marchioness? And then there was the question of Toby. Even if a duke wanted to marry a very ordinary widow, past her first youth, would he want to saddle himself with a common-born stepson?

On the morning of Cressida's thirty-fifth birthday, Maudie brought in a bouquet of pink roses. To her guests' astonishment, Cressida picked them up and dashed from the room, muttering something about putting them in water, so that Toby, who was knocking off the top of his boiled egg while chanting, "Hark, hark the lark, at heaven's gate sings," would not see the tears in her eyes.

Juno found her sitting on the bench in the conservatory.

"Was it the duke?" she asked.

"Who sent the flowers? I believe so, but I am not certain," Cressida said, putting away her handkerchief. She had not really cried, just shed a few tears.

"The Ashby whom you once loved! Lord Randal told me the duke had been in love a very long time ago, and had never really got over it. Cressida, I think he still loves you."

"Oh, Juno, you're too young to understand."

"I'm not as young as I used to be." Juno laughed and sat down next to Cressida. "I can't presume to advise you, but if you still care for him, I think you ought to do something about it."

"But what if he doesn't love me, but feels he must make amends—" She broke off, aware that she must not trouble the younger woman with her doubts and fancies.

"I think," Juno said sensibly, "that you should ask him." She went to the cupboard where the vases were kept and took one out. "If you don't, you'll always wonder. Women ought not to be in the dark about such things."

Cressida had never considered herself bold, but she was fired by the truth behind Juno's words. She went back to the dining room to tell Toby that she was going out and to ask the girls to mind him. Then she sent John Barleyman to the inn with a note, and went to the church porch.

The duke had made a considerable contribution to the fabric fund, and she was recording secretary to the ladies' committee. She hoped that anyone who saw them together would assume they were discussing how best to spend his donation.

He arrived quickly. "Is anything wrong?"

"No, nothing." Now, how to begin? "I believe we both recall events of some years ago. We speak of them as if they were long past, and if that is indeed the case for you, I ask only that you forget this meeting."

"To me they are as yesterday. But I cannot imagine how you feel. Cressy, I once gave you to understand I would be making—"

"No. My feelings have not changed, or rather they are rekindled, but my circumstances are different. There is still the question of my suitability to be your wife, and there is also Toby. Could you accept him as your son?"

"I never doubted that you would be the best possible wife for me. I was more concerned that I would prove a fit husband. Toby would be my child in every way. If you wish, I can adopt him."

"That isn't necessary," Cressida said, astonished at how quickly matters were proceeding. "I would like him to have his father's name. Oh, Chelmly, what if I have other children, and he is jealous of your heir."

"If I talk to Toby and he agrees not to mind not becoming a duke, can I finally ask my question?"

Despite her worry, Cressida was hard put not to laugh at the frustration she saw in his eyes.

A Maiden All Forlorn

A BRIGHT WINTER SUN sent its beams through the arched windows of Tilbury Manor, bathing the bedchamber in its ruddy glow and rousing Miss Katherine Tilbury, the youngest daughter of Baron Tilbury.

Blinking against a brightness for which she had longed through two days of snow, Katherine slipped out of the bed and, unmindful of the chill floor, dashed to the window. The ruins of Tilbury Castle, fallen long ago to the cannons of Oliver Cromwell's insurgent army, were a study in brightness and shadow. She was tempted to paint the ruins at once, before the sun destroyed any of the crispness, but she was equally tempted by the nymph in the fountain, for the snow around its feet had been shaped by the wind into waves. Katherine found herself torn between the dramatic and the romantic.

"I cannot do either until I dress," she murmured as she pulled on her clothes. She sent a wary glance over her shoulder. She had spoken out loud, a habit Miss Simpson, her governess, had decried.

"Other people will think you insane," that lady had said.

"But there are no other people, Miss Simpson," Katherine had reminded her. "My brothers and sister seldom visit here, and neither does Papa. Aunt Serena says I remind them of their mama, and they cannot forgive me for her death."

"Nonsense!" the governess had exclaimed. "What does that woman mean filling your head with such folderol?"

Katherine still missed Miss Simpson, but Aunt Serena had decreed that the governess must find a new post when Katherine had turned sixteen, and had spitefully forbidden any correspondence since then.

Katherine grimaced, wondering why she was spoiling this lovely morning by dwelling on thoughts of Aunt Serena. She would be here soon enough. Generally, Serena Rayburn paid quarterly visits, bringing a new volume of sermons and a few lengths of material to be fashioned into gowns for her niece. She had been expected in January. It was now the second of February, and she had yet to appear. Katherine sighed as she thought of the fabric. She had little doubt that it would be drab in hue and that her aunt would, as always, instruct the village seamstress to make a plain gown high at the neck, with long tight sleeves and narrow skirts—innocent of any decoration.

She had once asked for a ruffle round her skirt and had been chided for an unseemly display of vanity. Still, it little mattered what she wore. She went nowhere, not even to the village. At Aunt Serena's request, the seamstress came to the house to make Katherine's garments, and on Sundays the vicar arrived after conducting services at the village church and prayed with her. Afterwards, he generally lectured her on the error of her ways, evidently recounted to him by her aunt. Chief among those recent errors was the possession of a copy of Lord Byron's poem, *The Corsair*, sent to her by her great-aunt Blanche St. Denis.

When Aunt Serena had noticed the unfamiliar volume among the books, she had ripped out its pages and thrown them into the fire. Subsequently,

she had warned Katherine that if she were not
careful, she would follow in the footsteps of Blanche,
whose name she uttered like a curse.

"She wed a Frenchman, if you please . . . eloped
with him, an enemy of her country!"

Katherine was used to Aunt Serena removing
Aunt Blanche's gifts as unsuitable for a young girl,
but the destruction of the book set her back up. "He
was not an enemy of her country then," she had
dared to say. "We were not at war with France in
1774." For that spirited defence she had been
slapped on both cheeks and sent supperless to bed.

Still, Katherine, who had memorised several
stanzas of Byron's poem, could comfort herself by
recalling them when she was happily alone. And
why was she wasting the morning light dwelling
on Aunt Serena? It were better she dressed and
went outside.

Just then Jane, her abigail, came quickly into
the chamber, shutting the door behind her. "She be
'ere. Your aunt, miss."

Katherine winced. "Miss Rayburn has arrived?"
she asked.

"No, miss, not 'er . . . the other, 'er wot married
the Frenchman."

"Aunt Blanche!" Katherine cried. "But that's
impossible. She never comes here."

The door was flung open, and on the threshold
stood a fair slender little lady some fifty-odd years
of age. In a light voice, the lady said, "She is here
now, *ma petite*, and wishing to see you very much.
I have travelled all night to tell you my news."

She was across the chamber so swiftly that it
seemed to Katherine that her great-aunt had
floated rather than walked. Flinging her arms
around the girl, Aunt Blanche clasped her to her
scented bosom and then, moving back, regarded
her in amazement. "But you are so beautiful,"

she cried. "Your hair is such a ripe gold and your eyes . . . I think they are green, yes, green! And such lovely features . . . I cannot think whom you resemble. . . . Enough—why did your papa not tell me you are the beauty of the family? He told me so little . . . save that you are often in the company of your aunt Serena. And I told him—and her, to her very face—that no one should be in her company save harpies and dragons. She had convinced your papa that there was no need for you to come out, at least this year. But I said seventeen was too old to be buried in the country. And *voilà*, I have your papa's permission to take you to London. Now, I visit friends in the north, but when I return, you will accompany me to London."

"To . . . to London . . . ? My father wishes *me* to come to London?" Katherine said faintly.

"Alas, you are so surprised . . . That tells me much about your father."

"Aunt Serena has said that he could never forgive me for my mother's death," Katherine explained.

"Which, to be frank, was as much his fault as yours," Aunt Blanche snapped. "Certainly, you should not bear the flame for a tragedy that was none of your doing or desiring."

"Aunt Serena has told me I am a very poor exchange for my mother, and I am certain my brothers and sisters agree with her—for I never see them."

"If they do agree, they are quite as mad as your aunt, but I suspect that since they are all wed, they are just busy with their own lives. Your mother was, I understand, your aunt's sole joy in life. They were orphaned when Serena was nineteen, and your mother only five, and Serena, who, might I add, never found anyone fool enough to marry her and give her family of her own to occupy her, lived her life through your mother. You should have heard the tears when the poor girl announced she was going to marry your father!

"But let us not think of Serena . . . though I wish I had had the care of you . . . But there I was in Greece and Italy and . . . but you do not wish to hear of my travels." Aunt Blanche had not sat down, but walked rapidly around the room. She noticed that Katherine was standing, and waved her to a chair.

"Oh, but I do," Katherine said. "I would love to visit Italy and Greece."

"You will. Maybe your husband will take you on your honeymoon."

"But I have no husband," said Katherine.

"You will. Someone so beautiful will not emulate Serena in her single state . . . though it was a boon to some man that *she* never married. Ah, you smile . . . finally you smile, and such a lovely smile. You do resemble your mother, and how that fool Serena could have punished you for her death. . . . But again, that is at an end. In six weeks you'll be in London, and all the *ton* will be at your little feet."

Katherine gazed at her great-aunt incredulously. Aunt Blanche had spoken so quickly and said so much, that her spate of words had not quite registered—still, she *had* said they were going to London. Katherine said faintly, "I am not sure you understand."

"*Ma petite*, I am not a prognosticator, but I predict that you will be the toast of London, and not too far into the future. But first—let me see your gowns, for you may well need new ones for London. Serena's taste is abominable."

It took only moments for Aunt Blanche to condemn every garment Katherine owned. "As I feared. No matter. I shall remain a few days and my dresser, Simone, can make you a costume or two. Is there a dressmaker in the village?"

"Mrs. Harvey, Aunt. She makes all my gowns."

"The seams are fine enough, even if the cut is horrible. She can help Simone. I hate to think of you wearing any of these hideous garments again ... they should be burned, the lot of them. And that prune-coloured sack you are wearing."

Katherine tried not to laugh, but that was exactly the way she thought of the dress.

"Come, time to present me to your governess and tell her I shall stay until Thursday. And remind me to write to the Oliphants to tell them I shall be delayed."

"Miss Simpson left a year ago," Katherine explained.

"Serena let you live here alone? *Alors!* I shall tell Lady Oliphant to expect you as well! Is this your cloak?" She picked up a dull-grey cloak.

"Yes."

"Ah, it is shame and a disgrace to hide this golden light under such a bushel." She put the cloak around Katherine's shoulders. "Come ... my child, my coach is waiting."

"Where are we going?" Katherine asked, wondering if she was to be whisked off to the Oliphants' house without any breakfast.

"To the village. Mrs. Harvey must have some decent material in stock."

The next few days were full of heady excitement for Katherine. She was fitted for three new gowns. Once Mrs. Harvey had overcome her dismay at being instructed to work under a Frenchwoman, she was determined to keep up the British side, and produced several bolts of fine fabric. Simone fingered them and sniffed. "They will do to wear at home, I suppose. In the country," she pronounced.

When Katherine was not being summoned for fit-

ting, or being taken to the cobbler to be measured
for slippers, or driven to the market town to look
at the bonnets in the mantua maker's workshop,
she went on long walks with Aunt Blanche, who
chattered constantly about her travels; her son,
Jean-Luc, who was her only child; and her large
circle of friends, which encompassed an Egyptian
holy man, an Indian princess, and hundreds of more
ordinary people. Katherine soon came to the con-
clusion that Aunt Blanche did not need to sleep, for
she seemed to have lived two lifetimes in the space
of one.

When the gowns were finished, Katherine was
delighted. For mornings there was a gown of jac-
conet muslin with a ruff around the neck and a
flounce at the skirt. Katherine exclaimed, as she
examined the lacy garment, "This is much too fine
just to wear at home."

"You will not believe it so fine when you discover
what ladies of fashion wear in the morning," Lady
Blanche said, laughing. "Wait until you see dear
Lady Oliphant's daughters."

There was also a blue dress of French cambric,
collarless but edged about the neck with cambric,
which Lady Blanche said looked just like pointe
lace. A pale brown pelisse of fine cloth trimmed
with gold embroidery was also produced, and an
evening gown in a green muslin that, Lady Blanche
said, was almost the colour of Katherine's eyes,
though not as deep. Aunt Blanche had given Katherine two of her own bonnets, retrimmed by Simone, and a long cloak lined with swansdown.
There were also fine lisle stockings and little
leather slippers produced with amazing speed by
the local cobbler.

Katherine gazed at the garments with awe, saying, "I can hardly believe they are really mine."

"They are really yours, my love. And if you tell

me that you are living in a dream, I will tell you
that your life before this moment was an ugly
dream and you are now stepping into daylight.
Katherine, why do you frown?"

"I beg your pardon, Aunt, but I am a little overwhelmed. I have never met your friends Lord and
Lady Oliphant, and it sounds as if so many people
will be there. . . ." Katherine did not want to sound
ungrateful, but the prospect of a houseful of
strangers was more than she, who had only just
gotten used to having her great-aunt's company,
could face with equanimity.

"I understand perfectly, *ma petite.* You need a
little time to become used to the society of others.
A pity there is no time to arrange for a term at a
school. Ah! Of course, dear little Cressida!"

"Who is she?" Katherine asked.

"She is the child of my dear friend Mrs. Loop.
Her mother and I wrote each other often after I first
left England. After Mrs. Loop's death, her daughter, Cressida Trent, and I continued to correspond.
I have not seen her in years, but, in her letter which
arrived yesterday, she told me several young ladies—all near your age—are staying with her.
Would you be content to visit Mrs. Trent?"

Katherine, who had no intention of remaining for
the rest of her life at Tilbury Manor, and saw the
wisdom of first becoming acquainted with those of
her own years before venturing into Society, agreed
with relief.

"You will have a wonderful visit. Mrs. Trent lives
in the village of Valentine Parva, which is not far
from the city of Lincoln."

"Lincoln," Katherine repeated excitedly. "That
is where the great cathedral stands." She was enchanted with anything gothic. As a child she had
invented inhabitants for the ruined castle. Their
lives had been as romantic as anything Lord Byron

could have imagined. "I have always wanted to visit the cathedral."

"Ah." Aunt Blanche laughed merrily. "Truly, you are a revelation, *ma petite*! I promise you a whole new life, and you speak to me about a cathedral."

Katherine blushed. "It ... it is just that you mentioned Lincoln. . . . There is a book in Papa's library telling of its construction. I should love to paint it."

"You are an artist, then?"

Katherine said rather hesitatingly, "I am not an artist . . . but I enjoy painting. Miss Simpson taught me."

"Might I see these paintings?" Aunt Blanche asked.

"They are not very good," Katherine said deprecatingly.

"I beg you will let me judge for myself, dear."

Reluctantly, Katherine went to her chamber and selected several watercolours and a few sketches done in pencil. She diffidently proffered them to her aunt.

Aunt Blanche looked at them quickly. Far too quickly, Katherine thought, stifling an interior sigh. Probably she would like them no better than had Aunt Serena, who had chided her for wasting paint.

"But these are lovely," Aunt Blanche said firmly. "Such a fine use of colour and so discerning an eye. I have seen many paintings, many, and these, I tell you without prejudice, are very fine. *Mais mon enfant*, why do you weep?"

"I thought . . . She said . . ." Katherine shook her head.

"She being the dragon or, rather, the worm, as they were called in the old ballads. I wish Serena were a worm small enough to be trod upon." Aunt

Blanche stamped her foot. "Instead, she does the treading and the stamping. Enough, my love, we must leave this Serena-haunted mansion tomorrow at daybreak!"

"But do you not need to ask Mrs. Trent if I may stay?"

"Oh, that," said Aunt Blanche. "How long can it take to send a letter?"

It took, in fact, just three days for her groom to carry a letter and return with a reply.

Aunt Blanche ordered the preparations for their departure as soon as she received Mrs. Trent's invitation. They spent two days on the road, and two nights in small, clean inns. Katherine had the impression that Aunt Blanche only put up at night for the sake of Simone, and her coachman and footman. They passed through towns and tiny villages, open countryside, and miles of pastureland. Gradually, hills gave way to plains. Staring out of the coach window, Katherine felt as if she had entered a new world. Everything was new—stone bridges arching over rivers, market-town streets, muddy but full of tradesmen and farm wives at their stalls despite the cold weather—all new, and all wonderful.

And now they were on the outskirts of that little village with the lovely name—Valentine Parva! Soon Katherine would meet Mrs. Trent, and the three young ladies staying with her. She had a moment of fright, and wished she were back home. Then she remembered the day that Mark, her eldest brother, had brought his children to see the house and the remains of the castle. Then family consisted of two boys, a little older than she, and a younger girl. Urged by Mark's wife to join her little nephews and niece, Katherine had gone outside, only to have them make faces at her. The girl had thrown a rock. Mark had made them apologise to

her, but it had been obvious they had not meant it.
Later, as they were leaving, the older boy had asked
her, "Why do you not leave. If you were not here,
we could live here."

A frightened Katherine had replied, "Because
there is no place for me to go."

"I would find somewhere," he'd said scornfully.

Well, now there was a place for her. But it was a
place she would have to make for herself. For if she
retreated into a shell of fear, she'd be as trapped
here as she had been at Tilbury Manor.

"Mon enfant, voilà. We have arrived."

"Oh, it does look pleasant," Katherine said. They
had stopped in front of a large house, fronted by a
garden, winter-bound, but giving promise of flowers
in the spring.

As soon as the footman let down the step, Aunt
Blanche herself went to knock on the door. It was
opened by a middle-aged maid who showed them
directly into a double drawing room, and went in
search of Mrs. Trent.

Katherine was surprised to hear the sound of
birds coming from behind a heavy red curtain hung
across a doorway in the far part of the room. She
was about to draw Aunt Blanche's attention to it
when the door opened and a woman in her thirties,
her blond hair covered by a cap, came into the room
and was swept into Aunt Blanche's embrace.

"Ma belle Cressida!"

"Madame St. Denis, how pleased I am to see you.
I had thought you in Rome or Samarkand until I
received your letter from London. And I was so
pleased when you wrote again asking me to have
Katherine to stay. I take it that this is Katherine?"

"Yes, this is Katherine. I find her very pleasing,"
replied Aunt Blanche as Katherine made her curtsey.

"How you do you, Miss Tilbury."

Katherine noticed Mrs. Trent's gaze flicker between her and her aunt. Apparently Aunt Blanche noticed it too, for she said, "It is surprising, yes? She could be my Jean-Luc's sister. And can you believe, the boy has made me a grandmother?"

Mrs. Trent offered her congratulations and invited them to sit down. She seemed about to suggest some refreshment when Aunt Blanche said, "I vow you have not changed since I last saw you and you were a girl of fifteen!"

"It has always seemed to me that you must have found the fountain of youth, Madame. I am always amazed by the vigour your letters suggest."

"I refute that." Aunt Blanche laughed. "Come, let us talk of Katherine. She has spent her life shut away in an immense, gloomy mansion that smells strongly of rats."

"One never sees them, and they harm no one," Katherine said.

Aunt Blanche laughed. "Is she not a little love?" she demanded. "She tolerates rats and bears no ill will for as lonely an existence as I have ever seen, but you know that."

Mrs. Trent nodded. "I was much distressed by your letter. I hope I shall be able to provide some entertainment. It is fortunate she will be here for Valentine's Day." She turned to Katherine. "The village children put on a pageant, and I am helping to organize them. Perhaps we could enlist your aid."

Katherine could not imagine what would be involved in such an entertainment, but willingly said she would help Mrs. Trent in any way she could.

At that moment a small clock on the mantelshelf chimed four o'clock, and Aunt Blanche rose. "I must go. I hope to break my journey at the Golden Shilling, and it is yet some little distance from here."

"Can I not persuade you first to drink some tea?" Mrs. Trent asked.

"It is not possible, but I will be back in late March or early April and then, I promise, I shall have more time."

"I hope so," said Mrs. Trent warmly.

"I promise, I promise. And again, I thank you for accepting this child." Aunt Blanche sighed. "I think it was the work of the good Lord that sent me to visit her father—and to learn of Katherine's need for me. To keep a girl such as her in that ugly pile. Even when her dear mother was alive, and the house full of little children, it was gloom personified. And to leave the child alone save for the occasional visit from that bird of ill omen, Serena—cruelty of the highest order. Her father will hear from me regarding his lack of consideration." Aunt Blanche paused for breath, then added, "Oh, Cressida, I nearly forgot. Katherine is an artist. Could you take her to the cathedral in Lincoln? She wants very much to visit it and sketch some portions of it."

"I can understand her wish," Mrs. Trent said. "I have often wished I could draw some of the statuary, but I am not an artist. I would be happy to take her to see the cathedral. In fact, I think all the girls would like to visit it. We will go together."

"Oh," Katherine said breathlessly. "I would like that above all things."

"I am glad it will be so easy to please you, Miss Tilbury," Cressida said.

"Oh, she is very easy to please," Aunt Blanche said. She embraced her niece, then kissed Cressida. "I am so glad you can harbour Katherine. And please, I beg, neither of you come out to the coach with me. I always find it so painful when friends fade into the distance. Now farewell, my dears ... and may St. Valentine bring you your heart's desires. Cressida, do not frown so!"

"I am no longer sixteen," Mrs. Trent replied.

"And I will never see thirty-four again, but my heart is always filled with desire." Aunt Blanche laughed lightly as she hurried to the door.

"Thank you, Aunt Blanche," Katherine called after her. "And God speed you."

"I really am glad that you are here," Mrs. Trent said as the door shut. "Would you care to call me by my Christian name as do my cousins and Juno?"

"Yes, thank you," replied Katherine, feeling a little at a loss.

"Well, let us go upstairs and I'll show you your chamber."

Katherine followed Cressida up the stairs slowly. She was experiencing a sharp pang of regret that she had not been nearly grateful enough for all of the kindnesses Aunt Blanche had shown her. Kindnesses such as she had never known in all her days. As they came to the landing window, Katherine looked down into the lane and saw her great-aunt's coach disappearing around a bend in the road.

She sighed, and Cressida, coming to stand beside her, said, "It was a great pleasure to see Madame St. Denis again. She is like a breath of spring, and as spring never changes, neither does she."

"I wish I knew her as well as you do, Mrs.— Cressida," Katherine said softly. "But I am so glad that she came for me."

Cressida smiled. "You are very like her—an amazing resemblance, indeed. Come, this is your new room."

More than my new room, Katherine thought, *my new home, my new life.*

"Here you are," Cressida said, opening the door to a large, bright chamber, furnished with a bed, covered by a tree-of-life patchwork. Near the window was a table—and the light was excellent: she could draw her pictures here.

"Oh," she said. "It is lovely."

"I am pleased you find it so, my dear. Now I shall send my maid, Maudie Brick, up to unpack for you. We dine at five. If you wish to rest until then, do so. Otherwise, you may come downstairs and meet my other guests."

Eager to begin her new life, Katherine stayed in the room just long enough to remove her bonnet, then hurried downstairs.

Unfamiliar sounds woke Katherine the next morning. Somewhere dogs were barking, horses neighing, all the sounds of a village coming to life. She sat up in bed blinking against the sunlight, realised that she was in a strange chamber, and then remembered where she was. The remnants of sleep fled, chased away by memories of the previous day.

It had been such a strange, wonderful evening that her regret at her great-aunt's departure had actually been swallowed up in the excitement.

There were three girls here, a little older than she. Juno Rathbone had been polite, but Katherine wondered if Juno were as shy as she, for as soon as she could Juno had opened a large book and begun to read. Cressida's cousins were friendlier. They were very much of an age. Aquila Ware, the elder, was a lovely, elegant young woman. Her sister, Philomena, or Philo, as she was called, was also attractive, though very different from her sister. Aquila seemed cool and dignified, and Philo, Katherine remembered with a smile, very serious when asked about the birds she kept in the conservatory, behind the red curtain.

"They all sound different," Philo said, adding indignantly, "Someone said they all sounded alike and that I was wasting my time trying to breed the ideal singer."

"Whoever said anything so silly?" Aquila had demanded. Katherine realised that Aquila was very protective of her younger sister, and she found that fact very pleasant.

She found even more pleasant the fact that the sisters took pains to include her in their conversation and activities, and before long she found herself very much at ease in their company.

A few days later Cressida announced that she had arranged an outing to Lincoln for them. Since they would spend the middle part of the day there, they could also visit the lending library and the shops, and Cressida planned to call upon the dean's wife, who had recently had a baby and was recovering rather slowly. Libraries and dean's wives, however, meant very little to Katherine. It was the cathedral that loomed large in her consciousness.

On the day of the outing, Katherine dressed in her gown of French cambric and her new brown pelisse and took with her a supply of paper and sharpened pencils.

Cressida explained that she would accompany them to the cathedral and then spend the rest of the morning with the dean's wife, who lived in the cathedral close. They would all meet at one o'clock at the bookseller's, an easy place to find since it was at the bottom of the steep street that ran down from the cathedral.

Katherine was struck by the outside of the building, but Cressida hurried them all inside, telling Katherine that she could walk around at her leisure later. "I have arranged for one of the vergers, Mr. Pillpot, to show us around," she explained, "and I do not wish to keep him waiting."

Mr. Pillpot was a genial man, and began by asking if there was anything in particular that they wished to see. "The East Window, please," Katherine asked.

"The East Window, Miss Tilbury. You are fortunate that it is a sunny day. I shall certainly show it to you."

Aquila remarked that she had heard that the high altar was considered to be very fine, and Philo asked to see the statue of the Lincoln Imp.

"We can manage all that," Mr. Pillpot said. "It's a shame your visitors have so little time, ma'am. They could well spend two weeks here, not just two hours."

"Perhaps we can return after St. Valentine's Day," Cressida said. "I will have more time then."

Philo smiled. "I am looking forward to it." She turned to Katherine. "Aren't you?"

Katherine shook her head. "Why is that?"

Philo looked at her in surprise, but before she could answer, Cressida said, "I do not think that Katherine has ever received a valentine. I expect this year will be different. Now, Mr. Pillpot, you must not let us waste any more of your time."

The East Window was large. Katherine found its elongated shape and arched top a pleasing shape. There seemed to be all the colours of the rainbow in the glass panels: green, blue, yellow, purple, and red gleamed from the intricately worked figures. It was so beautiful that Katherine felt tears in her eyes.

As soon as Mr. Pillpot finished guiding them through the cathedral, Aquila and Philo began to discuss which shops they wanted to visit. Juno invited Katherine to accompany her to the lending library. "I hope to spend the rest of the morning there."

"I had hoped to stay here a little longer," Katherine said.

Cressida said, "I rather imagine that Katherine could spend all morning here. Aquila, why don't you and Philo walk with Juno as far as the library, and call for her there when you have finished shopping. Then we can all meet in the cathedral close at one o'clock. Katherine, is that agreeable to you?"

"Oh, yes, thank you," replied Katherine, and went at once to the East Window, where she began to sketch. At half past twelve she put away her drawings and walked along the nave, trying to form a unified impression of the whole cathedral. There were very few people about, and she imagined what the cathedral must have been like when it was first built. She wandered along the apse and into one of the side chapels. She was just about to leave when a man stepped in front of her.

"And where are you going, my pretty maid?" he drawled.

Looking up at him, she met bold dark eyes set under heavy brown brows. There was a broad smile on his lips, and without knowing quite why, Katherine found his presence intimidating. Perhaps it was the way his eyebrows met across his forehead. She moved forward, and he blocked her way, his arm across the narrow doorway.

"So beautiful and so unfriendly," he commented.

"I do not know you, sir. Let me pass," Katherine said, her voice quavering.

"Not yet . . . but that can soon be remedied. My name, sweetling, is Reginald Seton. And how are you called?"

Katherine ducked under his arm and hurried towards the outer door. She hoped that he would not follow her, but he did, saying, "You've not given me your name. I call that most unfriendly."

"I have no desire to be your friend," Katherine said. "Go away before I summon Mr. Pillpot." It was an empty threat. Neither the verger nor anyone else was nearby, and Katherine did not think she had the courage to shout in the cathedral. But what would she do if the dreadful man followed her all the way to the library? Perhaps he would not pursue her once she was outside.

He stepped in front of her again, and she stopped, not wishing to bump into him. As she stepped back, he moved forward, turning his steps so that she found herself backed against the curved wall of the apse. "But I do not wish to go away, not from someone so lovely."

Katherine took a deep breath and made sure she had a firm grip on the bag holding her drawing materials, intending to ram the bag into the man's knees and run for it.

"But the lady wishes you gone," someone said.

Katherine looked past her tormentor and met the gaze of a young man.

"What's it to you?" asked Seton.

"An intention to see the lady's wishes carried out."

There was a moment's silence. Katherine found nothing menacing in the newcomer's tone or manner, but Seton must have found him intimidating, for he shook his head and left.

"Oh," said Katherine, "I . . . I do thank you, sir."

"You are most welcome, ma'am."

Katherine swallowed to keep back tears. It was too soon to expect Cressida to be waiting for her, and she no longer fancied wandering about the cathedral alone.

"Are you here with friends?" the young man asked. "Do you live nearby?"

"I am staying with Mrs. Trent, in Valentine Parva."

"Do you mean Mrs. Homer Trent?"

Katherine did not recall ever having been told the Christian name of Cressida's late husband, but when her rescuer asked if Mrs. Trent lived at Hugh's Grange, she was able to answer in the affirmative.

"I know Mrs. Trent! I went to school with her brothers."

"We are to meet in the close at quarter to one," Katherine explained. "She is visiting at the deanery."

He held out a hand to take Katherine's bag from her. "Please allow me to walk there with you."

"No, thank you. I mean, it would be very kind of you to walk as far as the close with me, but I'd rather not go in the house. I don't know anyone there. If you could wait with me until Mrs. Trent comes out, I would be very glad. It will only be a minute, I am certain." She let him take her bag.

The man shook his head. "You are far too trusting, ma'am. I could be a wolf in sheep's clothing."

"I think not, sir. You are far too kind."

He sighed. "Where have you been living, child? In an ivory tower?"

"I am not a child," Katherine said. "I have turned seventeen."

"Have you? I think I shall hold to my theory of your childhood home."

"The manor where I grew up had nothing so romantic as a tower," Katherine said. As they walked quickly along, Katherine told him a little of her childhood. Rather than dwell on the loneliness she had often felt, she told him about the ruined castle and the hours she had spent playing among the fallen stones, peopling them with characters from her fancy.

They came to the end of the close and looked towards the city gate. "It is such a distance down," Katherine said. "It took us nearly half an hour to climb it."

"It's faster going down. This hill always reminds me of Sisyphus and his stone."

She laughed. "Poor Sisyphus, forever rolling a

stone up a hill, only to have it roll down again. What a punishment for a king."

"Fit for a king of his persuasion, I think. He was a true tyrant." He smiled. "You know your mythology."

"Oh, yes. I have always enjoyed reading about gods and heroes. There are all sorts of books in the library at home."

"Your father gave you much liberty, Miss . . ."

"My name is Katherine, sir. Katherine Tilbury."

"And mine is Anthony, Anthony Overton."

"I am pleased to make your acquaintance, Mr. Overton," Katherine said shyly.

"And I yours, Miss Tilbury."

"And you are right about my father. He never forbade me to read anything."

At that moment, Juno, Aquila, and Philo came into the close and hurried towards them. "Sir Anthony, I did not know you knew Miss Tilbury," said Aquila.

"I found her in the cathedral, Miss Ware," Sir Anthony said.

Before he could continue his explanation, Katherine said, "I . . . I stayed to sketch . . . and a . . . a person c-came up to me, and even when I told him to leave me he kept talking . . . and Mr. . . . Sir Anthony sent him away."

"Ever 'the gentil, parfit knight,' " Aquila said. "I did not know you were in Lincoln, Sir Anthony."

"I am delighted to see you again, and you also, Miss Philo. My uncle, who lives some distance from Lincoln, is not well, and I have come to keep him company."

"I am sorry to hear that," said Aquila. "I hope he is not seriously ill."

"The doctor says it is nothing serious. I believe my company helps my uncle find being bedridden a little less intolerable. Certainly it allows my aunt a few hours respite."

Aquila introduced the gentleman to Juno, then returned to the conversation. "I remember your uncle well. Be so kind, if you please, as to recall us to him."

"Of course, Miss Ware. I am sure he remembers you."

Katherine listened to this exchange with interest. Seeing Aquila smile at Sir Anthony made her conscious of an odd little pang—they did seem on such friendly terms. How long had Aquila known him? Philo was smiling at him, too, but he had not conversed with her. Obviously, he was Aquila's friend.

Cressida joined them, and greeted Sir Anthony warmly. Katherine noticed that he would have been willing to pass off his being there as a chance reunion with his friends, the Misses Ware, but truthfulness forced her to confess her part. Cressida accepted her assurances that she had come to no harm, then thanked Sir Anthony. "But I think that we had best be getting home again."

Sir Anthony nodded. "I am sorry I have not yet been to call upon you, ma'am. Miss Rathbone, Miss Ware, Miss Philo, your servant. And Miss Tilbury." He paused.

"I do thank you for your help in the cathedral, Sir Anthony," Katherine said shyly.

"I am glad that was I present," he said, frowning. "The utter insolence of that miscreant! Had we not been in the cathedral, he would have regretted his temerity, I can assure you."

"Gracious, Sir Anthony," Aquila said. "You are looking quite fierce."

"Are you all right?" Philo whispered to Katherine, who nodded.

Sir Anthony flushed. "He was a most unwholesome rascal, and I am sorry that poor Miss Tilbury had to suffer his outrageous advances!"

"So are we all," Aquila said. "And I imagine that I am partially to blame for the misadventure. We should not have deserted her."

"Oh, it was not your fault," Katherine protested. "I was so anxious to finish my sketching, and there was so much to see. I never thought harm could come to me in a cathedral—a house of God."

"Your innocence is refreshing, Miss Tilbury," Sir Anthony said. His gaze lingered on her face for a moment, then he said, "But I detain you ladies. And I must go."

"So must we," said Cressida. "The carriage will be waiting."

Sir Anthony, however, seemed reluctant to leave them. "Perhaps I may walk with you to your coach."

Cressida consented. He offered her his arm, and Cressida accepted. "Aquila and Philo, would you and Juno lead the way? Katherine, walk beside me, please."

They set out for the innyard where the carriage was standing.

"Miss Tilbury has been a great help to me with the pageant," Cressida said.

"Indeed. Are you enjoying it?"

"Very much. I'm trying to help the children learn their lines," Katherine said. "Do you know the legend, Sir Anthony?"

"All about King Alfred and the grant of land for Valentine Parva being presented on St. Valentine's Day? Yes, I have seen the pageant."

"Oh." Katherine was despondent. She had cherished a hope that he might come to see it.

"I see it every year, although I confess I enjoy the cakes that are sold to benefit the missionary fund more than the theatrical."

Katherine smiled.

"I'd lay two to one that anyone would say the same, Miss Tilbury. While the children are enchanting, the cakes are divine."

Cressida laughed. "We all know you are not a betting man."

"I may have changed for the worse," he said.

At that moment they entered the innyard and, after handing them all in to the carriage, Sir Anthony bade them good afternoon.

Aquila and Philo apologised again for leaving Katherine in the cathedral. "I had no idea you would be subjected to such an experience," Juno added. "It says much for the condition of our society that a man will listen to one of his own sex, yet ignore the reasonable request of a woman."

"Experience?" Katherine echoed, and felt herself blush. She had been watching Sir Anthony stride away, not attending to the other girls' words. "No, you are not to blame. It was my fault, and fortunately it turned out well."

Cressida spoke. "It was a most unfortunate occurrence, Katherine. When we are home, you and I shall talk about it. I am glad that you are not more upset, for it was not your fault."

"I never thought something like that could happen in a cathedral," Katherine said.

"It is open to all," Philo said, "saints and sinners."

"Well, that man was certainly a sinner," Aquila observed. "Does that make Sir Anthony a saint?"

"He is an extraordinarily fine young man," Cressida said. "I had no idea that you knew him, Aquila. He was a schoolfellow of my brothers, and, since he spent the holidays with his uncle, he was often at Hugh's Grange."

"We first met him aboard the packet from Ostend."Aquila laughed. "He was travelling with his uncle, who—like everyone else aboard save Philo and Sir Anthony and I—was seasick. After that we ran into him everywhere for a while."

"He is very kind," Katherine said softly. "I do not think I thanked him enough. I will send him a note."

"Why not send a valentine?" said Philo.

"A valentine . . . What exactly is a valentine?"

"Surely you know what a valentine is," said Aquila. "You must receive dozens every year."

"A valentine is a greeting—I'll show you some when we are home," Cressida said. "You must remember, Aquila, that until this year, Katherine was still in the schoolroom."

For the rest of the drive home, Katherine was silent, but her mind was full of pictures—for Sir Anthony would make the perfect hero.

Late that evening, Cressida spoke to Katherine about the man who had accosted her, and after she had advised her again against going alone into secluded places, she turned the conversation to Sir Anthony.

"I expect, Katherine, that he will call in a day or two, to see how you are, if nothing else. Certainly, he would call on me out of friendship for my brothers, but I believe he will want particularly to see you. When you are in London with your great-aunt, you will have many admirers."

Katherine had not thought of that before, and said that she did not expect to be a belle.

"With your birth and beauty, men will seek you out. I hope that a friendship with Sir Anthony will help prepare you for their attentions. Certainly, his company is worth receiving for its own sake, but it will do you no harm to become more used to gentlemen's compliments. But you must not take Sir Anthony too seriously. He is somewhat older than you, and used to the company of sophisticated ladies.

Certainly, he will not treat you dishonourably, but
his affections will not become engaged."

"I understand," said Katherine. It had not occurred
to her that Sir Anthony would have any interest in
her.

"I hope I've not put ideas into your head, Katherine."

"Oh, no, Cressida. If Sir Anthony wants to be my
friend, I will welcome it, but he knew Aquila first."

On the morning after her never-to-be forgotten visit
to the cathedral, Katherine sat at the table in her
chamber, looking at the two valentines given her
by Cressida. Both had charming little pictures on
them. One was of a fat cupid, wreathed with flowers. The other was adorned with roses framing the
words "Will you not be my valentine?"

Glancing at her watercolour, Katherine tried to
think of one for Sir Anthony. She had found his
direction by talking to Aquila and learning his ailing uncle lived in the village next to Valentine
Parva. She had easily made four, one each for Cressida, Aquila, Philo, and Juno, and a fifth, smaller
one for Toby. She thought again of the encounter
in the cathedral, of the brave way in which he had
faced down the horrible Seton. . . .

Two hours later, Katherine finished her picture
of a slender David, clad in a blue tunic, his foot on
a writhing Goliath, dressed in red. It was nothing
like the valentines she had seen, but she had tried
to mitigate the subject matter by delicately sketching flowers all around the card and by the small
heart she had placed at the top.

She had wanted to write "To my valentine," but
that had seemed far too bold. In the end she put,
"To a brave valentine," and wondered if Sir Anthony would guess the identity of the sender. Cressida had explained that valentines were supposed

to be anonymous. Of course, it was very unlikely that Sir Anthony would remember her at all. Probably, the whole episode had vanished from his mind, and he would be racking his brains wondering from whom the card came. For, no matter what kind words Cressida and effusive Aunt Blanche had said, Katherine knew she had no beauty. As Aunt Serena had never scrupled to tell her, it was well that she had a sizeable dowry, else there would be no incentive for anyone to offer for her at all.

Sir Anthony did call, but the drawing room was crowded with the girls and other callers. Katherine found herself too shy to do more than murmur conventional replies to his questions. After he left, she berated herself for her stupidity. Of course, she was too young and innocent to interest him, but if only she could command a little of his attention while she remained in Valentine Parva she would be content. Nightly she debated with herself the wisdom of sending the valentine. In the end she decided that she would rather send him an unrecognised token than ignore him completely.

On the night of February thirteenth, she joined the others in their Valentine's Eve game. Since Sir Anthony was the only man she knew, she wrote his name on one piece of paper and left several others blank. She watched the other girls encase their slips of paper in clay and take turns tossing them into the water. Even Cressida seemed to be enjoying herself. Katherine wondered if any of the others believed that they would marry the man whose name first floated to the surface. It seemed so foolish, and yet, if it really happened, so romantic. When she snatched Sir Anthony's name from the water, she had to tell herself firmly that it was only chance that had not left her clutching a blank scrap of paper. She was very glad that they had all agreed not to show each other the names.

Later that night she slipped out and left her valentines on the doorstep, happy at the thought she was rewarding, if anonymously, the kindness she had experienced in the house. The following day, St. Valentine's Day, was festive, but Katherine was constantly distracted by the thought of Sir Anthony receiving her valentine. What if he did not guess she had sent it? Worse, what if he did?

A few days later Katherine was sitting in her room, a shawl around her legs, since the morning fire had died hours before. She was carefully colouring with pencils the inked outline of the East Window she had started after breakfast. She was so engrossed in her work that she did not hear Eliza come into the room until the maid said, "Please, miss?"

Katherine looked up. "Yes, Eliza?"

"A gentleman's stopped by for you, miss. Sir Anthony Overton. He's in the drawing room with Miss Ware."

"Tell him I'll be down directly, please."

"Yes, miss." The maid curtseyed and withdrew.

There was a smear of ink on one finger. Was there also ink on her face? A glance in the mirror alleviated that fear. She poured a little water into the washbowl and scrubbed her finger. The ink wouldn't come off. She'd just have to keep her hand close to her skirt. She was glad she was wearing her blue gown . . . and her hair. What of her hair? Another hasty glance in the mirror showed her that her curls were tumbled. She ran a comb through them and hurried out of her chamber.

As she started down the stairs, she heard the sound of the spinet. She entered the drawing room and found Sir Anthony turning the pages for Aquila, who was playing a sonata. Katherine stopped just inside the door.

Aquila looked up and took her fingers from the keys.

"Oh, please," Katherine protested, "I beg you, do not stop. It was such lovely music."

"Good day, Miss Tilbury," Sir Anthony said. "You are an admirer of the works of Herr Ludwig van Beethoven, I collect."

Katherine had never heard of Herr van Beethoven. She was suddenly all too aware that she had never studied music. "Sir Anthony . . . I am . . . pleased to see you again."

Aquila put away her music. "Shall we sit down?" she asked.

"I trust you are quite recovered, Miss Tilbury," Sir Anthony said when they were all seated.

Katherine assured him that he was. "But I never should have gone alone into such a secluded place. It was very foolish of me."

Sir Anthony smiled. "But as Shakespeare says, 'all's well that ends well,' and with this particular end comes a beginning . . ."

"A . . . beginning, sir." Katherine looked at him in confusion.

He regarded her with a touch of surprise. "A beginning to our friendship. At least, I am in hopes that it was."

"Oh . . . oh, yes," Katherine said softly, and felt her cheeks grow warm. Then, aware that she might have spoken too boldly, she added quickly, "At least I hope . . ."

In the silence that followed, Aquila said, "Sir Anthony was telling me about his new horse. He rode her over. She sounds a beauty."

"Would you care to see her?"

"That is very kind of you, sir, but it is uncommonly sunny today, and I have a touch of the headache. I am sure Miss Tilbury would be interested."

"Are you an admirer of horseflesh, ma'am?" Sir

Anthony asked. "You would have to walk as far as the Valentine Arms to see her."

"I know very little about horses, but I would like to see yours," Katherine replied.

She ran upstairs to ask Cressida's permission.

"Take Kate with you," Cressida said. "And don't stay out too long."

As they walked down the lane, with Kate following them, Sir Anthony said quietly, "Do you know, Miss Tilbury, I am almost grateful to that rogue: his boldness gave me the opportunity to approach you, although, as it turns out, I would have met you through Mrs. Trent in time. Blast, I wish I had drawn a little of his claret!"

"His claret?" Katherine said, confused.

He flushed. "I did not mean to sound bloodthirsty, Miss Tilbury, but to see that impudent scoundrel make advances towards one so innocent and sheltered. Enough. We are here."

Katherine wished she could say something that would not sound innocent and sheltered. Unfortunately, those words described her exactly.

"Well," demanded Sir Anthony as he led a sleek chestnut mare from the stable, "what do you think of her?"

"She is lovely!" Katherine replied.

He smiled. "At the risk of sounding too proud, I must agree. This is Princess Gulnar. Look at her head, you can see the Arabian in her."

"She is splendid."

"I know. Would you care to ride with me some morning, Miss Tilbury? Miss Ware enjoys a good gallop. I could arrange a mount for you."

"I don't know how to ride," Katherine said, aware that she must be sinking lower than ever in his estimation.

"Then I must ask Mrs. Trent's permission to

teach you. A lady as lovely and as graceful as you are, Miss Tilbury, belongs in the saddle."

The whole way back to Hugh's Grange, Katherine felt as if she were floating.

Cressida was agreeable to Katherine's learning to ride, and Sir Anthony had promised to return after breakfast the next morning. Katherine stood by the landing window to watch him ride away. She wished that he could have remained with her longer, much longer, or better still, that she could have gone with him. It was very odd, she mused, she had seen him only twice, and yet she had the odd impression that they had known each other much longer.

She was suddenly reminded of Romeo and Juliet, who had met and loved immediately. Like Juliet, she, too, could say, "Gallup apace, ye fiery footed steeds . . ." Katherine shuddered. Their story had ended too tragically.

But it was foolish of her to harbour such fancies. She was not Juliet, and Sir Anthony was not Romeo. Cressida had warned her that Sir Anthony would not be interested in anything but friendship with her, but surely it would hurt nothing for her to love him a little. Even the tone of his voice had filled her with emotions, emotions she scarcely understood.

But every day she learned just how much it could hurt to love him. When they rode together he was a patient teacher, but even through the gloves she wore, the touch of his hands as he corrected her grip on the reins made her want to swoon. Often he would come back later in the day, to walk with her and another of the girls, or to sit in Cressida's drawing room, talking with her.

But she was constantly reminded that Juno and Philo had both found happiness in love. Katherine was feeling very left out. She wondered what names the other ladies had picked out of the water on Valentine's Eve and whether these had been the names of the men now pledged to them. Oh, she wished it were so, for then she would have reason to hope.

When, at Aquila's urging, she showed him her sketches, he admired them greatly. Only later did it occur to her that it might give him a clue as to the sender of the David and Goliath valentine, but he made no mention of it. Finally, she could stand the suspense no longer and, one evening, when he had stayed to dine with the household, she turned the subject to valentines. Sir Anthony enquired if she had received many, which gave her the chance to ask him the same question.

"Only one," he replied. "A very fine drawing of a biblical story, that of David and Goliath. I took it as a warning from a friend that I must not think myself too fine a fellow, or a David would cut me down to size."

Oh, dear, thought Katherine. He obviously did not connect it with her, but it was a shame he had so misunderstood.

"I cannot imagine why anyone would want to correct you, Sir Anthony," she said.

"Well, we all have our flaws," he said. "And the card was a change from all those flowers and cupids one sees every February. One could do without the reminder that it is true what they say about Eros' arrows. They do pierce the heart, and quickly." He frowned. "Come, Miss Tilbury, let us talk of something else. Have you considered my request that you draw Princess Gulnar for me? I promise you a box of bonbons as your commission."

"I'd gladly paint her, and for no reward," Katherine replied, "but I am not certain how true a likeness I would create. I've never drawn a horse all by itself."

She started the painting the next day. It was too

cold to spend long outside, but Katherine made some quick sketches and spent longer in the stable making studies of the mare's head. Sir Anthony kept her company while she painted. His uncle was up and about again, which let Sir Anthony more hours at his disposal. But it seemed that he still felt his presence was required, for he made no mention of leaving the area.

As Katherine had feared, her lack of experience drawing horses resulted in a picture that was not among her better efforts, but it gave them something to laugh at together. Sir Anthony kept his promise and brought her a very large box of bonbons.

"I am not sure I can accept, sir," Katherine told him, "since we are neither of us pleased with the picture."

"Then take the sweets as a present from a devoted admirer," he said, making her a sweeping bow.

Katherine did not reply, for that was exactly the spirit in which she wished to think they were given.

"Well, if you still demur," Sir Anthony said, "please present them to Mrs. Trent as a gift for her and her visitors."

Katherine knew she had been gauche, again, and feared he'd stop calling at Hugh's Grange, but his visits did not cease. After the sweets were eaten, Katherine appropriated the box they had come in and used it to hold her sketches of Sir Anthony.

It seemed to her that Sir Anthony found her very amusing, for he appeared to be content to listen to her chatter for hours. When she attempted to imbue her conversation with the elegance exhibited by Aquila, he'd laugh and turn the subject to history or mythology, and demand her opinions. Juno said she was fortunate to find a man willing to listen to her thoughts, but Katherine wanted to impress him, not amuse him.

And the time for Lady Blanche's return was drawing close. Soon she'd be whisked away to London. And if she saw Sir Anthony there, he'd be surrounded by a bevy of sophisticated beauties.

She was sitting alone in the drawing room one afternoon, reading a book of French fairy tales Cressida had lent her. There was a most engaging story about a girl and the prince who loved her. Katherine's fingers were itching to illustrate it. She drew herself as the girl, with Aunt Blanche as her fairy godmother, waving a magic wand and turning her rags into a silk gown. Katherine was pleased at the way the torn apron became an over-skirt where the fairy dust fell. Then she drew the Prince—Sir Anthony, of course. And then the wedding: she and Sir Anthony coming out of church, hand in hand. From there, it was an easy step to write the sort of letter the prince might have written, proclaiming his love.

She'd throw the pictures and the letter on the fire before the others returned. Cressida had gone to make some calls, and Philo had gone for a walk with Toby. Aquila, who had lightly said she would remain at home with Katherine in case any beaux came to call, was the only other person in the house, save for Kate. John Barleyman had taken Mrs. Barleyman to the market, and Maudie Brick and Eliza were in the village collecting the shirts sewn by the Dorcas Society for the heathen.

There was the sound of a carriage pulling up in the lane outside, and Katherine quickly gathered up her papers. Suddenly a familiar voice shouted, "I said the carriage was to wait here, you fool."

Katherine, still clutching the papers, ran into the hall just in time to see Kate opening the front door to Aunt Serena. "How . . . ? Why . . . ?" Katherine was at a loss.

"I might ask you the same questions," said Aunt Serena, pushing past Eliza, who was trying to tell her that Mrs. Trent was not at home.

Without thinking, Katherine held open the door of the drawing room, and her aunt stalked over to the fire. "I might well ask you the how and the why of it—why you are here instead of at the manor where you belong, and how you came here—had I not heard the whole of it from your sister Elizabeth. Fortunately she learned of your location when Blanche St. Denis asked her to help with your Season. Blast and damn the creature for her interfering ways. Your father said I was to have the raising of you! Were it not for dear Elizabeth, I might have travelled all the way to the manor in this vile weather. Katherine! You are to pack whatever garments you need for our journey to London. We must leave at once. Time is of the essence, and the clouds are gathering. There might well be a snowstorm. Go! Hurry!"

"London . . .," Katherine repeated, confused. "I do not want to go to London with you."

"You have no choice in the matter. A marriage has been arranged. Negotiations have just been completed. Your groom is an old friend of mine, a widower, wealthy and titled. His name is Lord Haversage. The marriage will take place within the month."

"No," cried Katherine, clutching her drawings to her bosom.

"Give those to me, and go at once!" Aunt Serena snatched the papers from Katherine's grasp. "What have we here?" she demanded as she looked at them.

"They are mine," Katherine cried.

"They are immoral," shouted Aunt Serena. "Pictures of yourself as a bride, and Blanche as a witch. And this evil letter. 'I cannot live without you, my beloved.' Who wrote this to you?"

"I wrote it myself, as a game," Katherine said.

Aunt Serena folded the papers and stuffed them into her reticule. "Your father will want to see these, I think. What has been happening in this household?"

Katherine was frightened. While Aunt Serena had often flown into rages, there was an intensity about her now that Katherine found frightening. "I'll go to my chamber," she said, planning to run and find Aquila. Perhaps she would know what to do.

But Aunt Serena was suspicious of her sudden acquiescence. Grasping Katherine's arm cruelly, she said, "I will accompany you. And remember, Katherine, should you try to resist me, the postilions will obey my orders."

Just then, Aquila entered the room. "I thought I heard voices," she said blandly.

"Are you that Trent woman?" demanded Aunt Serena.

"Actually, I am Miss Ware. Mrs. Trent is not in. Who are you?"

"This girl's legal guardian, come to take her home."

"I don't have to go," cried Katherine. "Papa gave his permission for me to be here." But even as she spoke, she was not certain. Aunt Blanche had said that she had Katherine's father's permission to take her to London for the Season. She did not know if Aunt Blanche had informed him of Katherine's removal to Valentine Parva.

"And I am shocked to find her alone in the house, reading this rubbish!" She poked at the book of fairy tales so hard that it fell to the floor. "I shall tell the world the sort of woman Mrs. Trent is. Allowing young girls in her household to receive blasphemous love letters! I wonder what liberties she has allowed you, Miss Ware."

"I think, ma'am," said Aquila in icy tones, "you had best remain here until Mrs. Trent returns. You will find her quite respectable. Her reputation is beyond reproach. She is the daughter and widow of clergymen, and her brothers are clerics also."

"Not all who wear the cloth are saints," cried Aunt Serena. "There are sinners everywhere."

"No doubt," said Aquila as she left the room.

Katherine felt abandoned. She let Aunt Serena draw her from the room and order Eliza to bring Katherine's cloak. "We will leave your clothes," she informed Katherine. "Bride clothes can be made in London."

Aquila hurried up the back stairs and snatched up her cloak. She found Kate in the kitchen and charged her to tell Cressida exactly what had happened the moment her mistress returned. Then she slipped out the back door. She doubted that Katherine's self-proclaimed guardian would remain any longer than it took to pack a few articles of clothing into a portmanteau. Even if the woman had a legal right to remove Katherine, Aquila thought she must be mad and had no intention of simply letting her vanish with Katherine.

As she came into the lane, she took careful note of the coach standing there. It was green, with a black top, and the coachman and postilions wore black and green livery. The vehicle was drawn by four horses—one black and the other three chestnut. Despite her concern, she was pleased that at least the coach was easily recognisable.

Fortunately, Cressida had mentioned the names of the ladies on whom she planned to call. Aquila did not bother to go to the houses of the first two ladies, reasoning that Cressida would be finished there already. She had to knock on only two front doors before she found her. Naturally, Cressida's first assumption upon being told that there was a domestic emergency was that something had happened to Toby, but Aquila was able to assure her that he and Philo had not yet returned. Cressida made her good-bye as quickly as possible. As they walked along the frozen road, Aquila told her what had happened, and that she feared Katherine would be gone when they returned.

"How long since you left the Grange?" Cressida asked.

"It will be a good half hour by the time we return," Aquila replied. "But perhaps they will still be there, after all, even if this women is unbalanced, she wouldn't expect Katherine to leave without bidding farewell to you." However, the cheerful tone of her words was belied by a worried frown.

As they turned into the lane that ran in front of Hugh's Grange, they saw that the green and black carriage was gone, and knew the worst had happened.

"What if Lord Haversage has obtained a special license?" asked Aquila, her forced cheerfulness gone.

"Even if her father consents to the marriage, it cannot take place if she does not consent as well," Cressida said. She kept to herself her fears that Katherine might well not know that, or might be so overwhelmed and frightened that she simply agreed to the marriage. "However, that woman, and I think she must be Katherine's aunt, Miss Serena Rayburn, is wrong in saying that Katherine's father would not approve of Katherine's being here. It is true that Madame St. Denis did not obtain his permission before bringing Katherine here, but I have since had a letter from him, consenting to the arrangement. From remarks in his letter, and from others made by Madame St. Denis when she wrote to me about Katherine, I believe Lord Tilbury no longer wishes his sister-in-law, Miss Rayburn, to play a large part in Katherine's life."

Kate must have been watching from the hall. She ran out in the lane to tell them that Katherine had been bundled into the coach only moments before they returned. "I made ever such a fuss about Miss Tilbury going off without luggage, ma'am, and I offered the lady refreshment and said I'd put a few things in a bag for Miss Tilbury, but before long she—she's Miss Tilbury's aunt, ma'am—said Miss Tilbury would have to manage with what she had. And she ordered me to take the bag out to the carriage, so I didn't fasten it, and dropped it all down the front stairs—for she had me by one arm and Miss Tilbury by the other, and we was all crowded together. But she just went out and called her servant in to take the bag and made me and Miss Tilbury shove everything inside while he waited. And Miss Tilbury, she said don't try to stop the lady, so I didn't."

"You did very well, Kate," Cressida said, urging them into the house, but the door had not even closed behind them when Aquila spotted Sir Anthony striding up the lane and hurried to meet him.

"Is this true?" he demanded of Cressida as soon as he was close enough to call to her.

"I'm afraid so."

"Haversage's reputation equals, even surpasses that of Old Q! A ravisher of innocents, and three times Miss Tilbury's age! I would not be surprised if he took steps to ensure that a wedding must take place. Damn the viper who took her from us. Mrs. Trent, we must recover her. How long have they been gone?"

"Close on ten minutes."

"But there is only one road from here to the highway. If I leave for my uncle's house at once, Mrs. Trent, I can be back here in twenty minutes to take you up. Miss Rayburn will have half an hour's start, but my cattle are fast goers, and the phaeton is made for speed."

He ran toward the Valentine Arms, where he had stabled Princess Gulnar.

Cressida glanced at the sky. It was dark, full of the promise of snow. "I'd best get a warmer cloak. And put on another pair of stockings."

Aquila offered her a fur-lined mantle. "You should take Philo's as well, for Katherine," she said. "Or perhaps I should go in your stead, Cousin. It will be cold, riding in an open carriage, and coming back, you will all be very crowded."

"No, you are too young to be considered a chaperone. But I'll gladly take the cloaks. I hope Philo will bring Toby back before the snow starts. Ask Maudie Brick to look after him. I must write to the magistrate—tell Kate to take the letter and then go home. And when Mrs. Barleyman returns—"

"Cressida," Aquila interrupted her gently, "don't worry. We three can look after the house while you are gone. I expect you and Katherine will be back here before we've had dinner cleared away."

The heavy coach lurched over the frozen ruts in the road. Outside the sky grew darker.

"Fine weather indeed," Aunt Serena muttered. "Everything to do with you has to be such a trial. What a dance you've led me, you little wretch. And as for that creature your great-aunt, it is a pity she cannot be imprisoned for abduction!"

Katherine was tempted to retort that Aunt Blanche had not kidnapped her. That crime should be laid at Aunt Serena's door. However, she did not want to give her aunt any occasion to scold her. She wanted to hear as little of that hectoring voice as possible. Clutching at the strap at her side, she braced herself against the motion of the carriage. It was just like Aunt Serena to make Katherine ride with her back to the horses when there was ample room for two side by side on the forward-facing seat.

She stared out the window, seeing nothing as the hours passed. Aunt Serena had ordered the coachman to keep a steady pace, but not to tire the horses. Perhaps she did not plan to stop anywhere, even to change horses. Well, Katherine did not care. It made no difference to her whether they hurried towards London or took a week. At the end of the journey was inescapable marriage to a man she had never seen.

As Cressida suspected, Katherine did not know that she could not be forced into marriage.

Images of Sir Anthony filled her mind. Sir Anthony, who was lost to her forever. If Aunt Serena had not arrived, she would have had a few more days to enjoy his company, and the illusion that there was something more than friendship between them. Katherine wondered if Aunt Serena could understand that by taking away those few days, she had initiated the ultimate punishment for what she saw as Katherine's great sin—killing Serena's sister.

"I did not ask to be born," Katherine had once cried to her aunt.

She had received the bitter answer, "It was the devil's work, and yours, you whelp of Satan!"

How typical that her sister Elizabeth had been the one to tell Aunt Serena where she was. Even if Elizabeth hadn't known that Aunt Serena wanted to take Katherine to London for her wedding, she would have passed on any information Aunt Blanche had given her merely to make mischief.

Katherine conjured up an image of her oldest sister, the daughter who had been the closest to their mother. She remembered the mixture of anger and disdain Elizabeth had regarded her with when she had visited Tilbury Manor with her husband, Lord Northcott.

He had been kind, Katherine remembered. He had brought her a present—a doll. He had teased her gently and hugged her goodnight, just as he had his own little girl. Katherine had even heard him castigate Elizabeth for the unkind words she had directed at her little sister. But Elizabeth, sobbing in her husband's arms, had recounted the death of her mother.

"It is not the fault of the child, my love," he had said.

"If she had not been born, Mama would still be here," Elizabeth had replied.

They had cut their visit short, leaving after only two days, instead of remaining for their projected week's stay. And Katherine's half-unthought dream that Lord Northcott might want her to go live with him and his daughter went with them.

Better not to think of that. Better to think of London, and her marriage. In fact, it was a kindness that she was being married so quickly. It would give her less time to brood over Sir Anthony.

"Shall I be wed tomorrow . . . no, this shall forbid it . . . lie thou there . . ." Juliet's words. Juliet, who would have stabbed herself had Friar Lawrence's draught failed her. And in the end, she had died rather than face life without the man she loved. But Juliet had known that Romeo loved her; had spent a few days as his wife. And Katherine knew that Sir Anthony did not, could not love her.

She had best put him out of her mind and face the rest of her life.

But instead she daydreamed. Aunt Serena would stop at an inn. While she slept, Katherine would slip from the chamber and make her way back to

the Grange. Sir Anthony would be there. And he
would declare that she, Katherine, was in fact the
most bewitching woman he had ever met. He no
longer found her naive. And he wanted to marry
her. . . .

"It has started to snow." Aunt Serena's words
broke into Katherine's thoughts. "My bones ache.
I'll be glad when you're off my hands. You'll not be
able to play such tricks with your husband."

Husband, husband. Katherine sighed. So much
for her daydream that Sir Anthony would offer for
her. And once she was married, she'd have to guard
her mind strictly against any such thought of him.
He was gone. Lost in the whiteness that swirled
around them. And if he had gone to Hugh's Grange
to see her, as he often did in the afternoon, he'd
learn that she had left without even saying good-
bye.

There was the sound of a carriage behind them.
Aunt Serena leaned forward to peer out the window. "Some fool in a phaeton. Driving much too
fast. It's dusk."

Katherine caught a glimpse of the vehicle as it
passed them. Suddenly there was a lurch. Aunt Serena pitched towards her, then fell back.

"Passing on such a road," she shrieked at the top
of her voice. "They nearly grazed our wheels!"

The coach jolted as it came to an abrupt halt.
This time Aunt Serena pitched onto the floor. She
pulled herself to her feet and opened the trap in the
roof. "What happened?" she shouted at the coachman.

"There be summat in the road, ma'am," he called
back.

"Drive round the obstruction," she ordered. "Or
over it!"

At that moment, one of the postilions opened the
carriage door. In the pale glow cast by the riding

lights, Katherine could see a well-muffled woman standing by the doorway. "The obstruction will be removed when Miss Tilbury is returned to my care," the woman said.

"Cressida!" cried Katherine, leaping to her feet.

"Are you Mrs. Trent?" demanded Aunt Serena. "Sit down," she ordered Katherine. Then she returned her attention to Cressida. "What right have you to interfere with—"

"I might ask you the same question. You have seen fit to abduct a young woman placed in my care by her relatives."

"By her great-aunt, who has no rights over her. Katherine was placed in my care by her father. She has always been my charge."

"I have a letter from Lord Tilbury consenting to his daughter's visit. Have you any proof that Lord Tilbury has given you permission to take Miss Tilbury to London, or for her to marry Lord Haversage?"

"That is no concern of yours," snapped Aunt Serena.

"But I think it is," said a familiar voice. Sir Anthony stepped into the circle of light. "The local magistrate has been informed of your actions. If you have legal grounds for your removal of Miss Tilbury, you had best apply to him. Meanwhile, she will return with Mrs. Trent. And," his voice was louder, "anyone who aids you in carrying Miss Tilbury beyond this point will himself face criminal charges."

Sir Anthony came forward to let down the step. "Miss Tilbury?"

Katherine put her hand into his and stepped out. To her relief, Aunt Serena did not clutch at her.

"Right is on my side," Serena shrieked. "I shall return with her father!"

"Good night," Sir Anthony said civilly, and slammed the door in Aunt Serena's face.

Katherine felt as if she were in a trance as she watched him tip one of Aunt Serena's postilions, who was holding his horses. "We'd best put you in the middle, Miss Tilbury," he said. "You look done in."

He boosted her into the high seat. "Have a care for your balance," he cautioned. "And now you, Mrs. Trent."

"Are you all right, Katherine?" Cressida asked once she was settled.

"Yes. Thank you. Won't Papa be angry?"

"If he is angry with anyone, it will be with me. But I rather suspect he'll approve of what we did. You had best slide closer to me, it will be a squeeze. And Aquila has sent you a warmer mantle. Stand up for a moment. It is rather chilly riding so high. I had never thought to be driven by a gentleman in one of these carriages. The speed was astounding, although I expect Sir Anthony will drive more slowly now that it is dark."

Katherine sat back down carefully and let Cressida tuck a rug round her legs. The phaeton lurched as Sir Anthony pulled himself onto the seat, then shouted for the postilion to let the horses go.

There was no conversation as they made their slow way home. Sir Anthony did not come into the Grange. Philo and Aquila were waiting up, but as soon as they had assured themselves that Katherine had come to no harm, they acquiesced to Cressida's suggestion that it had been a long day and they all needed some rest.

Katherine went up to her chamber, but as soon as she heard Cressida walk from Toby's bedroom to her own, she went and tapped on Cressida's door.

Cressida opened the door. She had unpinned her

cap and taken down her long blond hair, but was still dressed. "Is something wrong, Katherine?"

"No. It's just that I did not thank Sir Anthony. I cannot imagine how I could have been so remiss."

"You can thank him tomorrow. I am sure he understands how overset you were. And Katherine, my dear, while you should be guided by your parent in your choice of husband, your father cannot force you to marry. You do understand that?"

"Yes, Cressida. I'm sorry I disturbed you. Good night."

Unfortunately, Katherine thought, *my father cannot make anyone want to marry me, either.*

Sir Anthony did not call the next day. Katherine was crestfallen. Perhaps he was disgusted with a girl who always needed rescuing. Perhaps he was put off by her bad manners in neglecting to thank him.

The following day brought a note from him. He apologised for not having paid a call, but explained that he had not wanted to postpone a visit to London and had hesitated to call on her so soon after her ordeal. Katherine put his letter in the bonbon box along with her sketches of him, and tried not to think about him.

During the next few weeks, while Aquila taught her to waltz, Mrs. Barleyman showed her how to make sponge cake, and Katherine gave drawing lessons to Toby, she tried not to think of Sir Anthony.

She made calls with Cressida, drew portraits of everyone in the house, and tried not the think of Sir Anthony.

Once in a long while she gave way to temptation and thought about him, but doing so always brought tears to her eyes. If only she had been older, possessed of what Aquila called town bronze. If only Sir Anthony had loved her.

Even the news that Aunt Serena's health had suffered and Elizabeth had taken her to Bath did not distract her. Though she was relieved to hear that Lord Haversage, when he learned that Lord Tilbury had not consented to the match, had withdrawn his claim.

Katherine had since vowed never to marry, but to love Sir Anthony always.

But, one morning, she heard something that did thrill her. Aunt Blanche had returned, and Katherine all but ran into the drawing room where, Eliza told her, Madame St. Denis waited alone to greet her.

"Let me look at you, *ma petite*. I vow, you have grown. Wait until you see all the gowns Simone has ready to fit on you."

"And Aunt Blanche, you look so lovely all in pink."

"Thank you, my dear," she replied, sitting down and beckoning Katherine to sit beside her. "And you will never guess why I am so late in calling for you. I have been in London."

"In London," said Katherine. Even the mention of the town where Sir Anthony had gone was enough to set her heart racing.

"Yes. The Oliphants were dull. Since your letters sounded so happy, I decided to leave you here a little longer. But in London I saw all sorts of men, one of whom might make an excellent husband for you."

"But I have no wish to marry," Katherine exclaimed.

"What!" cried Aunt Blanche, throwing up her hands in mock alarm. "Have you never seen a man who took your fancy?"

"Only once," said Katherine sadly, "and he never loved me."

"Tell me," said Aunt Blanche. "Tell all."

And so Katherine did. "I do wish I was the sort of woman Sir Anthony could love," she ended sadly. "Of course, I can only wish him happy, but I fear that one day I shall hear that he has wed, and I think my heart will finish breaking."

"Fah," said Aunt Blanche. "You are only grateful to him because he rescued you from that Serena creature."

"No, Aunt Blanche. I loved him long before that. He is so gentle and kind. And I've seen him with little Toby, and know what an excellent father he would make. . . . "

"But would you not rather have an earl or a duke? He is only a baronet, and not a very wealthy one."

"I would rather have him than anyone," Katherine insisted, "if I thought he cared for me."

"But a title . . ."

"It is not the title, but the man," Katherine said passionately. "Believe me, Aunt Blanche, he is like no one else. I love him for his sake, not from gratitude."

"Well," said her great-aunt, "then I have a lovely surprise for you." She went to the red curtain that separated the conservatory from the drawing room and drew it aside. A slightly abashed-looking Sir Anthony stood there.

"You have your answer, young man. Now I expect you have a question of your own to ask." Aunt Blanche swept out of the room, closing the door firmly behind her.

"I am sorry, Miss Tilbury. I did not mean to eavesdrop, but I was so afraid that you might listen to my suit only because you felt an obligation to me. When I confided that to Madame St. Denis, she said she could prove that was not so, provided I gave her my word to obey her. And I was so eager to learn the truth, I fear I was less than a gentle-man."

Katherine cared nothing that some might fault his behaviour. All that mattered to her was that he was with her and wished to be. Boldly, she invited him to sit by her.

"I suppose you are wondering how I came to be here today in the company of Madame St. Denis. I met her in London. I went there to ask your father for permission to court you. I feared that Lord Tilbury might in fact arrange a marriage for you before I had time to make my feelings known. I saw Madame St. Denis at a ball, and knew at once that she must be related to you. And you know how charming and perceptive she is. Within the hour of my being presented to her, she had the whole story of our friendship. I confessed my feelings to her, and my concern that you were too young to desire my suit. Madame St. Denis then pointed out that you were almost eighteen, and that while long engagements are not the fashion, we could do as we pleased."

"But I thought you loved older women, older than I, that is. And you have always said I was too sheltered and innocent."

"My dear Miss Tilbury—would I be very forward to call you Katherine?"

He took her nod as permission and continued.

"My dear Katherine, the sort of woman a man flirts with is not necessarily the sort of woman he wishes to marry. Until I met you, I had no wish to wed, but within moments of our acquaintance, I knew that sophistication could not hold a candle to your charm. However, I was afraid that too bold an approach might frighten you. I had planned to wait until after you had had your Season—or were at least well into it—before I even approached your father. But I get ahead of myself, and I find I have no need to wait." He took her hands in his. "Katherine, will you marry me?"

"Yes, Sir Anthony."

"Yes, Anthony.

"Yes, Anthony. My beloved."

"That is better. So you will be Lady Overton, wife to Sir Anthony and, one day, mother to Sir David."

"Sir David?"

"Well, I have no wish to call my firstborn son Goliath. But if it will please you, dearest . . ."

A Talk with Toby

THE DUKE OF TYNE knew very little about children, but he recalled from his own boyhood a strong love of sweets and a hearty dislike of being talked down to. He invested in a bag of bull's-eyes from the village shop, then walked with Cressida on his arm up to Hugh's Grange. They found Toby watching as Katherine drew pictures of castles for him.

Toby was willing to show the duke his bedchamber and toys. After he had admired the rocking horse, Tyne offered Toby a bull's-eye and sat down on the straight-backed chair by the bed. Toby sat in one of the nursery chairs.

"So," said the Duke, "do you know what a duke is?"

"You're one, sir. That's why grown-ups call you 'your grace.'"

"Dukes, Toby, are otherwise ordinary men whose duty it is to sit in parliament and advise the king as best they can. They also have large estates, and many people who rely on them."

"Like a bishop and his flock, sir."

"Very, except dukes take care of everyday things, like ditches and roads and people's houses. Do you know how one becomes a duke?"

"Shoot lots of Frenchies," Toby replied with blood-thirsty zeal.

"That is one way," agreed the duke. "But it is most uncommon. I am a duke because my father

was, and his father before him. And my son—when
I have one—will also be a duke. A boy, like you,
whose father was not a duke, could never be one."

Toby sat patiently, bored but attentive.

"Let me try again. If I were to marry your
mother—"

"I could have a pony!"

"I beg your pardon?"

"Mama said that I can't have a pony because
there is no one to teach me to ride. Neddy's papa is
teaching him."

"Yes. If I marry your mother, you may have a
pony, and I shall teach you to ride." The duke found
the idea rather pleasing. "But if I marry your
mother, and we give you a little brother, *he* will be
the Duke of Tyne after me, not you."

"But," said Toby, "you already said I couldn't
ever be a duke. As long as I get my pony, I won't
mind."

"I see that you take after your uncle Randal already."

"Who is he, sir?"

"A great gun who doesn't mind about not being
a duke either. Is it all right if I leave you alone
here?"

"I'd rather go back to Miss Tilbury, sir."

The duke took Toby back to the sitting room, and
asked Cressida if she would accompany him. It
seemed that every room they came to had someone
in it already, so finally they went out into the garden.

"Your son is content not to be a duke—having
pointed out to me that he'll never be one regardless
of whom you marry. So, my dear Cressy, will you
marry me?"

"Of course, Chelm—Tyne."

"I think," said the duke, taking her into his arms,
"you had better call me James."

Cressida leant against his chest, feeling as if she had found home after many years of wandering. "May I confess that I always have in my heart?" She raised her head for a kiss. "Remember, dear James, to remind me to tell you about a most interesting Valentine's Day custom. . . ."

*R*egency...

HISTORICAL ROMANCE *AT ITS FINEST*